Published by Pink Tree Publishing Limited in 2023

All characters and events in this publication, other than those clearly in the public domain, are fictitious and any resemblance to real persons, living or dead, is purely coincidental.

Copyright © Pink Tree Publishing Limited.

The moral right of the author has been asserted.

All rights reserved. This book or any portion thereof
may not be reproduced or used in any manner whatsoever
without the express written permission of the publisher
except for the use of brief quotations in a book review.

For questions and comments about this book, please contact
pinktreepublishing@gmail.com

www.pinktreepublishing.com
www.agathafrost.com

WANT TO BE KEPT UP TO DATE WITH AGATHA FROST RELEASES? *SIGN UP THE FREE NEWSLETTER!*

www.AgathaFrost.com

You can also follow **Agatha Frost** across social media. Search 'Agatha Frost' on:

Facebook
Twitter
Goodreads
Instagram

ALSO BY AGATHA FROST

Claire's Candles
1. Vanilla Bean Vengeance
2. Black Cherry Betrayal
3. Coconut Milk Casualty
4. Rose Petal Revenge
5. Fresh Linen Fraud
6. Toffee Apple Torment
7. Candy Cane Conspiracies

Peridale Cafe
1. Pancakes and Corpses
2. Lemonade and Lies
3. Doughnuts and Deception
4. Chocolate Cake and Chaos
5. Shortbread and Sorrow
6. Espresso and Evil
7. Macarons and Mayhem
8. Fruit Cake and Fear
9. Birthday Cake and Bodies
10. Gingerbread and Ghosts

11. Cupcakes and Casualties
12. Blueberry Muffins and Misfortune
13. Ice Cream and Incidents
14. Champagne and Catastrophes
15. Wedding Cake and Woes
16. Red Velvet and Revenge
17. Vegetables and Vengeance
18. Cheesecake and Confusion
19. Brownies and Bloodshed
20. Cocktails and Cowardice
21. Profiteroles and Poison
22. Scones and Scandal
23. Raspberry Lemonade and Ruin
24. Popcorn and Panic
25. Marshmallows and Memories
26. Carrot Cake and Concern
27. Banana Bread and Betrayal
28. Eton Mess and Enemies
29. Pumpkins and Peril

Other

The Agatha Frost Winter Anthology

Peridale Cafe Book 1-10

Peridale Cafe Book 11-20

Claire's Candles Book 1-3

1

"Where are they?" Dot's voice rose over the hum of conversation at the table nearest the counter. "They should have arrived by now."

"Maybe they're caught in traffic?" Percy, her husband, suggested, shuffling his deck of playing cards. "Or perhaps they're struggling to find the place?"

"Traffic? In Peridale? On a Monday?" Dot rose from her chair to peer out of the café window. "What if they've driven headfirst into a ditch?"

Julia stifled a laugh as her gran's dramatic suggestion silenced the teeming café. It was a mild day in the second week of September, and a dry day was a relief after the summer's relentless downpour.

The crowd gathered outside while preparing the morning's bakes had been so dense that Julia had called her sister, Sue, in on her day off. The sisters hadn't stopped serving cups of tea and cakes since flipping the sign, rare for even a dry Monday morning.

"Is it me, or does everyone look more dolled up than usual?" Sue observed as she collected the day's first tray of used cups and plates. "Never seen this much lipstick smudged on the rims either. And what is that smell?"

Julia inhaled as she carried a tray of Victoria sponges to the window table, trying to identify the sweet and floral scent masking the rich coffee and sweet cakes. As she weaved through the tables, it seemed everyone had bathed in perfume that morning.

"Have you been telling people about this documentary?" Sue asked.

"Barker told me to keep it quiet."

Behind the counter, the sisters turned to look out over the sea of back-combed perms and glittering accessories. Their gran, Dot was hard to miss, sporting a crimson beret, white blouse, pleated navy skirt, and fur-lined coat.

"Gran?" Julia called, and Dot left the window with a reluctant huff. "Did you perhaps let slip that a film crew is coming here?"

"Wasn't I supposed to, dear?"

Julia pursed her lips at her gran, replying, "I said to keep it within the family."

"Did you?" Dot said airily. "That detail must have slipped my mind."

"To everyone in your phonebook?"

"To one or two people, Sue."

Even if that was true, they all knew how Peridale worked. You told 'one or two' people something, and by the time it circled back to the source, so much had been embellished that the original story might as well never have existed.

"Which do you think is my best side for the camera?" Dodging their glares, she turned her head from side to side. "Percy says both are as beautiful as the other, which I almost agreed with, but on closer inspection, I think I look best from the left."

"I maintain both sides are beautiful, my dear," Percy said, fumbling with his cards. "But if you prefer your left side, so do I."

Sue cleared her throat and called, "Good morning, everyone. How many of you are here for the film crew?" When no hands shot up, she added, "They've asked us to compile a list of interested names."

Almost every hand shot up except for Shilpa from the post office next door, who was too busy sniffing the woman beside her. The mere mention of the film crew escalated the hushed chattering into an indistinguishable buzz.

Julia's husband, Barker, was absent. When the cameras showed up, they'd be lucky to get a clear shot of him with the sea of aspiring starlets to fight through.

"I wonder where he is," Julia said as Sue restocked the coffee machine. "It's not like Barker to be late, though the documentary people were expected to be here half an hour ago."

"Time to check the ditches, I guess," Sue offered with a shrug.

Another half an hour passed, and with no one willing to leave until they'd had their shot at stardom, people began standing in the spaces between the tables and chairs. Julia's daughter, Jessie, the last member of the café trio, joined them behind the counter for a late breakfast with a preview copy of the next issue of *The Peridale Post*. The headline read: 'Greg Morgan MP Promises to Regenerate Left Behind Areas.' Jessie slurped her coffee, splattering drops on the pages. She looked up as the door opened, and Ethel White breezed in, bypassing the counter to join Dot by the window.

"Should I play referee?" Jessie asked, flipping the page. "It's only a matter of time until one of them has the other in a headlock."

"Leave them to it, I say," Sue suggested. "With a crowd this big, a show is just what they need to entertain them. Who knows, the cameras might arrive by the time they're rolling around on the floor?"

Julia had never seen them in actual headlocks—or rolling around on the floor, for that matter—but Ethel and her gran butted heads whenever they were within spitting distance. Once the leader of the Peridale Eyes neighbourhood watch group, Ethel had been Dot's rival since Dot started the Peridale Ears group. Both groups had since disbanded due to infighting and poor management, but their rivalry remained.

"Are you pulling my leg, Ethel?" Dot exclaimed after some muttered back and forth. They mirrored each other with their hands planted on their hips. "I've graced the stage, ladies and gentlemen!" Her voice was filled with theatrical grandeur. "I am *the* actress around here."

"You were in *one* nativity play," someone called from the crowd.

"And you *shot* that man halfway through!"

"Wasn't she *arrested* before the play even got to the ending?"

"A setup, I assure you all," Dot proclaimed, as though speaking to her adoring fans. "All in the past, and they dropped *all* charges. I also used to work in a theatre in my youth."

"Weren't you the girl who took the coats?" Jessie asked.

"Whose side are you on?" Dot cleared her throat, her gaze drifting off into her memories. "Ah, those were the days. I met my first husband, Albert, in that theatre."

"Your husband was *never* an actor," Ethel said. "I refuse to believe it."

"He was a plumber, there to fix a broken pipe," Dot admitted, pursing her lips. "But he was as handsome as *any* actor. The most handsome man I'd ever laid eyes on. No offence, my love." She glanced at Percy, too engrossed in making a coin disappear in and out of his nimble fingers. "Had I not left the theatre to marry and have my son, Brian, I could have been the biggest star this country has ever seen."

"Ah, yes, everyone," Ethel said, her tone brimming with mock agreement. "That well-known coat-check-to-famous-actress pipeline."

"There's still *every* chance my Dorothy could be a star," Percy said, rising to Dot's defence as the coin rolled across the floorboards. "She'll be an overnight sensation when the camera lands on her."

Dot folded her arms with a satisfied nod as though her husband's approval settled it. However, from Julia's vantage point, Ethel and the rest of the room weren't as supportive of Dot as she might have hoped.

Jessie passed a small packet of caramel-coated popcorn between them, and the trio continued watching the spectacle.

"*I* was on the small screen," Ethel announced, her gaze distant. "It was a rather glamorous affair. The lights, the camera—"

"The *action*?" Dot interrupted. "Prove it, or I don't believe you. Jessie, get your phone ready to look up her credits."

"Fine! It was an advertisement," Ethel admitted. "And it still aired on television."

"Nationally?"

Checking her nails, Ethel muttered, "Regionally."

"And what were you advertising? Bags to hide one's face, perhaps?"

Ethel held up her hands. "Luxurious hand cream. These mitts were the most famous pair in the Cotswolds for 1972."

A couple of people turned to examine Ethel's once-famed hands as she flaunted them at the crowd, twisting them this way and that, but most returned to their conversations. Ethel stuck her tongue out at Dot, who reciprocated the gesture. Again, Julia wondered when the pair would realise that they might be best friends if they could refrain from acting like children whenever in each other's company. Dot marched towards the counter, and Julia was about to share her observation, but her grandmother remained enamoured with stardom.

"Will this documentary air on television?" she asked, adjusting her beret in the glass of the revolving display cabinet. "Or will it be more of a feature film?" Excited by her suggestion, she added, "Oh, do you think there'll be a premiere?"

"Small indie director," Jessie said.

"And they're not even here," Sue added.

"And neither is Barker," Julia concluded.

Leaving her grandmother to continue with her daydreaming, Julia went through the beaded curtain and out the back door to find the actual star of the show.

The search was brief, and she found Barker in the first place she looked. He was in his basement office under the café, a den of dark wood, rich fabrics, with a red leather Chesterfield sofa covered in more lines than Dot and Ethel's faces combined. He was reading over something, only glancing up to greet Julia as she crept down the wooden staircase. Perhaps he was going over his notes from his current PI case. His hunt for the arsonist, Arthur Foster, had consumed much of the past fortnight since the fire at the Knights' home. But by the speed of his pacing, she guessed he was going over the latest version of his new manuscript, which still wasn't ready for her to read despite him having declared it as finished over a month ago.

"Lost track of time?" she asked.

Barker shook his head, placing the papers down on the large mahogany desk taking up the centre of the room. He snatched off his reading glasses and blinked up at the ceiling as the floorboards creaked, and it sounded like Dot and Ethel were wrestling for real.

"I think I might just cancel," he said.

"I believe that ship has sailed."

His face fell.

"Are they here?"

"Not yet. They must be running late."

"Then there's still time." He opened his laptop at his desk. "I don't know why I agreed to this. I should have ignored the email." Fingers typing, he added, "On second thoughts, I should never have spent so much time writing this book. It's not even like I'm going to publish it, so I won't need a documentary to promote it, and—"

Julia reached across the desk and closed the laptop.

"Any chance this is just pre-show jitters?" she asked, her tone soft. "You were excited last night. Relax. See how the day goes. I'll be there every step of the way."

They looked up as an engine rumbled somewhere above, and Barker groaned in a similar tone. Julia walked around the desk and wrapped her hands around him, resting her chin on his dark hair.

"She wants to read the book for context, but it's nowhere near ready."

"She?"

"Anwen Powell, the director. *Award*-winning director. You should read her emails. She's the real deal. I'm just some guy."

"Some guy with a bestselling book," Julia reminded him.

"*A* bestselling book," he said. "Singular. And if you recall, I couldn't handle the stress of the publishing industry."

"And became a successful private investigator in your own right," she said, ignoring his pessimism; she knew it was just the nerves talking. "And after a successful two decades in the police. A worthy subject for any film." She paused, kissing his hair, more salt and pepper every year. Car doors slammed, and his hands grabbed hers. "Upstairs has turned into a *Peridale's Got Talent* audition holding room, so there'll be someone to point a camera at if you don't want to go through with it. But at least meet Anwen. You've been planning this over emails for weeks now."

Barker kissed Julia's hands, and without another

word, he slid the manuscript into the top drawer and made his way to the stairs. Julia followed and felt a sudden rush of nerves on his behalf and even a little of her gran's reverence.

Her husband in a documentary?

Not too shabby at all.

2

Anwen Powell won a handful of awards for her *To Frack or Not to Frack* documentary in 2015 and a couple more for *Secrets of the Urban Fox* a few years later. The first followed a group of environmentalists protesting a proposed fracking plant in Lancashire, the second a literal fox roaming around London. Neither had been Barker's cup of tea subject-wise, but they were well made enough that he hadn't thought Anwen was a total hack when conducting his research.

Not that he thought she was a hack as she bustled across the café, squeezing between the sea of people waiting for her arrival. But she was nothing like Barker had imagined from reading her emails, either.

He'd envisioned she'd have a serious air about her. She always replied promptly and directly, her tone never stepping over the line of proficient politeness.

"So sorry to have kept you waiting!" Anwen called around the full café, her accent distinctly Welsh. She licked what looked like red strawberry jam from her lips before offering him her hand. She stared at it, wiping more jam on her baggy pink linen trousers. "Barker Brown, it's a pleasure to meet you finally. To say I was a huge fan of your book would be an understatement."

The crowd parted around her, and Julia hadn't been joking about the audition holding room comment. Percy clanked two spoons against his knee like a musical instrument, and those who weren't checking their reflections in compact mirrors seemed ready to pounce on her as she took in the café, busy on a Monday on her behalf.

Dot scanned Anwen's mismatching clash of bright clothes as though she'd expected someone else, but Anwen continued to shake Barker's hand obliviously. The messy brunette bun hanging off the back of her head sagged side to side with each swish of her head. She finally let go and made an effort to prop it back up, but it deflated again. He'd have put her in her mid-forties, give or take a few years.

"And you must be Julia," Anwen said, moving on,

bubbling with excitement. "Or should I say Julie North? It's truly an honour to meet the real-life inspiration behind Barker's novel. If I'd known your café was a real place, I might not have stopped off for breakfast on the way." Licking the other side of her lips, she gave the café another scan. "It's exactly as you described, Barker. Truly remarkable if I—"

"Dorothy South," Dot interrupted, jutting her hand into Anwen's, her accent taking on a transatlantic tilt. "Professional actress, at your service, anything you need, I—"

"Ethel White." Ethel reached out, and Anwen crisscrossed her arms, shaking both hands simultaneously. "Actual actress. Have you heard of Bronsworth's Luxurious Hand Cream?"

"Oh, I—"

"Anwen?" Julia called from the beads, already parting them. "If you'd like to come through?"

Played off by Percy's rattling spoon concert, Anwen hurried behind the counter, still looking around the café as though she couldn't believe she'd entered his book. Barker wondered if he'd slipped in with her; the morning was turning out to be quite surreal. He'd been so caught off-guard by the whiplash of the woman he'd been expecting shattering that he'd forgotten to keep up his nerves.

"People are very friendly around here, aren't

they?" she said, taking a stool at the stainless-steel kitchen island. Her Welsh accent had a rhythmic, hypnotic quality to it that Barker found himself drawn to.

"Tea?" Julia offered.

"What's that tea Julie North always drinks in your book?"

"Peppermint and liquorice," Barker replied, pushing forward a smile. "And yes, it's real."

Julia excused herself to make a cup.

As Anwen dug through her bag, Barker couldn't help but notice a small mountain of foil wrappers spilling over the top.

"I can put these in the bin for you?"

"Oh, would you?" Anwen's round cheeks darkened a shade. "So friendly. This place reminds me of my grandparents' home village, Portmeirion."

"Do you still live in Wales?"

"Ah, I wish," she replied with a wistful sigh, pausing to dig out fistfuls of protein bars mixed in with chocolate wrappers. "Once I got my BA in Film Studies from Bangor University, I ran off to make my first film. I live on the road, you could say. Until this documentary is finished, my address is Peridale, and what a place it is."

Barker felt anxious at the thought of her pinning

her immediate future on him. "That's quite a lot of faith to put in a stranger."

"Well, you're hardly a stranger, Barker," she said, pulling out an original hardback copy of *The Girl in the Basement* and a pen. "Would you?"

"It would be my honour."

Barker scribbled his signature on the inside cover of the well-read book, feeling a jolt of excitement.

"Wanted to get that out of the way first," she admitted in a whisper. "But I'm not just here as a fan of your work. I'm here *to* work. I've been hunting for my next project for a while, and when I came across your book and did a little digging into your background, I realised your story is unique. And not just you, but this village, the place behind Perington in your book." Swapping the signed hardback with a binder, she opened it and primed the pen. "The village is the inspiration for your next book, too, I presume?"

He nodded. "I based it on a cold case from late last year. A body was found in a time capsule dug up at the school just around the corner."

Julia returned with Anwen's tea and offered her a slice of double chocolate fudge cake, Barker's favourite.

"Oh, how lovely," Anwen said, her eyes lighting up. "I think I'm going to like it here." She took a bite and, through the mouthful, said, "After I fell in love with your book, I started researching the area. There have been many strange cases, and the two of you—PI and café owner—seem to crop up a lot. Quite the duo."

"The documentary is about Barker, though," Julia said, her tone uneasy.

"Of course," Anwen assured her, "but you're a part of Barker's life. A huge part." Her accent missed the first letter, making it sound like 'uge.' "Not just his wife, but his muse. It would be strange if you weren't to appear at all?"

Barker shot Julia a reassuring smile. "We do make quite the team."

Julia considered her options, but Barker widened his smile, knowing she wouldn't turn it down if she thought it would help him. And it would. The thought of having Julia by his side eased the last nerves clinging on from his tense morning in the office.

"I suppose I wouldn't mind appearing in a few sections."

"You'll be fantastic," Anwen assured her. "I have a very naturalistic filming style. We point and shoot, capturing what's happening, and then the narrative is stitched together in the editing bay. I oversee every cut. Nothing is forced or set up, which seems to be the way these days. Every documentary is a shocking ten-part story about who killed who and what big scandal can be re-examined again, and again, and *again*." She feigned a yawn. "Call me old-fashioned, but I prefer the *real*, and I want to capture what your lives are like here. And what's easier than acting like yourselves?" She took another bite of the cake and said, "This is delicious, Julie."

"Juli*a*," she corrected.

Anwen laughed, shaking her head at her mistake. "Sorry, that'll take some getting used to. You are exactly as Barker depicted. Don't suppose you have Eton mess on the menu? I know it's not much of a cake, but my grandparents used to make it for me every time I visited."

"Then I'll put Eton mess on the menu tomorrow," Julia said.

"Really, too kind." Anwen licked the chocolate cake crumbs, consulting her binder. "We'll start tonight."

"So soon?" Barker asked.

"I work quickly, and there's no time like the present." She glanced up with a sympathetic smile. "Don't worry, Barker, I won't throw you in the deep end. We'll begin slow. B-roll and texture shots to get you used to the camera. Speaking of which, the crew should be checked in at the B&B by now. Wait till you meet them. They're excellent. Fresh out of film school

19

and eager to prove themselves."

Barker hesitated. 'Fresh out of film school' wasn't what he'd expected based on their email correspondence, and his surprise must have shown on his face.

"Not to worry," Anwen said quickly, standing up. "Some of the best people I've worked with were fresh out of film school. That's when they're hungriest and most passionate. My entire *To Frack or Not to Frack* crew were recent graduates. So, shall we meet back here at seven? No better place to start than the heart of the village."

The three of them agreed to meet at seven, and as she left, Barker felt a mix of excitement and apprehension. His concerns were overshadowed by a new text message.

> DEREK KNIGHT (ARSON PI CASE)
>
> ARTHUR FOSTER SPOTTED AT B&B!! Must be around the village. Family shaken up. Please visit ASAP. Thanks. Derek.

He showed the text to Julia, and her brows furrowed with worry.

"Evelyn said the Knights were staying at the B&B?"

Barker nodded. "And Arthur Foster made sure they didn't have a thing left after he burned down their house, so what's he doing sniffing around their new temporary home? I should check how they're doing."

Leaving through the back, Barker found Anwen reversing a beat-up Volvo that had to be from the 1990s out of the space behind Julia's vintage car. She rolled down the window, and it jammed halfway.

"What did I leave?" she asked. "I'd forget my head if it weren't screwed on."

"I'm going to the bed and breakfast, too," he said, nodding up the road to Evelyn's B&B. "My latest client is staying there. They're having some trouble."

"Active PI *and* author? I smell awards on you already, Barker Brown." Leaning across the car, she opened the passenger seat. She brushed food wrappers off the seat into the footwell and said, "I'll drive slowly. Please tell me all about this new book of yours. When can I get my hands on it?"

"Soon," he replied, climbing in, the foil crinkling under his shoes. "It'll be ready soon."

After filling Anwen in on the case rather than talking about his book, Barker exited the rust-riddled Volvo, staring up at Evelyn's B&B.

Made of golden Cotswold stone and flanked by a garden humming with life, it was the sort of place pulled from a postcard. Across the road, the village police station, Barker's former workplace, contrasted with the whimsy of the B&B. Next door, The Plough's sign creaked gently in the summer breeze above a smattering of people enjoying lunch on the benches outside.

Detective Inspector Laura Moyes was one of them. Her lunch partner, Roxy, had her back to Barker, but Laura nodded to him, and Barker returned it. They'd been building a friendship since she arrived in the village for the time capsule cold case. Anwen joined him on the pavement and made a soft sound of approval.

"Everything around Peridale is so special, isn't it?" she said, her accent dancing around the words like the bees and butterflies around the wildflower garden. "It's like stepping into another time."

At the front door, Anwen yanked on the doorbell chain. A melodic series of chimes rang out inside, another detail that amused her. The sound had barely faded when the door swung open, revealing Evelyn.

"Ah, Barker, do come in," she said, stepping back and gesturing with a sweep of her flowing emerald green kaftan. "And if I'm not mistaken, you're Anwen? Please, come this way."

Evelyn swept down the hallway into the sitting room towards the soft strumming of a guitar.

"How did she know that?" Anwen whispered. "I didn't so much as get out of the car when I dropped the crew off."

"Psychic," Barker said, though he wasn't a believer. "And I'd stay away from her 'special tea' if I were you."

They followed her into the homely sitting room, where the walls were adorned with framed photos and eccentric knick-knacks from her travels. Sitting by the bay window was Evelyn's grandson, Mark. His fingers strummed over an acoustic guitar resting in his lap, filling the room with a soft tune. Mark glanced up from under his black hair, his sleepy eyes lined in charcoal black, offering them a tight smile before returning to his strumming. The tune changed, taking on a haunted edge.

"Hang on," Anwen said, pointing around the B&B like a penny had just dropped. "Evelyn, a bed and breakfast and a boy with black hair? Is this..." She looked up at Barker, and he offered a nod. "*The Girl in the Basement*."

"*The Girl* being my mother," Mark said, his fingers freezing on the guitar. "And I'd rather not talk about it."

Evelyn reached over, patting Mark's arm. "Now, dear. Barker did a splendid job honouring Astrid's legacy with his first book. I believe it brought much closure to many of us."

Mark forced a laugh. "*Closure?*"

Taking his guitar with him, he left behind more than the absence of his music. Evelyn seemed unusually rattled and wanted to follow him but stayed put. Barker wasn't sure what that was about. He'd talked to Mark during the writing process and was more than willing to help back then.

"Are you here to discuss the book?" Evelyn asked. "That could be a fine feature for your documentary, Barker."

Anwen nodded appreciatively, but Barker interjected, "I'm here to speak with the Knights, and you were right about Anwen being here to check in."

"Ah, yes, the Knights," she said with a sad sigh. "They're shaken after Arthur was spotted at the B&B earlier. I sensed something untoward would happen the moment my eyes opened this morning. One of the guests noticed him creeping by the window over breakfast, and he's hardly a man you can miss."

Arthur Foster was easily recognisable, his features marked by a prominent scar on his left cheek. Barker had only seen it in pictures, still no closer to tracking down the man he'd been tasked with finding.

"Where are the Knights?" Barker asked as Evelyn was on her way to the check-in book in the hallway. "I'd quite like to speak with them again."

The garden behind the B&B was as charming as

the front, a flourishing landscape of wildflowers swaying gently under the afternoon sun. The Knights were crowded around a rusting wrought-iron table in the overgrown grass, a pot of tea going untouched. The Knights all looked alike in some way, all linked by dark red hair passed down from their mother. Even Derek had a whisper of red in his thick, greying crop.

"Sophia," Barker began with the family matriarch at the head of the table. She clutched her crystal pendant around her neck, as lost in the stars as Evelyn. "How are you all doing? I heard Arthur was here?"

"He was, Barker," Derek replied for his wife. "Spotted over breakfast."

Derek sighed, his weathered hand squeezing Sophia's. Barker had found him to be a pragmatic man in the two weeks since Derek met with him at the office following the fire. A history professor at Oxford University, he starkly contrasted Sophia, a reiki healer and yoga instructor.

"We still don't know it was Arthur," Faith, their only daughter, said, arms folding. "He was seen leaving the scene, not starting the fire."

"Get real," Sam muttered, an artist and the eldest of the three siblings. "It was him."

"It was," a quiet teenage voice echoed. Nathan, the youngest, clenched his jaw as he met Barker's eyes. "I thought we were safe here, but we're not, are we? He's come to finish what he started. He wanted to kill us all in that fire. I know it."

Sophia whimpered like she was about to faint, and Barker once again wondered what the family weren't telling him. He'd met with Derek three times, Sophia twice, and their three children only once. Each time, all five insisted they had no connection to Arthur. Barker had never believed them.

"I still think all of this is ridiculous," Faith muttered, picking at her nails. "One witness statement isn't proof that Arthur set the fire."

"Shut it, Faith," Sam snapped, standing up. "You can't see the whole painting because you're still only obsessed with the pink shade, even after everything."

"That's enough, Sam!" Derek's rebuke silenced them all. "Barker is here to find Arthur. That's all."

Barker made a mental note to investigate a possible romance between Faith and Arthur if that's what Sam had meant by 'pink shade.' Faith, an accountant, was in her early thirties and would be around the same age as Arthur.

"I *felt* him, Barker," Sophia muttered, eyes trained on something far in the distance. "His aura has always been so dark and filled with malice, and I felt him here. He came back to do us harm, I know it. I should have trusted Evelyn's warning that she sensed something would happen today."

"Evelyn predicts many things," Barker assured her. "Ask her about the weather, and there's half a chance the opposite will happen within the hour."

"You don't understand." Sophia clenched her eyes, both hands going to the crystal.

"And why would Arthur come here?" Barker asked, trying to steer the conversation back to the facts. "If this was a random attack like you claimed, Derek, why would he want to? What was it you said, Nathan? Finish what he started?"

Faith stood abruptly and stormed off, leaving a bitter silence in her wake.

"Thank you for coming, Barker," Derek said, joining his daughter in standing. "Arthur was thankfully scared off before he could cause more trouble. If you'll excuse me, I think I need to lie down. Too much excitement for one day already. The police have been informed about his appearance, so I trust you'll continue your search. I don't trust them to find their own feet."

Barker assured him that he would before Derek made his way up the garden path, followed by Sophia. The brothers, Nathan and Sam, separated by at least fifteen years, remained at the table, each staring off in opposite directions. Barker almost stayed behind to continue quizzing them about their connections to Arthur, but as Derek had pointed out, Barker hadn't been hired to find out why Arthur started the fire at their family home. The police were taking care of that; Barker only had to find Arthur, and his appearance at the B&B window over breakfast was the closest he'd got to the elusive arsonist.

As Barker walked away from the wildflower garden, he recalled the sight of what was left of the Knight's home. He'd visited with Derek to gauge the situation as the last fire engine drove down their private driveway. Once a grand detached house with a plot of land on the village outskirts, little had survived. The ornate wooden frames were charred beyond recognition; the lush greenery turned to blackened stubble. The fire had been merciless, leaving behind only a skeletal smouldering structure.

"Find him, Barker," Derek had said, thrusting a photograph of the family posing in front of the house one Christmas, smiling in a way he'd yet to see. "I don't care what it takes, what it costs. Find the monster that did this."

Making his way back through the B&B, Barker's path was intersected by Evelyn's grandson, Mark. Usually shy and reserved, Mark glared at Barker, eyeliner accentuating his piercing gaze.

"Keep your documentary crew away from me,"

Mark stated, his voice trembling with emotion. "I won't be part of anything else that exploits my mother's memory."

He walked around the check-in desk and slammed the door to the 'STAFF ONLY' quarters. Barker was left standing in the quiet hallway, Mark's words echoing. Evelyn emerged from around a corner with a soft smile despite the tension.

"It would have been Astrid's fortieth this week," Evelyn explained as haunting music filled the B&B again. "Mark means nothing by it, Barker. I promise. I predict he'll be back to his old self by the weekend. Healing is a journey, not a destination." She presented Barker with a crystal. "Amethyst, for luck with the documentary."

Barker rolled the purple stone in his palm, the cool touch strangely comforting. "Thank you."

"And I'd be happy to participate if needed," she added. "Your book brought me closer. Astrid was an avid reader. She would have loved it too."

Barker pocketed the crystal, thanked Evelyn, and left the B&B, wondering again about his involvement in the arson case. This was more than a typical PI case chasing infidelity and shady business partners.

The Knight family needed peace after losing everything. He couldn't restore their home, but he could help their healing journey by finding Arthur

Foster. Walking back to his office under the café, he pondered whether distractions like the book and documentary had hindered his search.

3

Walking up the creaky metal steps snaked against the back wall of Katie's Salon on Mulberry Lane, Jessie paused to look above the door with quiet satisfaction, and not just because she'd been the one to help Veronica hang the small 'The Peridale Post' sign above the fire door. She'd never expected her troubled path would lead her to write for the newspaper, but here she was.

Inside the white box of an office with two desks, two chairs, and a water cooler, the paper's editor since spring, Veronica Hilt, was holding wallpaper samples against the wall with a cocked head. Below, the sound of Katie's singing, jarring and off-key, rose through the floor with the hum of her nail drill.

"Ah, you're here," Veronica said. "Thought you might have ditched me for the documentary crew."

"As if."

"Funny, there was almost a documentary *The Peridale Post* before Johnny left." Veronica tilted her head at the samples, beckoning Jessie. "What do you think? Is it too jazzy?"

"Way too jazzy," Jessie said, letting the door slam behind her. "And so are the fish. I think they might drive me mad."

"The white walls are driving me mad," Veronica said, discarding the samples to scratch at her short grey hair, always jutting in every direction. "But you're right. Might be too much pattern to stare at every day, and they are a tad random."

"Did you call me here to talk about wallpaper?"

"Of course not." Veronica peered over her oversized frames, always a different colour. They were a dark maroon today. Nodding for Jessie to follow her to the desk in front of the window. "If you're still not interested in covering Greg Morgan's conference at the library later this week, I have a more exciting lead that might interest you."

"Yeah?"

"A tip-off about the Knight fire," she said, raising her brows. "Your dad still looking into it?"

"Last I heard."

"Good, you've already got a foot in the door," she said. "A contact of mine thinks the fire might be linked to gang activity."

Jessie's brow furrowed. "Fern Moore?"

"No, not a bunch of kids in tracksuits with nothing better to do. A real gang by the name of the Cotswold Crew, and yes, I know, it's a terrible name." Veronica spun in her chair, casting her gaze through the window at the pink glow of the salon's neon sign. "But as bad as they were at naming themselves, they've managed to evade the police for years."

"Years? Damn."

"You name it, they've been linked to it," Veronica said. "Bank robberies, intimidation, even murder if my police contact is to be believed. No one knows where they're based, who all the members are, and they move in the shadows."

"Then how do you know Arthur is connected to them?"

"I don't." She shrugged. "It's a tip-off."

"Why would this Cotswold Crew want to go after the Knights?"

"That's what I want you to figure out. Talk to your dad. See if there's any truth to this." Veronica glanced at her newly painted yellow nails, then back up at Jessie. "What do you think? Katie did these on her lunch break. She practically pinned me down."

33

"She's growing on you."

Veronica protested deep in her throat, glancing at the floor as Katie bravely attempted a squeaky high note. "We'll see. So, are you up for the assignment?"

"I can poke around between café shifts."

Veronica looked at her thoughtfully. "Don't go hunting for the gang, okay? We need some information."

"Grew up on the streets, remember?" Jessie reminded the editor, her gaze steady. "I'm not dumb enough to wander into a gang's lair. I can handle myself. I'm not here to chase storms. I'm here to find the stories. Leave it with me."

4

*J*ulia's gran's dining room remained as frozen in time as during Julia's childhood living there. The floral wallpaper was unaltered, the furniture still traditional polished dark wood, and the air retained that distinctive scent she'd never been able to identify, except as 'gran's cottage.' Only the chalkboard hidden behind rich red curtains hinted at its past dual purpose as the official investigation board of the Peridale Ears neighbourhood watch.

At the table, Dot rummaged through a rustling tin filled with neatly cut-out newspaper articles. Their dogs, Lady and Bruce, were curled up together underneath, and a crossword had Percy scratching his bald head at the head of the table. Olivia, Julia's youngest, played on her mat by the sideboard, stacking wooden blocks in a tower-like configuration. The articles, some yellowing with age, detailed cases Julia and Barker had tackled.

"Will these do, love?" her gran asked, handing over a pile of papers. "Gertrude Smith's stabbing after that awful review of your café, and oh, here's one about Katie's brother being pushed through that window at the manor. And remember Mabel, my dear old friend, falling out of the ceiling at Barker's first book launch?"

Waving his pen, Percy added, "And don't overlook my brother's murder at our wedding. Going headfirst into that vat of dry ice was nasty. And the Ronnie Roberts case at the food bank this past summer."

Julia wasn't one to wander down memory lane when it came to the cases they'd put to bed, but as she scanned the headlines, it was strange to consider how many incidents they'd been involved in.

"I suppose my days of sleuthing are behind me now," Julia stated, placing the papers into her handbag. "I've got my family, the café, and Barker needs my support for the documentary right now."

"If you say so, dear," Dot replied, patting her cheek. "And bring those back, won't you? I like a complete record. Does that mean you're going to be in the film? Any word on the premiere?"

"Since shooting hasn't started yet, no word," Julia said, laughing. "And I might appear in a few scenes. Anwen thought it would be strange if I didn't, given that I'm part of his life. We're starting tonight."

"Oh, dear." Dot examined Julia's chocolatey brown curls and her usual vintage dress. "So, there'll be hair and make-up provided?"

"No, Gran."

"What about us?" Percy called out, tongue poking as he worked on the crossword. "Anwen might not have liked my spoons and cards, but we're part of Barker's life, too."

"That's right!" Dot gave a satisfied nod. "Would be strange if I—" She looked back at Percy, glancing up at her, and corrected, "If *we* weren't a part of it too."

"Gran, I promise I'll ask her," Julia said, looping her bag over her arm with a glance at the antique clock on the mantelpiece. "But try not to hog the spotlight. Anwen said she wants to capture our *real* lives. Berets, fur coats, and musical spoons might not be needed." Both sighed but nodded. "I need to go. Barker and Anwen will be waiting." She bent down to kiss Olivia, who was engrossed in playing with her blocks. "I'll be back in a few hours to pick you up, sweetheart."

Across the village green, Julia could see the hubbub of the small crowd gathered outside her café, lit up in stark white light from an attachment atop a camera balancing on a young woman's shoulder. Anwen stood just behind the camera, another crew member holding a fluffy microphone on a stick. Walking across the green, Julia remembered Anwen say she wanted to capture the village as it was. She supposed the old ladies in their cardigans and skirts vying for the limelight were part of the village. Leading the accidental circus was Ethel White.

"Can you believe *I* was once one of their suspects?" Ethel bemoaned. "Picture the scene. Last year, spring. The former leader of the Peridale Eyes neighbourhood watch group had her head bashed in at that graveyard just over there by her very own husband. It just goes to show you can't trust anybody. As you can imagine, it was quite the scandal."

Julia couldn't help but admire Anwen's patience as she nodded, eyes fixed on her watch. She let out a relieved sigh at Julia's arrival.

"And *cut*! I think we got everything we need from this segment," Anwen called out as the light cut off. "Excellent work, everyone. You gave us some good stuff there."

The group didn't scatter, and Anwen motioned for Julia to follow her down the alley between the café and the post office. Barker was already there, deep in conversation with Jessie.

"Anwen, this is our eldest daughter, Jessie," Barker introduced her.

"*Daughter*?" Anwen shook Jessie's hand. "Beautiful, too. The camera will love you."

Staring down her nose at the director, Jessie gave the camera a dismissive glance, and without another word, she retreated through a side door of the post office to her flat above. Anwen stared after Jessie like an intriguing narrative had been snuffed out like a candle in the wind.

"Camera shy," Barker explained with an uncomfortable laugh. "So, what's first?"

"Perhaps we move somewhere quieter?" Anwen suggested, the rabble having taken to retelling stories without the need of the camera. "A clear night is forecast, along with a beautiful full moon. Ideal for b-roll footage and initial interviews to see where to take things." She glanced around the dark alley and asked Barker, "You said the school the time capsule was found at was only around the corner? Could be a good place to start?"

"Sounds good to us," Barker agreed, nodding at the crew. "Aren't we going to be introduced?"

"What am I like?" Anwen chuckled, pointing to the young woman with the camera. "This is Ava Edmonds, an outstanding budding camera operator." Ava, whom Julia had noticed wore trousers too short with mismatching bright socks, gave a small wave of acknowledgement. Anwen then motioned towards the bald man with the quirky round glasses. "And that's Rupert Jones. He's our assistant director, cinematographer, and sound guy."

"Hi," Rupert said, his voice terse.

With introductions out of the way, Anwen announced, "And *action*!"

The light blinded Julia as it flicked back on, the camera pointing at her and Barker. Anwen gave them an encouraging nod, so Julia followed Barker around the corner, and they walked along the path next to the field behind the café. Despite their initial stiffness, Anwen encouraged them to relax and pretend the camera wasn't there. With the brightness of the light, Julia wasn't sure that would be possible.

"So, tell me about how you two first met," Anwen prompted from behind the light. "In the book, Detective Inspector Robert Greene was a new face in Perington who met Julie when he moved into his cottage."

"Sums it up," Barker began. "My moving van was blocking the road, and Julia was trying to make her way to the café in her car. It was my first day in the village. I wasn't the politest, especially after a dreadful introduction at the station. There were quite a few people who thought they should have been promoted internally."

"I didn't know that detail," Julia said. "I thought you were just a stuck-up city boy."

"Well, I was that, too."

Anwen's eyes sparkled with delight. "That's incredibly romantic. Building a life and solving mysteries together, starting from a chance meeting. *Perfect!*"

After a brief pause outside St Peter's Primary School, where Barker detailed the significance of the time capsule case, the crew took a detour into the graveyard to capture some footage of the gravestone Penelope had been found near, to add 'texture' to Ethel's retelling of the Peridale Eyes story.

"Are there any landmarks in there?" Rupert asked, dropping the microphone momentarily as he looked off to the forest's dense edge at the graveyard's far side. "Something that would add to the atmosphere? The full moon is lighting the place in a way you'd pay a fortune to recreate."

"There's Howarth House?" Barker suggested. "It's an old derelict building near the edge."

"Perfect!" Anwen exclaimed, clapping her hands. "A full moon, an old house, what more could we ask for? Shall we set off?"

The group crossed from the quietness of the

graveyard into the stillness of Howarth Forest. The silver sheen of the full moon seeped through the dense canopy of gnarled oaks and delicate birches. Anwen cleared her throat after a few paces, and the camera shone on Julia. She no longer winced whenever its unblinking light swung towards her, though she couldn't ignore it as she was supposed to.

"So, what drives you to investigate?" Anwen asked. "What is it about a mystery that pulls you in?"

After pondering her answer, Julia reached into her bag and handed Anwen the snippets. "These might be useful, and my gran will murder me if I don't ask if she can feature in the documentary somehow. She's rather eager to get in front of the camera, so could you indulge her?"

"Of course," Anwen said, nodding. "The question?"

"Right," Julia said, taking a moment to think about it. "I suppose I like to put things right. Perhaps a little too much at times. A case, to me, is like a recipe. Get the right ingredients, and everything falls into place."

"Excellent!" Anwen encouraged. "Now, can you repeat it all but incorporate my question at the beginning? 'I'm driven to investigate because...'"

Julia did as she was told, uncertain how natural it was to repeat herself.

"And Barker?"

"I guess I'm driven to investigate because I was hooked on murder mysteries as a kid," he said, stepping over a fallen log. "Probably read them much younger than I should have. But I loved how the bad guy always gets caught at the end. Howarth House is just up here."

∽

Barker's steps crunched on the forest floor as they walked closer to the ruins of Howarth House. The once-grand edifice was now an emblem of desolation, surrounded by overgrown bushes, thorny brambles, and tall grass that swayed softly in the evening breeze. The wooden window trims were either decayed or missing entirely, and the windows were shattered or covered in a shroud of dusty cobwebs. Vines clung lovingly to the brickwork as though trying to hold together the crumbling structure.

Turning to the camera, Barker's face softened. "I've loved this place since I first came across it. She might look dilapidated now, but there was a time when this house must have been the envy of the village."

"Know anything about its history?" Anwen asked.

"I heard it was built by a man named Duncan Howarth."

"I came across his name while researching the

village," Anwen said excitedly. "An entrepreneur who tried to bring the industrial revolution to the Cotswolds in the 1800s."

"Tried and failed," Barker recalled. "I think his trade was wool, but this house is his last remaining mark on Peridale. He built this place for his love."

"How romantic," Anwen said, clapping her hands together. "When are you building a house for Julia, eh?"

"If Julia wanted a house, I'd build her one," he said, smiling at Julia, who'd stepped out of the spotlight. "But Mr Howarth's love died before the house was finished, and he spent his days here heartbroken and alone, going completely mad until consumption got him in the end."

"Oh," Anwen said, a little less excited. "Less romantic, but great storytelling, Barker. We'll cut there, and Rupert, do you want to frame this next shot?"

Rupert carefully arranged them, using the dilapidated house as a chilling backdrop, and Barker noticed how at ease he was starting to feel with the camera's presence. With Julia by his side, the earlier nerves were a fast-fading memory. When pacing his office that morning, he imagined he'd freeze the second the camera landed on him. He'd enjoyed the single press tour he'd done after his first book became an overnight sensation, but he'd had a publicist prepping him for every question, coaching his every response.

"Try to look solemn for a moment," Rupert said, disappearing around the camera. "Anwen, do you want to ask them more questions while they're here?"

"Sure..." Anwen agreed, her gaze narrowing on the house. "Ava, just kill the light for a second."

Like two startled deer, Barker and Julia swivelled towards the house to see what had captured the director's attention as Ava lowered the camera.

"I see a light in there," Julia announced. "Should we go and see what it is?"

"Could be squatters?" Barker speculated, though his seasoned Detective Inspector instincts were kicking in. "Everyone stay here. I'll go and have a look."

He shoved open the decrepit wooden gate and ventured forward. A glimmering light seeped from one of the bay windows on the left side of the main door. Missing glass panes, moss and ivy had infiltrated the stony structure. He stepped past the oversized arched door, dangled from its hinges. Though the elements had taken their toll, remnants of its former glory still lingered. An ornate chandelier, now home to several bird nests, hung from the high ceiling. Wallpaper, with its faded floral patterns, peeled from the walls, revealing the layers of history beneath. He ran his fingers along a dust-covered bannister as the rotting floorboards protested under his weight. A flickering light beckoned him from one of the adjacent rooms, an invitation he couldn't resist.

What he found was far from a squatter.

A man lay on the floor in the centre of what he guessed was once a grand dining room. Beneath another crystal chandelier, now masked by cobwebs, the man was ringed by a constellation of tealight candles. They danced like minuscule lighthouses, guiding Barker closer. Symbols etched in white chalk adorned the floorboards around him. As the passing clouds moved, moonlight poured through the shattered window, illuminating the silver coins resting on his eyes.

This man was not a stranger to Barker. He'd only glimpsed him in photographs, but the deep purple scar on his left cheek was the giveaway. The crew's light invaded his space as they tiptoed behind him.

"What the…" an unfamiliar voice, likely Ava's, muttered behind him. "Are you seeing this?"

"I'm seeing this," Rupert confirmed. "Keep rolling."

"No," Anwen intervened, and she guided the camera down. "Someone should call the police."

"The scar," Julia said. "Barker, is that…"

"You know him?" Anwen questioned. "Who is he?"

Barker gulped as he squinted at the scribbled symbols, trying to make heads or tails of them. "That's Arthur Foster. I was hired to find him, and I suppose I have."

5

Outside Howarth House, the scent of earth and pine filled the cooling evening air, punctuated by the chilling stillness. Julia, her fingers intertwined tightly with Barker's, felt her heart race as they watched the flickering glow of the candles inside the house, the image of the man engrained in her mind. His arms and legs had been spread out like arms on twisted clocks, the numbers replaced with candles and strange symbols. Blood had pooled on his chest, a possible cause of death. And most chilling of all, the silver coins resting on his lids—fifty pence pieces—had stared up at the cracked ceiling like unblinking robotic eyes.

Out of the forest shadows, an out-of-breath police constable ran towards them, a torch flickering as it scanned the trees. PC Jake Puglisi emerged, his enthusiastic jog slowing to a breathless crawl. He dragged his radio from his vest.

"DI Moyes, I've made it. And you were right, it's them two."

Barker and Julia exchanged glances, knowing they had to be 'them two.'

"I was patrolling near the farm when the call came through," PC Puglisi explained, casting an arm off yonder before grabbing one of Barker's hands in both of his. "Always a pleasure, Mr Brown. How's that second book coming along?"

"Hardly the time, eh, Puglisi?"

"No, you're right, Sir. Is it as freaky in there as they said over the radio?"

"Afraid so," Barker confirmed. "Arthur Foster. Stabbed through the chest, by the looks of it, and there's…" He paused as though searching for the words. "Strange things are decorating the scene."

Puglisi took in the sight of the house, hands on his hips as the colour drained from his cheeks after his sprint. "Your new book should be nearly finished? If you need someone to give it a once over, I'd be happy to."

Puglisi's gaze wandered to the crew, who were taking the young PC in with curious stares. The camera was on Ava's shoulder, pointed right at him, though the bright light wasn't blaring.

"We're filming a documentary," Barker explained. "About me, about the village, and what we just stumbled upon was unexpected, to say the least."

Anwen, her bubbliness muted since their discovery, stepped forward. "Constable, our footage may be of some help. We've captured quite a lot already since our arrival this morning. Perhaps we've picked up something of interest?"

"A documentary, eh?" Puglisi's boyish smile returned, and he flattened his short brunette hair. "That's Mr Brown for you. Always putting Peridale in the spotlight." He patted Barker's arm as though they were best friends. "And DI Moyes will want to review whatever you have. But Barker, any initial thoughts on this? I mean, you write this stuff."

Before Barker could share his thoughts, more police officers emerged through the woods with torches, commanding them away from the scene. They ventured into the house, led by Puglisi, leaving them to stand back and watch as torches flashed around the dilapidated house.

"Shocking stuff," Anwen said, her arms folding tight as the officers came out one by one with the same shocked expression. "We're documenting real-time events right now, capturing actual history in the making. When life gives you lemons—"

"You keep the camera rolling?" Barker asked with a hint of disapproval. "This was supposed to be a light-hearted, feel-good documentary, and what we just found in there is anything but."

"The nature of filmmaking is being adaptable," Anwen said, though she lowered Ava's camera again. "Though, you're right. For now, I think we have everything we need. How long until the Detective Inspector shows up on the scene?"

Barker wasn't sure, though he didn't want to stick around in the woods. After giving their initial statements to the responding officers, they left Anwen and the crew behind to share their footage with the police. Julia followed Barker back through the forest and out into the graveyard, the full moon lighting their way.

"What was Arthur doing in there like that?" Barker said as they weaved in and out of the gravestones. "This doesn't make any sense."

Barker had encountered many strange things in Peridale, but this one took the cake. Leaving the mysteries of the night to continue unfolding without them, they were pulled towards the closed café.

∽

In the stillness of the café, Julia and Barker huddled around the table nearest the counter, with only the display cabinets for light. The once vibrant and bustling space was eerily quiet, the soft hum of the fridge in the kitchen replacing the radio. The lingering scent of coffee and cakes did nothing to comfort Julia; the candles and symbols still swirled in her mind. They cradled steaming mugs of hot chocolate, though neither had taken a sip.

Outside, the street was filled with onlookers, their murmurs and footsteps a constant reminder of the investigation unfolding in Howarth Forest. The blinds were pulled down, shielding them from prying eyes. Julia didn't have the energy to cater to her customers, not tonight. She wondered about the future of the documentary and whether it would continue at all, despite Anwen's claims that they had an opportunity to 'capture actual history.' Taking her first sip of her hot chocolate, Julia hoped the whole situation was nothing more than a sinister prank.

Lost in her thoughts, she was startled when a shadowy figure appeared at the window in the door. As the figure came into focus, she recognised the familiar face of Detective Inspector Laura Moyes peering inside. Barker rose from his chair, his movements slow and deliberate. He unlocked the door, allowing the detective inside. The smell of the night air wafted in as she stepped in, followed by a faint scent of menthol, the remnant of her last puff on her electronic cigarette. She entered the café, her eyes meeting theirs with stern concern. The quiet night was about to become even longer.

Barker offered a nod. "Evening, Laura."

"You, of anyone, should know it's Moyes when I'm on the case," she said with a smile, though her husky tone was annoyed.

"Coffee?" Julia asked without her usual enthusiasm. "There's some chocolate cake left if you're hungry."

"Forget coffee and cake, Julia. Why am I not surprised to find the two of you in the middle of another mess?"

"We've already given our statements," Barker replied, sounding as tired as he looked. "It was a coincidence. We were filming for the documentary in the forest with Anwen's crew. We were only at the house because it looked cool."

Sighing, Moyes looked like she wanted to pull up a chair at their table. She glanced at the door and remained standing. "A documentary, Barker? Really? Didn't have you down as the fame-chasing type."

"It's for my book."

"And you just *happened* to be there?"

"That's exactly it," Julia interjected, her voice

strained. She sipped the hot chocolate, the sweetness unpleasant against the dryness of her mouth. "We filmed in some other places too. There was no way for us to know we were walking into a murder scene."

"One of the stranger murder scenes I've seen," Moyes said with a sigh. "Freaked me out, to tell you the truth."

"You and me both," Barker added, his eyes fixated on the blinds as though he could see the forest. "Any idea what those symbols around him meant?"

Moyes leaned against the counter, chewing the inside of her lips. "From our initial analysis, they seem to be linked to the moon's phases. There was some text written in a language none of us recognised."

"Cause of death?" Julia asked.

"Stabbed right through the heart." Moyes ran her hands through her dark blonde hair a few times before tucking it behind her ears and stuffing her hands into her trouser pockets. "From the looks of it, it seems to be some ritualistic killing. It's like nothing I've ever seen in all my years."

"Me neither," Barker agreed.

The trio stewed in the silence of the suggestion that the killing could be part of some strange ritual. Julia had considered it, and Barker must have too, but neither had said it out loud until Moyes.

"But in Peridale?" Barker sighed, scratching at his

stubble. "Nothing like this has ever happened here before."

"That we know of," Moyes corrected. "As I said, none of us recognised the language, and I have a few linguists on the team. We could be dealing with something old. Really bloody old."

The door opened, left unlocked by Barker. Julia stood to tell whomever they were that the café was closed, but her gran hurried in, slamming the door shut before the bell had time to finish its tinkle.

"Have you *heard*?" Dot cried. "Some man's been found in the woods, and from what I just eavesdropped from Ethel White telling Amy Clark, and given my *expertise*, I hate to be the bearer of bad news but I think we need to pack our bags and head for the hills. It seems there's a cult running around the place."

"Expertise?" Moyes asked.

"My gran means she's seen a documentary," Julia corrected apologetically. "And yes, we've heard."

"Two documentaries," Dot corrected, holding the corresponding number of fingers. "And what else could it be? A man was found hanged, drawn, and quartered in a room filled with thousands of candles, symbols smearing the walls in his blood. If that's not a cult, I'll eat my beret."

"Word does travel fast around here," Moyes said.

"Dot, as much as I respect your *expertise*, jumping to conclusions isn't helping anyone, especially based on wild rumours." She checked her watch and sighed. "If that's how the story has transformed after an hour, what will it be by tomorrow morning?"

"Throw in some levitation and maybe a couple more bodies," Julia said. "And a dozen people will claim to have seen the whole thing happen."

Dot huffed. "You'll see. There's something ominous happening around here. Don't be surprised if a portal appears on the village green to drag us all down to hell!"

"You first," Barker muttered with a dry smile.

"Mark my words," Dot continued, undeterred. "If that man was sacrificed to some ancient goat god or who knows what, there's no telling which of us will be next." Her eyes cut to the blinds, and she returned to the door. "Oh, dear. I should never have left Percy at home with Olivia. His soul is too pure. He's certain to be next in line for a sacrifice."

Julia and Barker exchanged glances. As much as Julia wanted to dismiss Dot's declarations as bizarre ramblings, the scene she'd witnessed made it difficult.

"Dot might not have got the details correct," Barker said, the one to vocalise the unspoken. "But given the evidence so far, she might not be too far off."

6

The familiar warmth of the B&B felt different than it had that afternoon; the comforting ambience was replaced by tangible tension. The ticking of the grandfather clock echoed through the quiet sitting room. The lamps dotted about failed to lift the shadows. Evelyn moved restlessly, adjusting trinkets and frames after they refused her several tea offers.

Barker occupied a plush armchair. Across from him, Derek sat in the middle of the sofa, leaning on his knees, stoic following Barker's revelation that he'd found the man who'd burned down their home. Nathan, the teenager who must have been around eighteen, perched as though on pins in the corner of the sofa, chewing his cheeks, eyes darting between his father and brother. Leaning in the corner with crossed legs and folded arms, Sam was lost in his thoughts, gazing out the window at the full moon.

And between them, as Evelyn fussed around, a giant elephant occupied the room.

"Considering your history with Arthur," Barker began, "it's only natural you'll be considered suspects."

"Yes, I assumed as much," Derek replied, sitting up straight as he cast an eye to the door. "I'm sure it's only a matter of time before the police come to question us."

"Ridiculous," Sam snapped, kicking away from the wall, arms wide. "We had nothing to do with this farce."

"I'm glad he's dead," Nathan muttered, eyes staring through the coffee table scattered with tarot cards. "I might sleep tonight."

"Watch your tongue, my son," Derek instructed. "You wouldn't want to say anything like that around the police."

Caught between his past detective career and his current private investigator path, Barker was about to advise the same, but he had no way of knowing if Nathan was innocent, and statements like that didn't help.

"The way Arthur was found was a little peculiar,"

Barker said, gulping the lump in his throat. "He was arranged in a circle of candles, coins on his eyes, surrounded by symbols corresponding to the moon's cycles, and an as-yet-unidentified language." Pausing, he inhaled, knowing the next part still sounded bizarre. "It seems as though Arthur was killed as part of a ritualistic killing."

Evelyn gasped, floating through to the dining room with a hand clasped at the gem in the middle of her turban. The three Knight men didn't offer a glimmer of a reaction to the news.

"Given the circumstances, I don't suppose you know what that could be about?"

"None at all," Derek answered instantly. "Arthur is dead, and like my son, I won't pretend that doesn't fill me with a certain type of morbid joy. However, I recognise that our troubles are far from over. How seriously do you think the police will treat us as suspects?"

Barker considered his options. If he'd been the DI on the case, knowing that Arthur had been behind the vicious attack on their home, he'd have already been at the B&B to check out their alibis. He told them as much, and Nathan twisted in his seat.

"I was walking along the canal in Riverswick," Nathan confessed, glancing at his father. "I go there whenever I need to clear my head."

"Did anyone see you?"

"Not that I noticed."

A heavy sigh escaped Derek, the lines on his face deepening at his son's confession. The unsaid implication hung heavy in the room.

"Derek?" Barker prompted. "Where were you?"

"Visiting what was left of our home," Derek revealed. "And before you ask, I was alone and didn't notice anyone there either. I felt drawn back to the house after Arthur dared to show his face so close to us this morning." Gritting his jaw, he looked sharply at Barker and said, "I grew up there, you know? It was passed down to my parents from their parents and eventually to me. All three of my children were born in that house. All my books, our photographs, my wife's research—"

"My artwork," Sam added, back to staring at the moon. "My first ever painting was in there. Burned to dust."

Barker pushed on. "Where were you tonight, Sam?"

"Here at the B&B," he said. "Alone in the back garden, trying to paint. I've been suffering from a block since Arthur destroyed everything, but you know what? I think my block may be over. If you'll excuse me."

Sam walked to the dining room, leaving another

unconfirmed alibi in his wake. Barker watched him walk down the garden path through the dining room windows towards an easel near the shed at the far end of the garden. A gnawing mistrust manifested within Barker.

"Sophia and Faith?" Barker asked.

"They got an early night," Derek replied, rubbing his temple as if to ease the pressure building within. "It's probably best we wait until morning to disturb them with this news. After the garden meeting, we all needed some space. I assume they were here at the B&B."

Nathan slipped away without uttering a word, leaving Barker alone with the man who'd hired him.

"We'll need to try and confirm everyone's alibis," Barker said, meeting Derek's gaze. "Once we know the window of Arthur's time of death, perhaps the police can track down some witnesses to put you all where you said you were."

"You're speaking as though you do not believe us."

"It's not that," Barker said, choosing his words carefully. "I'd be careless to ignore how this could look. You're an intelligent man, Derek, an Oxford professor, and you said yourself you wouldn't be surprised if the police turned to you."

"I understand," Derek said, pushing himself up with his hands on his knees. "You're still on the case,

Barker. Like I told you before, I no longer trust the police. Please help us prove our innocence. I know my family had nothing to do with this." His gaze faltered, landing on the patterned carpet beneath their feet. "But I also know how all of this appears."

Sensing an opportunity for openness, Barker took another stab in the dark. "The candles, the coins, the moon drawings?" he asked, watching Derek's reaction closely. "Are you sure you don't know what this could mean?"

A moment of unease flickered across Derek's face, but a frown replaced it. "As I told you, I know nothing about that." With a final, weighty sigh, Derek moved to the door, signalling the end of the uncomfortable conversation. "Goodnight, Mr Brown. I expect you'll be in touch soon."

Left alone, Barker faced a mystery that deepened with every passing moment. The quiet ticking of the clock was the only sound that accompanied his thoughts, the rhythmic beats echoing the unsettling undercurrent that had become a part of the Knight family's existence.

Barker considered Derek's denial, and he wasn't easily fooled. He'd observed enough liars across interview desks to recognise the twitching, the glances, the avoidance. For a scholar, Derek had shown no interest in such bizarre circumstances.

Given his pragmatic nature up to this point, Barker found his denial too rushed, too final.

As he sat pondering the implications of Derek's reaction, Evelyn, who had been lurking half-hidden in the dining room, stepped into the glow of the lamps, her eyes wide and unsettled.

"Could you be talking about..." Evelyn's voice trailed off, her eyes going to the ceiling as the floor creaked. "Perhaps I'm mistaken."

"Evelyn?" Barker pushed, rising from his chair. "What do you know?"

"Nothing," she said, never one to shy away from sharing her thoughts. "Most likely nothing."

"And if it isn't nothing?"

"I... I... I must get to bed." Evelyn swept across the sitting room, holding the door open for Barker in an unexpected move for the ever-so-polite hostess. As Barker walked past her, she rested a hand on his shoulder, and the two stood frozen in the doorway momentarily. Leaning into his ear, with the scent of a strange tea blend on her breath, she whispered a single word. "*Lunara!*"

Evelyn refused to elaborate further, and as he walked away from the B&B for the second time that day, Barker once again had more questions than answers. Staring up at the icy full moon shining down on the village, Evelyn's utterance was another twisted thread in the tapestry of the increasingly complex case.

~

The scent of houseplants filled Jessie's small flat above the post office, mixing with the sharp tang of day-old takeaway. Clothes were strewn across the place, and clutter seemed to cover every surface. But Julia wasn't there to remind Jessie that tidying up was free to do.

Julia cradled Olivia deep on the sofa as she slept, a peaceful image contradicting the night's events. By the window, Jessie looked down at the village green that refused to quieten down. Jessie had been the one to call Julia there.

"What's on your mind?" Julia pushed.

"Veronica had this tip about the Knight fire," Jessie began, still staring out into the night. "She seems to think Arthur could be to a gang. Ever heard of the Cotswold Crew?"

Julia shook her head.

"They sound pretty hardcore." Jessie turned away from the window, smiling at the sleeping sight of Olivia. "Veronica suggested this tip-off could mean they're involved in the fire. Maybe even what happened to Arthur in the forest." She paused and added, "I bumped into Dot out walking the dogs earlier. Is it true what she said you and Dad found?"

"Maybe a quarter true."

"But a cult?" Jessie arched a brow. "In Peridale?"

"We don't know that for sure."

"Sounds like it, though, doesn't it?"

Inhaling deeply, Julia nodded, unable to deny how things looked.

"Maybe this Cotswold Crew are into more than bank robberies and intimidation?" Jessie threw herself into a bean bag in front of the black-screened TV. "Veronica asked me to talk to Dad about it. See if there's any connection in all of this."

"She wants you to look into gangs?"

"*One* gang," Jessie corrected. "And don't worry, Veronica already made me promise not to go looking for them. I need to find some connections, that's all. I told Veronica I was chasing stories, not storms."

Julia nodded that she understood, but it didn't ease the knotting in her stomach. Julia had seen how quickly stories could turn into storms, but she wouldn't waste her breath trying to convince Jessie not to do her job. At twenty-one, Jessie could decide, and Julia was proud that she was juggling working at the café with the paper. She'd never expected the café to be Jessie's forever career when she'd first taken her in off the streets, but at least at the café, she didn't have the risk of crossing a potentially deadly gang.

"So," Jessie said, picking up the remote control but only whipping it around in her hand. "I assume you and Dad will dive into this headfirst tomorrow?"

"Only if a portal doesn't appear on the green at night to drag us all down."

Leaving Jessie to watch that afternoon's episode of *The Chase* on catch-up, Julia cradled Olivia closer as she descended the stairs from the cluttered flat. The pulse of the village beneath was abnormally active for as close to midnight as it was. She felt the same tug the late-night bystanders did as she leaned against the corner of her café at the top of the alley, her gaze drawn towards the intense crime scene lights bleeding through the stillness of the distant forest.

She'd told her gran she was out of this game only that evening. But there it was again, the all-too-familiar draw of a mystery, the ingredients laid out before her:

One cult.

One gang.

One dead arsonist.

A dash of a devastated family.

And a sprinkle of a torched house.

Julia tightened her grip on Olivia, kissing her forehead gently, turning to another light leaking into the night. She walked around her café and pushed on the wooden gate to her yard, the field behind a silent constant. Taking the steps to Barker's office carefully after letting herself in with her key, Julia was pleased to find her husband behind his desk. She could tell the same question occupied him that was spinning around in her mind.

Who had killed Arthur Foster, and why had they chosen to do it in the way they had?

"So," Julia asked, pulling up a chair beside him after settling Olivia under a blanket on the creaky leather sofa. "What do we have so far?"

7

"Are we doing anything for your birthday, Julia?" Barker asked in the kitchen at their cottage the following day over breakfast.

"Ah yes, the most pressing matter," Jessie said, flicking through the latest issue of *The Peridale Post*. "Get a load of this headline: 'Moonlight Mystery Madness: Cults in the Cotswolds?' Veronica's got a knack for headlines. I'll give her that. Bumped that Greg Morgan redevelopment piece off the front page, at least." Shutting the paper with a grin, she added, "And who knows, Mum, if you're lucky, maybe you'll be sacrificed for your birthday?"

The three of them laughed, and Olivia joined in. Barker was leaning against the breakfast bar, engrossed in either the latest draft of his book or case updates while sipping his coffee. Julia was across from him, next to Jessie, gently assisting Olivia with her scrambled eggs. She was too preoccupied with the unsettling events of the night before to think about her birthday.

"Nothing special about forty-two," Julia said. "Let's keep it a quiet affair."

"So, that's a 'no' to sacrifice?" Jessie asked, pretending to take a note. "I'll make you a cake if I don't get kidnapped by a cult or a gang before then." This time, they didn't laugh, only Barker's coffee slurp filling the quiet. "Got it. A single sacrifice joke is okay. A kidnapping joke is too far. So, what does everyone have? I could have had toast and coffee at my flat."

Julia and Barker exchanged glances, and Barker closed the lid of his laptop.

"This gang," Barker started, his fingers knitting together in a tight clasp. "The Cotswold Crew, as they're calling themselves. We don't think you should be getting involved."

Julia sipped her peppermint and liquorice tea, busy wiping Olivia's chin. She'd suggested they 'have a word' with Jessie about the gang, but they'd agreed he would lead, given Barker's background. Too much of a cheerleader, Julia had never been very good at talking Jessie out of things. However, from her peripheral vision, their daughter's stare was firmly planted on her as she encouraged Olivia to eat alone.

"What is this? Good cop, bad cop?" Jessie said, forcing a laugh. "I'm not getting involved. It's a little investigative journalism."

"Investigating the wrong group of people," Barker replied.

"But it's okay for you two to stick your noses in whenever someone keels over?" Jessie challenged, letting her words linger for a moment. Neither of them denied it. "But one little gang, and—"

"They're not a *little* gang," Barker interrupted, his strict manner unbroken. "Right around the time I quit policing, we were starting to hear whispers about them, and none of it was anything you'd want to be involved in."

"I'm going to quote you on that," Jessie said, her fingers tapping at lightning speed on her phone. "*The Crew have been active since at least the tenure of Detective Inspector Brown, who said—*"

"Jessie..."

"Dad..."

Olivia slapped her hands on her plate with a cackle, scattering the leftover eggs onto the floor. Glad for something to do so she could stop avoiding eye contact, Julia darted to the kitchen tiles as Mowgli, their fluffy smoky grey Maine Coon, skidded from the sunspot he'd been curled up in by the fridge.

"Jessie," Barker began again with a gentle sigh. "They're thugs for hire. They move discreetly and don't take kindly to people sniffing around in their business. If they were easy to catch, the police would have done it already."

"I'm not trying to catch them," Jessie said, her typing speeding up. "This is some good stuff. Don't suppose the Knights have mentioned them?"

Flaring his nostrils, Barker tossed his leftover coffee in the sink as Julia cleaned up the plastic plate. They shared a 'Should we give up?' glance, to which Julia could only shrug. Jessie was headstrong and more determined since Veronica had taken her under her wing at the paper. And Dot's tin of scraps from that paper had proved Jessie was right about them sticking their noses in.

"The Knights haven't mentioned much," Julia said, leaning on the breakfast bar. "Barker seems to think the daughter, Faith, might have had some personal connection to Arthur, and the youngest son, Nathan, seems desperate to confess something, but his parents aren't letting that happen. If the café isn't too busy, I will try and talk to them today."

"Good idea, good cop. If they mention anything about the Crew, let me know." Jessie stuffed the toast into her mouth and said, "And bad cop? What are you up to today if not answering my pressing questions?"

Barker gave a conceding sigh. "I'm not sure. I want to speak with the sons more than anything."

Jessie kissed Olivia's head before dragging her denim jacket off the back of the breakfast stool. "And I'm off to Fern Moore. Veronica thinks it's a dead-end, but where else do you start looking for a gang if not there? Stay away from people in black cloaks carrying daggers."

Jessie left the cottage with a slam of the door.

"Well, we tried," Julia said.

"We'll have to keep an eye on her."

"Might be easier to trust she won't get herself into anything she can't handle," Julia said, feeling no easier about it. "Hopefully, Fern Moore is a dead-end like Veronica thinks. We have the Knights to deal with."

"And Evelyn." Staring out to the garden as flies buzzed around in the morning light, Barker reached into his trouser pants and pulled out the purple stone. He'd rolled the thing around in his hand for most of their initial fruitless digging online about 'Lunara' in his office the previous night. "She seemed so frightened that she was even saying the word to me."

"I'll talk to her," Julia said, squeezing his shoulder. "We'll get to the bottom of this."

He kissed her hand before turning and knitting his hands around her waist. "The weather is nice. Let's walk—"

Two quick rings at the doorbell cut Barker off, and they walked into the hallway. Julia wondered if it might be her gran, but it wouldn't be like her not to let herself in. Cupped hands and a smiley face appeared through the frosted glass.

"Isn't this just the quaintest little cottage?" Anwen called before they'd reached the door. "Make sure you get a clear shot, Ava. The sky couldn't be any brighter."

"Is it bad that I forgot about the documentary?" Barker groaned, pausing by the nursery door. "Do you think she'll go away if we don't answer?"

"We're not ignoring her, Barker. We committed to this," Julia said, handing over Olivia. "And no, I don't think she would. The sooner we give her what she wants, the sooner she moves to her next project. Besides, it will be great promotion for your book Any idea when I can read it?"

Grumbling something as he took Olivia into her nursery, Julia greeted Anwen and the crew. Ava and Rupert were as quiet as they'd been the day before, but Anwen was as chatty as ever, apparently refreshed by the countryside air.

Already dressed for the day in pale yellow—she'd

picked the colour hoping it would cheer her up—Julia managed to keep the crew on the doorstep despite Anwen trying to step around her to get some 'context shots' of the inside of the cottage. Ava zoomed in on Veronica across the lane with nothing else to film. She was too engrossed in reading a gardening book as she hovered over her unruly rose bushes to notice.

"And you have a little one, too?" Anwen beamed, crouching to Olivia as Barker pushed her out of the cottage in a pram. "Isn't she just the most precious bean you've ever seen? Ava, get a shot of—"

"How about we keep the kids out of it?" Barker said, breezing past the camera and holding the gate open for them. "It's not like Olivia can sign the release form, and I think we have more than enough to be shooting with what's going on."

"Then I'm glad we're on the same page," Anwen said, hurrying through the open gate. "A murder on your doorstep is too good an opportunity to pass up. It's not good for the victim, but you know what I mean. Gives our story an extra punch we weren't expecting."

"How about we film something further down the lane?" Julia suggested, clipping the gate shut behind them. "We told the story of how we first met yesterday. It's just around the bend."

"Excellent idea, Julie," Anwen declared, clicking her fingers at Ava to go ahead. "And *action*!"

Julia almost corrected her, but she decided it would be a waste of breath. Thinking of first meeting Barker, being called the incorrect name was almost nostalgic, though she'd suspected the new DI in town had purposefully called her Julie to wind her up as they'd clashed over the Gertrude Smith case all those years ago. Anwen didn't seem to have a malicious bone in her, too lost in Barker's story world.

With the sun warming their backs and a gentle breeze rustling the leaves dotted along the other side of the low stone wall, they stopped at the last house on the lane. It was a stylish, sleek, newly built bungalow fronted with golden Cotswold stone and had yet to be filled with furniture.

"How fancy," Anwen exclaimed as Rupert arranged Julia and Barker in front of the new stone wall, wrapping around the perfect rows of fresh turf. "You must have been on quite the salary when you moved here, Barker."

"Not quite. My cottage was destroyed by the same storm that cracked the flagstones that uncovered the basement under the café." Barker starred off to the telegraph pole that had crashed through the sitting room of the long-gone cottage. "This belongs to James Jacobson, not that he's moved in yet. Built just last year. We were all surprised by how sensitive the design was to the landscape when the scaffolding came down."

"An actress tried to build a huge glass monstrosity there in the interim," Julia pointed out. "The Peridale Preservation Society didn't like that too much."

"Don't stand in the way of a small village and its heritage, right?" Anwen chuckled. "I've only been here for a few days but keep hearing about that Jacobson man. Who is he, and do you think he'll be willing to be interviewed for the documentary?"

Just mentioning James Jacobson made Julia squirm as Barker explained he was a property developer. She'd last seen him standing in the same spot the previous summer after his property development almost destroyed the village's public library. He'd relented on his plan, and after Julia and Barker helped him prove he hadn't been the one to shoot his wife, they'd all parted as friends. Despite saying he'd been ready to settle down, he hadn't been seen in the village since. He had, however, been the secret investor behind Benedict Langley's recent scheme to turn the flats at the Fern Moore estate into holiday lets. A scheme that had put Benedict behind bars after he poisoned two people for standing in his way. Since finding out that James had fed Benedict funds, Julia had hoped she wouldn't see the elusive man in the area again. However, she maintained her smile for the camera while Barker explained a sanitised version of the story.

"Cut for now," Anwen declared once Rupert was satisfied they'd captured the best angles of Julia and Barker's first meeting spot. They set off down the lane towards the village green, and Anwen turned her attention back to their discovery in Howarth Forest. "How have you two been? I haven't been able to shake the image of that unfortunate man sprawled out in that ring of candles. We went to The Plough last night, and the place was buzzing with talk of an ancient cult returning to claim the people of the village."

"Peridale does like to gossip," Barker said. "Hear any mention of Lunara?"

"Lunara? Not that I heard," Anwen whispered, leaning in. "Why, do you know something?" She gasped, clicking her fingers together. "Wait, are you two on the case?"

Julia and Barker exchanged glances.

"Oh, this is *too* good. For the documentary, I mean. What will be better than following Julie North and DI Robert Greene—Julia and Barker—solving a murder in Perin—Peridale? It's just like your novel, Barker. What better way to sell the next one?"

"*If* we solve it," Barker corrected.

"So, you are investigating?" Anwen bit into her lip,

pausing at the corner of the green where Dot and Percy were throwing tennis balls for Lady and Bruce. Their eyes went straight to the camera, Dot adjusting her brooch, Percy checking his bowtie. "Given how eager the villagers have been to get in front of the camera, I think I could use it to interview around for more information."

"That could be useful." Julia couldn't argue with Anwen's reasoning, but the lights were already on in the café, and she wouldn't leave Sue to the morning's baking. "Now, if you'll excuse me, I have to get to work. And I have some Eton mess to prepare."

8

*J*essie arrived at the Fern Moore estate a little after ten. Technically part of the village but disowned by its residents thanks to its troubled reputation, the housing estate sheltered hundreds of low-income families. It comprised two utilitarian blocks, each filled with cramped, tiny flats. As Jessie parked her yellow Mini Cooper in a small car park facing the central concrete courtyard, she absorbed the sight before her. The courtyard with the wooden play park served as a focal point for the estate, but it stood in stark contrast to the pristinely manicured village green outside their café. Still, it was better than what had almost happened over the summer.

Holiday lets at Fern Moore?

Dumbest idea ever.

Jessie stepped out of her car, scanning the groups loitering in front of the row of shops, their vape clouds rising like factory plumes. A quick scan confirmed they weren't who she was looking for. She made her way down a graffiti-covered alley towards the metal shutters of the food bank.

Inside, she found Billy Matthews, her ex-boyfriend, spraying the bare walls in swathes of bright colour from a can in his good hand. His other arm hung by his side, still cast after his electric scooter crash and scribbled with signatures and drawings. Jessie's signature was on there somewhere. He was creating a mural of the estate, where a portrait of the late Ronnie Roberts shone from the sky. After what Benedict Langley did to the former fundraiser, Jessie hoped he was rotting in his prison cell.

"You've come a long way from tagging the stairwells with 'Billy Woz Here,'" Jessie announced as Billy added bold strokes to the tower blocks. "How's it going?"

Billy stopped spraying and spun around with a grin. "Jessie! Didn't expect to see you here. And thanks. Hilda wanted to paint them white, but I thought I'd put my cans to good use."

"And what a marvellous job you're doing," Hilda, the food bank's owner, called from the back, where she was organising the shelves. "How's your mum, Jessie?"

After some small talk, Hilda let Billy take a break, and Billy and Jessie found themselves on the swings at the park eating chicken wraps from McSizzle's Chicken Shop around the corner. For a moment, it felt like they were back to the teenagers they'd once been. But Jessie wasn't just there for a chicken wrap and a catch-up. After some chitchat about how Billy was getting on in his new job working full-time at the food bank, Jessie filled him in on the reason for her impromptu visit.

"Yeah, I've heard of the Crew," Billy said, crinkling his foil wrapper and tossing it at the bin. He missed. "You don't want to go messing with them. They're the real deal."

"You sound like my dad." Licking the extra mayo from her lips, Jessie threw her wrapper and hit the target in one. "I'm not trying to mess with them. I just want to know about them. If you've heard of them, I'm going to guess they're around the estate?"

"Too much for my liking."

So much for Veronica thinking Fern Moore would be a dead-end.

"Are they based here?"

Billy shook his head, the uneasy look remaining. "They come sniffing around the place regularly. Someone always needs cash, and they always have stuff that needs doing."

"Thugs for hire, according to my dad."

"That about sums it up," he said, kicking his shoes against the woodchips. "Like I said, Jessie, you don't want to mess with them. Tommy G from flat 38 had both his knees broken when he grassed them to the police after they didn't pay him for delivering something on their behalf. And they stuck a fire bomb through Gina's letterbox at 29 when she asked too many questions about her missing cousin."

That did sound like the real deal.

"Hear about that guy found in Howarth Forest yesterday?" Jessie asked, and Billy nodded. "A chap by the name of Arthur Foster. He might have been working for the Crew. Burned down a house. The family who lived there are distraught. If there is one, I'm just trying to figure out the connection. From what you just said, they aren't into random attacks?"

"Not their style. You can tell them apart because they wear suits. Proper fancy blokes to look at, and they drive nice cars with blacked-out windows. I saw some of them around here a few nights ago."

"Whereabouts?"

"Round the back," he said, nodding off. "Might be worth a shot?"

They jumped off the swings just in time for some children who should have been at school to take over. They set off across the courtyard and past the food bank as Hilda handed out parcels. At the end of the row of storage units, they turned right and right again into an unfamiliar long alley. Graffiti lined the walls, less refined than what Billy had sprayed in the food bank. Murmurs of banter echoed as they approached a hooded group, their faces lit up by phone screens. A head nod from Billy settled their glares long enough for them to pass without trouble.

They rounded the corner of the block, the sprawling fields behind the buildings leading right back to the village. A sleek black car with tinted windows was parked in the shadows of the blocks, starkly contrasting the grimy surroundings. Two tall figures in black suits were next to the vehicle, silhouetted against its gleaming paint. They were beating a young man against the wall, the rhythmic thuds of their fists punctuating the otherwise silent afternoon.

Adrenaline surged through Jessie as she took a step forward, but just as she was about to shout, a firm hand tugged her back into the tunnel.

"Billy?" she whispered. "Get off."

"We can't get involved," he replied. "You wanted to know about the Crew? That's them. Two of them, at least, and two might as well be twenty. They'll be armed with more than fists."

Jessie stared into Billy's eyes, full of cautious fear, and took a deep breath that did nothing to calm her. She lunged forward again, and Billy pinned her against the wall this time.

"This isn't a game," he said, almost in a growl. "You're my mate, Jessie, but I won't jump in after you if you get involved." Letting go, he ran his good hand over his stubbly jaw and said, "I... I have a girlfriend now."

The sudden revelation surprised Jessie. She almost forgot about what she'd just witnessed. Gulping, Jessie managed an unsteady smile.

"That's great, Billy."

"Yeah, it is," he said with a shrug. "Look, we should get out of here before they figure out they've been seen. They won't like that."

The weight of Billy's sudden confession had knocked Jessie a little sideways. But she wasn't ready to give up, not when she'd already got so close to the elusive gang. Pulling her phone from her pocket, she adjusted the settings to turn off the flash.

Billy's eyes widened. "Jessie, are you mad? If they see you—"

"They won't."

Without making a noise, she leaned just enough to snap a quick picture of the two suited men, ensuring the shiny black car was in the frame. Pulling away from the wall, she stashed her phone securely in her pocket.

"No licence plate. Bit odd."

"We should get..." Billy's voice trailed off as he turned. Two more suited men were at the alley's far end, silencing the lads who could only stare at the floor. "Bloody hell. We're screwed."

"There must be another way?"

Billy clenched his eyes as though tracing the estate's layout, and Jessie couldn't recall ever seeing him look so scared.

"A few steps back, a stairwell to the left leads down to a service basement and comes out on the other side of the block. We can slip out there, but if it looks like we're running..."

Jessie grabbed his hand and dragged him away from the opening. "Head down, quick steps. You know the drill."

The men in suits weren't paying them much attention, too busy talking in whispers that the walls didn't pick up to echo. Once they reached the stairwell, Jessie dared a glance, neither of them recognisable to her. They looked like clones of the other two, still landing punches in the man's guts if his whimpers were anything to go by.

Taking the steps two at a time, they descended the cold, concrete staircase into the ground, the echoes making Jessie more anxious with each step.

"So, a girlfriend?" Jessie said. "What's she like?"

"I'm with Paige. We're giving it a proper go."

Jessie nodded. Paige had been Ronnie Roberts' neighbour during the holiday lets scandal. A feisty mother of two with cherry-red hair, she'd been one of the prime suspects. Billy had been sleeping on Paige's sofa the last Jessie heard. He'd befriended Paige's boyfriend in the army before a landmine wiped him out of the picture. They'd seemed close when Jessie had visited Billy at the hospital after he broke his arm. She should have known.

"I guess that makes you a stepdad?" Jessie said, the chicken wrap not sitting right in her stomach. "Looks like you got everything you wanted."

"I guess I did," Billy replied, looking thoughtful. "What about you, Jessie? What do you want if not to get yourself killed by the Crew?"

Jessie hesitated as they hit ground level, the dampness of the basement thick in the air. "Right now, I want to discover the truth about their connection to Arthur."

"Well, that was too close for my liking. You've got some nerve."

"And I got some evidence."

"Yeah?" Billy let out a strained laugh. "You might have just put a target on your back, too. And mine."

"Nobody saw us, and—"

"You don't know that!" Billy snapped, turning to face the rumbling generator. "A lunch break, you said. You might not have anything to lose right now, but I do." Billy's words stung, and he sighed as though he knew he'd gone too far. He rested a hand on her shoulder. "You're not going to take down the Crew, and whatever they wanted with this fire family, maybe it's best to leave it alone. Keep yourself safe, yeah? I don't want to have to be worrying about you."

"You don't have to, mate," she replied, shrugging his hand off her shoulder. "Thanks for the info. I'll let you get back to your spraying."

They stepped out into the brighter world above and parted with a quick hug. Jessie felt Billy's silent plea not to go looking for the Crew in his lingering stare before he returned to the food bank. Alone in her car, Jessie looked over the picture again. She hadn't expected to get so close so soon, but what did she have outside of a picture of some guys in suits next to a black car? She hadn't even captured the poor fella getting the wind beat out of him.

Still, Jessie sent the picture to Veronica and reversed out of the car park, ready to return to Peridale. She'd take her chances with a cult over the Crew.

9

*I*n the shadowy office beneath the café, Barker sat across from Wanda, a dishevelled but spirited woman with a bandage around her head. Her gigantic Doberman, Hercules, drooled all over Barker's leg. Behind them on the leather sofa, DI Moyes watched with amusement.

"So, Wanda," Barker said, going over the notes he'd made, "you were walking Hercules in Howarth Forest, and that's when you saw the cloaked figure?"

"That's right," Wanda exclaimed, her eyes wide with excitement. "I was minding my own business, trying to stop Hercules from chasing squirrels, when I saw exactly that. A cloaked figure dressed in all black. It was like something out of an old Hammer horror film!"

"And this cloaked figure was carrying someone over their shoulder?" Barker clarified, trying not to laugh at the image in his mind. "A man, you said? How did you know it was a man?"

Wanda nodded vigorously, her hand going up to the bandage as though doing so had made her dizzy.

"Because he was alive and groaning like he'd had one too many at the pub," Wanda said. "Honestly, I thought they were off for some how's-your-father if you catch my drift, but then I thought to myself, 'Why the cloak, Wanda?'"

"Why the cloak, indeed," DI Moyes echoed.

"And what happened next?"

"That's when I ran off to raise the alarm, but I tripped on a root, twisted my ankle, and bumped my head on a rock," Wanda explained, pointing to her bandaged head. "The next thing I remember after that is waking up in the hospital this morning. Hercules is such a good boy. He ran home and led my husband back to find me passed out in the forest. I could have been killed too."

Barker pushed the tissue box across his desk before giving Hercules a congratulatory scratch between his eyes. He thanked Barker with more drool. Wanda pulled out several tissues, blowing her nose so hard she was forced to clutch her bandage again.

DI Moyes rose from the sofa. "Thank you for

sharing your story, Wanda. Unless Barker has further questions, I think you should go and lie down."

Wanda hoisted herself up from the chair, but Hercules had other ideas. With a sudden pull, the enormous Doberman dragged Wanda up the stairs leading out of the office. Barker glanced down at the shiny trail of drool Hercules had left behind. He plucked out a tissue and dabbed at his trousers.

DI Moyes moved to occupy the now-vacant chair across from Barker.

"So," she began, leaning back, "twenty-three locals came forward with their versions of the event, all claiming to be the star witness. But Wanda's story is the only one correlating with the evidence."

Barker raised an eyebrow, intrigued. "Do explain."

"Arthur had a head injury, which explains the groaning Wanda described," she said. "We're still trying to figure out what he was struck with. The coroner placed his time of death between 5 and 5:20 p.m., aligning perfectly with Wanda's timeline."

Barker leaned back, tossing the tissue into the wastepaper basket by his vinyl player. "The tealight candles, the cloak... It's all a bit textbook. And Arthur over the shoulder must rule out anyone without the upper body strength?"

"I wouldn't be so sure. The man was five feet three inches and weighed nine stone. I could have picked him up without much effort." Moyes smirked, moving to get up. "Thanks for the Lunara lead. After bringing you Wanda, I'd say we're square. But keep me posted if you come across anything more."

"Found any connection with the Cotswold Crew?"

DI Moyes's eyes widened slightly, and she sat back down. "Nothing concrete, but Arthur was picked up a few times for arson over the last few years. Nothing like what he did to the Knight's residence, but going over his case files, he didn't seem like the brightest bulb in the bunch. He admitted to enjoying starting fires in his last interview. Should have locked him up then, but the judge gave him a suspended sentence and a slap on the wrist, even though, to DI Christie, it was obvious he wasn't targeting random people, despite his admission."

"He never gave up a name?"

"Loyal to a fault. Nothing connects the Crew's activities with the Knights or Arthur Foster, but they are good at that. They're old school. Everything is offline, non-digital. Hard to trace. I heard they don't even have names to give up."

"What've they got you on another Peridale job for, anyway? Riverswick must be missing its new DI?"

"You're not in the loop anymore, are you?" Moyes laughed, pulling her electronic cigarette from her pocket. She took one quick puff. "They're saying your old position is cursed. No DI has lasted more than a few years, and nobody wanted the internal promotion after they sacked DI Christie for blundering the festival case." She motioned to the field behind the café, tucking her vape away, a smile softening her face. "They offered me a pay rise to transfer after we closed the food bank case, so I asked for a little more, and they bit my hand off. And, I suppose, Roxy lives in the village, and she's why I decided to stop travelling after years on the road solving cold cases. But if things keep up like this with capes and cults, I might start believing in those curse rumours."

"We'll have to go for a celebratory drink soon if people in cloaks don't come for you first."

"If you can pull yourself away from writing."

"The draft is somewhat finished, and since you brought it up," Barker said, opening the top drawer to pull out a copy of the manuscript. "I know you're busy, but would you do me the honour of giving it a scan? I wouldn't ask, but you were the officer on the capsule case. As much as I love Julia and Jessie, I need brutal honesty. I have a feeling it's naff."

Moyes flicked through the manuscript, but her sigh let him know it was more a burden than an honour. "If I have time to read it, you owe me another one." She stuffed the manuscript into her bag and finally stood, checking her watch. "I need to get to the

B&B to interview Sophia and Derek again. I don't know what, but I'm sure they're hiding something from me."

"Not just me then," Barker said, saluting as Moyes made her way to the stairs. "Let me know about that drink."

Before Barker could return to his notes, footsteps pounded down the staircase before Moyes could close the door. Anwen charged into the office, the camera already lit up behind her, her face alight with anticipation.

"I've had some promising conversations with locals who claim to have seen the whole thing happen, but it seems you've got more to tell after a meeting with the DI. Got a minute to update the viewers?"

Before Barker could protest, the camera was again in his face, and he didn't try to mask his annoyed expression.

∽

Leaving Sue to manage the chaotic café, where regulars were lost in loud debates about 'the moon cult', Julia sought clarity from the Knight women.

Upon entering the B&B, Evelyn, dressed in flowing

black, guided Julia upstairs to the floor the Knights occupied exclusively. The room resembled another realm, adorned with delicate pink curtains dancing in the gentle breeze, celestial paintings, and crystals covering every wooden surface. An Eastern-sounding instrument hummed softly in the background.

Sophia, cross-legged on the edge of the bed, her dark red hair cascading over her shoulders, was deep in meditation. Faith sat on the windowsill, gazing out at the garden. Despite Julia having called ahead, neither woman turned to greet her. Evelyn excused herself to serve lunch, leaving Julia in the doorway, and she stepped in, clearing her throat.

"Thank you for speaking with me," Julia began, her voice drawing Sophia back to reality. "I brought you some Eton mess, made fresh this morning."

"Did you use organic and locally sourced produce?" Sophia asked.

"Always." Julia left the tray on the dresser, sure it wouldn't be touched. "I know we haven't met, but my husband, Barker, mentioned your distress after Arthur's appearance. How are you both this afternoon?"

"Fine." Sophia uncrossed her legs and said, "The police have already talked to us. Faith and I were together the entire night after Barker's visit."

Julia raised a brow at Faith, still staring out the window. "Did you both sleep in the same room?"

Before Faith could respond, Sophia interjected, "Given Arthur's threat, it seemed safest."

Julia's eyes darted between the two women, sensing unspoken tension.

"Do you have any other connection with Arthur besides the fire?" Sophia began to shake her head, but Julia focused on Faith, "Faith?"

"No,," Faith whispered, hesitating slightly. "Just the fire."

"And the way he was killed?" Julia continued, approaching the dresser covered in crystals. "The forest, the candles, moon symbols... Does the 'Lunara cult' mean anything?"

"Please don't touch my crystals!" Sophia cried, standing up to guide Julia away. "I don't want your distrustful energy on them, especially now."

Julia reflected on the accusation and acknowledged her scepticism. Barker had warned her that the family was guarded, and she sensed the same. Sophia's answers felt rehearsed, though she may have exhausted spontaneity with the police.

"The cult?" Julia pushed.

Sophia tutted, joining her daughter at the window. "What a preposterous statement," she muttered. "They're not a cult. They were a Celtic religious sect."

Julia's eyes narrowed, "How do you know this?"

"My husband is an Oxford professor. We are educated. Do you have a background in education, Julia?"

Sophia was deflecting, but Julia stood firm. "I studied patisserie and baking at college and enjoyed it very much." Julia sampled one of the untouched desserts. "Did you tell the police about this religious sect?"

"It hardly seems relevant."

"A man was murdered yesterday, surrounded by moon symbols," Julia countered, licking the cream from her lips. "Seems relevant to me."

"Yes, I'm sure it does." Sophia turned to Julia, clutching a crystal around her neck. With a huff, she said, "I should help Evelyn with lunch. If you'll excuse me."

And with that, Sophia swept out of the room.

Julia wasn't going to follow her. Sensing an opportunity, Julia closed the door and picked up another glass of Eton mess with a spoon. She perched on the windowsill next to Faith and passed her the dessert with a smile. Faith returned the smile and accepted the offering. She stirred the spoon around the top layer, but none reached her mouth.

"Have you been eating?" Julia asked.

Faith shook her head, but she forced herself to

take a bite. She chewed it slowly and swallowed hard before placing the glass on the floor.

"Faith, there's more to this story, right?"

Faith's eyes glistened with unshed tears; her posture deflated. She looked heartbroken, and Julia wondered if the rumours about her connection to Arthur were true. Julia had never lost a partner, but she'd lost a mother and hadn't been able to eat then either. With the soft hum of meditation music, Julia was determined to uncover some of the veil of secrecy before leaving.

In the silence, while she let Faith warm up to her presence, Julia noticed something that didn't add up—a contradiction between husband and wife. Derek had been clueless about the Lunara cult when he spoke to Barker, but Sophia seemed well-versed, almost confident, claiming she'd learned the information from Derek. Both could have been lying, but Sophia's explanation felt far too convenient.

"Your mother spoke with some authority when talking about this Lunara religious sect," Julia began, breaking the silence. "She almost seemed offended that I'd dare refer to them as a cult."

"We're not in a cult," Faith muttered, resting the side of her forehead against the windowpane. "I think it's what people are probably saying. It's the picture the police were trying to paint. It's ridiculous."

Julia tilted her head to meet Faith's eyes. "How does your mother know so much about the Lunara sect then?"

With a sigh, Faith left the window and searched several drawers. She pulled out a manuscript, bold in purple, its title embossed in gold.

The Lost Religions of the Cotswolds.

The author's name?

Sophia Knight.

"My mum wrote this," Faith admitted. "My dad stumbled upon some old academic papers about lost religions in the area, stuff that isn't even online, and she became consumed by it. She's spent years digging through old papers in private libraries, using all my father's contacts to write this thing. I haven't read it, but Lunara should be in there."

Julia's fingers itched to peruse the pages. "Can I borrow this?"

Faith clutched the book closer. "It's an advanced copy. The publisher isn't in a rush to get it out there. Mum would kill me if it went missing. She'd kill me if she knew I'd even told you about it, but I'm tired of pretending."

"Pretending about what?" Julia sensed the walls rising again, so she cut to the chase. "Faith, were you and Arthur involved?"

Faith's eyes widened. She seemed stunned by the

bluntness of the question. Yet, as the seconds ticked by and she didn't deny it, her red, swollen eyes and the tears threatening to spill over told Julia all she needed to know.

"He was different around me," Faith finally whispered, placing the manuscript on the windowsill. "When it was just us, you'd never know he was the same man. People never saw that side of him. He felt trapped, said he was with the wrong group, and wanted out. I tried to help him. I was so close, but he got cold feet, and—"

"The Cotswold Crew?"

Just as Faith looked set to answer, the bedroom door creaked open, revealing Derek's livid face, his cheeks as crimson as Faith's hair.

"Enough, Faith," he said, silencing her like a talkative teenager in a lecture. He turned his fierce glare on Julia. "My business is with your husband, not you. I'd appreciate you keeping your meddling nose out of our affairs."

The implied threat hung between them. Julia wanted to push the subject of the gang further, but there was nothing more to be gained without stepping on Barker's toes. Nodding curtly, Julia stood, but not before slipping the manuscript into her bag.

Away from the prying eyes of the lunching guests, Julia settled on a step and flipped open the book. She was about to delve into the Knights' secrets, the Lunara sect, and possibly the key to Arthur's death. Her hands trembled as she ran her finger along the table of contents. Despite Sophia's insistence that they weren't any such thing, 'Cult of Lunara' was listed on Page 28.

Julia found herself drawn to a detailed passage describing one of their full moon rituals, which she realised bore a startling resemblance to the haunting scene at Howarth House:

The Sacrifice of the Moon's Beloved

...their rituals were dictated by the lunar cycle. On the night of the new moon, the darkest evening, they would gather in sacred stone circles deep within the Cotswolds' rolling hills. There, under the star-studded sky, they would ask for Lunara's guidance, offering libations of mead and promises of devotion. But they held the most chilling of rites on the night of the full moon. According to local legends, the Cult of Lunara believed that human life was the most precious offering to their goddess. They thought this supreme sacrifice would imbue the community with Lunara's blessings, providing bountiful harvests, protection from enemies, and favour in love. Each full moon, a member of the cult, was chosen to be the Moon's Beloved. It was seen as a great honour, a sacred duty to their deity. The selected individual would be lavishly feasted and celebrated in the lead-up to the full moon. When the night came, under the brilliant lunar glow, they would willingly meet their fate, their life offered in service to the moon. Despite the horrifying nature of their rituals, the Cult of Lunara saw themselves not as bringers of death but as disciples of a cycle of life and rebirth. They believed that those sacrificed to Lunara would be reborn under her glowing light, living on as part of the moon that watched over—

Before she could read further, a familiar voice interrupted her.

"Julia," Evelyn cleared her throat pointedly, her hand outstretched. "I believe you have something that belongs to Sophia."

Julia looked up, startled. Evelyn wasn't someone Julia would have associated with such a secretive group, but as Julia met her gaze, she remembered an offhand comment Evelyn had made the previous month. She'd spoken about the powers of the full moon and how it charged her crystals. She'd even mentioned the word 'cult' before Julia's gran had abruptly changed the subject. Dressed all in black, like the cloak the witness had seen, Evelyn looked uncomfortable, her usually warm eyes clouded.

"I was given the book to preview," she admitted. "Sophia and I became friends after we met at a yoga retreat. We've been quite close since."

"Evelyn, do you know more about this? About the Cult of Lunara?"

Evelyn cast a wary glance around the hallway. "Not here. I'll meet you at your cottage after I finish dinner service."

10

Barker stared at the frozen image of his former publicist on his laptop in his office. He snapped the lid shut, ending the video call. Izzy had been frozen for at least thirty seconds, but she'd said everything he needed to hear.

"Mystery Triangle Publishing doesn't have any interest in even reading the manuscript," Izzy had said after their initial catch-up. They hadn't seen each other since the press tour she'd arranged for his first book. She'd placed him and his book before thousands, securing him spots on television and radio talk shows nationwide. "Sorry, pal. I'm sure you've written something good enough so I could put some feelers out. But... they said you were 'difficult', and the publishing world isn't big enough for something like that not to have spread around. There's always self-publishing?"

Barker leaned back in his leather chair with a sigh. The sting of rejection was hard to shake off, although he hadn't been too surprised given the disastrous end of his Mystery Triangle collaboration. They'd snapped up his first book without hesitation, offering him a three-book deal on the spot. The first book had been smooth sailing, but they'd rejected his following two attempts at a second book before he'd abandoned writing to focus on private investigating.

Before Barker could dwell on doubt, Anwen popped up on the intercom screen. The director had only been gone for a few hours after her last exhausting round of interviews about the case, but he couldn't turn her away. He let her in with a press of the button and waited.

Letting in some of the setting sun's rays through the door, Anwen carried the camera—its light off—but she was otherwise alone.

"Given them the night off," Anwen said, setting down the camera on his desk. "They've gone for a drink at Richie's Bar."

"Aren't you joining them?"

"I'll have drinks when the shoot is finished," she said, her smile tight. "If you aren't in a rush to get home, I thought we might have a deeper chat without the distractions. I'm curious to know more about the case that inspired your first book." She gestured towards the tall potted plant. "That's where she was found. Evelyn's daughter?"

Barker turned to the corner of the room, nodding. The plant had grown strong, its green fronds reaching the low ceiling. Tiny, shining crystals were wedged in the soil, brought in semi-regularly by Evelyn, a silent reminder of what happened there before it became Barker's office. Evelyn would stop by, spending moments in quiet reflection beside the plant. For her, it was sacred; for Barker, it symbolised one of the most challenging cases he'd witnessed as a DI.

"That was a difficult time for everyone," Barker recalled as the camera light turned on. He was getting used to ignoring it. "Evelyn's such a light around this village and that was her darkest hour. She says my book brought her closure, but I don't know…" He glanced back at the plant. "I suppose that whole ordeal sent me on the journey I've been on since. I don't think I'd be sitting here at this desk if not for that case. That storm destroyed my cottage and a little of my faith in humanity. If not for being head over heels in love with Julia, I'm not sure I would have stuck in Peridale after that."

"And yet here you are, with another book on the way."

Barker laughed, unsure if he should reveal Izzy's call to Anwen or the camera. He held his tongue, retrieving the fresh manuscript. He'd been resisting sending Laura Moyes a text message all afternoon.

"I suppose it's an outlet," he confessed. "A way to make sense of it all. My first book wasn't written for the market or the publishers. I think I wrote it because I needed to."

"You said you were inspired to solve mysteries because of reading mysteries with your mother? Do you want to go deeper into that?"

Among his wedding picture, a photo from the first scan of Olivia, and a shot of the whole family at Dot's from the previous Christmas—Jessie had two fingers held up behind his head—the mahogany frame encasing the picture of him and his mum stood alone; she was the only person photographed he hadn't seen for years. The stark contrast between her frailty and radiant smile was always a heart-wrenching reminder of the strength she'd carried, even on her deathbed when the picture had been taken. His older brother, Casper, had been behind the camera, insisting Barker should take the picture, the silent agreement between them all that it would likely be the last.

Barker smiled at the photograph. "Peggy Brown. Swore like a sailor and had a heart of gold. She would have given you the shirt off her back before you even needed to ask for it. It's coming up on a decade without her. I don't know where the years have gone."

"Never gets easier, does it?" Anwen said with a sigh, her bubbly personality absent. "I don't have any family left."

Barker paused. "What about your grandparents back home?"

"Long gone," Anwen admitted. "Why do you think I'm never in a rush to go back? Grandad went first, and then my gran not too long after. Haven't been back since her funeral." She paused, and he squinted behind the camera, pushing the box of tissues forward. They went unclaimed. "I... I wasn't even there when they died. I was filming, too busy to go back to see them. I knew I should have, but I just didn't. I suppose you always think you have more time, even at the end. But I know they're looking down on me, guiding me in the right direction."

The admission caught Barker off guard, and he felt closer to the director.

"I'm sorry to hear that," Barker said, smiling towards her shadow beyond the light. "And you're right, it doesn't get easier. I suppose I haven't been back home since either."

"You've made yourself a fine home here, Barker," she said, smiling. "And your mother gave you a gift.

She inspired your love for mysteries. Those trips to the bookshop you told me about?"

Barker reminisced about those childhood Saturday afternoons, where mysteries were more than just stories. They were bonding moments, experiences shared between mother and son. The light scent of old book pages and the muffled sounds of chatter would surround them as they'd become engrossed in the new arrivals at their favourite bookshop, an old rundown place tucked down a backstreet in his hometown of Sheffield. His mum had despised the modern places laid out like supermarkets. Books in hand, they'd walk back to the bus stop to read those first few lines together while they waited for their bus back home.

"I'd give anything to have one of those Saturdays again," Barker said, frowning into the darkness after the story spilt out. "It wasn't about the books, really. I have three brothers: a set of younger twins and an older brother, so I was the middle child, but Mum always made time for those book trips."

"And what about your father? I noticed you had your mother's maiden name?"

A lump hardened in Barker's throat.

"Could be anyone," he stated, teasing the edge of his manuscript. "Mum took that secret to the grave with her. Next question."

A moment of silence settled between them, and Barker could feel Anwen trying to figure out which angles to pursue. Glancing at the camera, he wished he hadn't shared any of it. He wasn't sure he had more questioning in him. Suddenly, all he wanted to do was go home to be with the family he'd built in Peridale, so he was glad when another buzz at the door interrupted them.

Barker sat upright, swallowing the lump as he blinked at the video screen on his desk. Two young men waited outside, one red-haired and the other with jet-black hair and lined eyes.

"Rupert and Ava, by any chance?"

"No," Barker said, his finger hovering over the unlock button. "Case related, and I'd rather my private meetings stayed out of the documentary."

"Understood," Anwen stood up, hoisting up the camera. "We'll continue our chat another time. And Barker, that was some good stuff. I know digging in the old memory banks can be difficult, so well done."

Anwen left, and Mark, Evelyn's grandson, and Nathan, the youngest Knight, entered. Nathan looked around the room with an impressed nod, but Mark lingered on the stairs.

Barker couldn't blame him. Mark was born in that room, then snatched from his dying mother to be raised by someone claiming to be his mother for twenty years. And then some bloke wrote a book about the whole thing and made the place his office.

"You wanted to know where it was," Mark said, his eyes fixed on the plant in the corner. "Here it is. I'll wait outside."

Mark slipped out of the office as Nathan flicked through the vinyl records at the player by the filing cabinet. Barker usually enjoyed some jazz spinning, another leftover from his mother, but the office had been quieter than usual lately, something he attributed to book stress.

"I had a collection at home before the fire," Nathan said, selecting an Ella Fitzgerald record. "All gone now."

Barker glanced at the door, half-expecting Derek Knight to run down and wrap a hand around his son's mouth. As Nathan continued to peruse the records, Barker realised they were alone for the first time and that Nathan's visit wasn't about the records.

"Do you ever feel alone?" Nathan began, his voice small as he examined the record. "Like surrounded by family constantly, but so utterly isolated?"

Barker frowned, echoes of his conversation about his family still rattling around the place. He offered Nathan the chair across from him, ready for the young man to open up.

"Sometimes," Barker admitted. "Why do you feel that way?"

"I'm not like them." Nathan exhaled, his gaze drifting to the far wall. "The fire destroyed more than my vinyl records. I'd been collecting beetles for years. I had types from around the world: Sun beetles, stag, rhinoceros. I spent so long taking care of them. They were like friends to me. All gone. Destroyed. Because of him."

"Arthur?"

Nathan hesitated before nodding. "He was making my life hell."

"How?"

"He'd been cyberstalking me for months," Nathan admitted. "Using fake names, fake profiles, ridiculing me everywhere. Beetle forums, music blogs, and all my social media profiles. I couldn't escape him. I didn't know it was Arthur at first, but he kept mixing up 'you're' with 'your', that sort of thing. I didn't put it together until I saw the same writing in text messages to my sister."

Barker's brow furrowed. "Why target you?"

"I still don't know," Nathan said, his tone bitter. "He targeted Faith, too."

Barker recalled what Julia had discovered at the B&B earlier. Faith hadn't admitted to being in a relationship with Arthur, but she might as well have.

He glanced at the door again, but still no sign of Derek.

"Arthur was never into her, not really," Nathan whispered. "It was all just to mess with Dad. Faith has got this thing with guys. Ever since her first bad-boy boyfriend, Faith's always gone after men she thinks she can fix. Arthur was just her latest project, but she couldn't see that she was his project. Just a pawn in his game."

Barker leaned back, absorbing the information. "But what game, Nathan? Why would Arthur want to target your family?"

"I don't know," he said. "Not for certain."

Sensing there was more, Barker leaned forward again.

"And if you were to make an educated guess?"

Sighing, Nathan said, "Dad inherited more than just the house from Grandad. Some land, not too far from here. It's useless. It's too narrow to build on. It's been in the family for generations, but as all of this has happened these last few months, my parents keep mentioning it."

Barker raised an eyebrow. "And where is this land?"

"I'll show you," Nathan said, standing. "It's not far from here. Should be able to see it before the sun goes down."

More than a little intrigued, Barker followed Nathan up the wooden stairs and into the yard behind the café. Through the kitchen window, Barker saw Sue, Julia, Jessie, and Olivia sharing a moment of happiness. His heart swelled, yearning to join them. The sight of Mark perched on a crate, lost in the shadows, brought him back to the moment.

Barker joined Nathan on the narrow path between the back of the café and the vast field, a sprawling carpet of untrimmed green punctuated by the occasional dandelion. Barker inhaled deeply, the scent of damp earth and fresh grass filling his nostrils.

Memories of the Cotswold Crowd Pleaser Festival still lingered in the air. Barker could hardly believe how alive the place had been exactly a year ago when the festival and a record number of tourists had descended on the village. He could almost smell the popcorn Julia had sold behind the café where they were standing. The festival might have gone off without a hitch if not for the power blow-out that had killed the headliner's lead singer at St. Peter's Church during rehearsals. Riots had followed, and upset music lovers had ripped the village to pieces, the café included. But the trampled field had since returned to its natural state, the café had been refurbished, and Barker hadn't heard anyone complain that Peridale had been chosen as the location in a while.

For Julia and Barker, the field was more than just the tragic landmark of the festival. It was where they often stared out after busy days, letting the breeze carry away their stress and worries. For most locals, it was a place to walk their dogs and lay picnic blankets when the green was packed with tourists.

"See those trees far in the distance?" Nathan asked, pointing to the far edge of the field. "There's a road on the other side that never used to be there. The council forced my grandfather to have the road put through the middle of his farm. I think he ended up selling off most of his land, and the farmhouse was knocked down years ago, but for some reason, he clung to two strips of land that ran on either side of the road. My dad inherited them with the house."

"And why are they important?"

"That's why I came to see you," Nathan said with a shrug. "I thought maybe you could figure it out. I keep catching my parents whispering about the land when they think no one is around, but we're practically living on top of each other at the B&B, and the walls are as thin as paper. I finally asked him why he kept bringing up the land over dinner, and he refused to discuss it. He only does that when it's something important. He didn't tell us about Grandad's cancer until the end, and he won't let us talk about Arthur to the police. I think he thinks he's protecting us. We've lost everything."

"You still have each other," Barker pointed out, resting a hand on Nathan's shoulder. "Your parents won't be around to keep tabs on you forever."

Barker was glad Nathan had come to see him to get some burdens off his chest, but he wasn't sure how they connected. The cyberstalking was something, as were the two strips of land far off in the distance, but he wasn't sure how they all connected to Arthur and the cult.

"Thank you, Nathan," Barker said. "I appreciate you coming to see me tonight. You've given me a lot to investigate. A sight more than your father has. If there's nothing else, I'll let you get back."

Nathan signalled for Mark, who got up from the crate, looking equally downtrodden.

"Mark?" Barker called as the two walked through the gate, hoping to bridge their gap. "Can we talk before you go?"

But Mark left without a word.

Barker sighed. For now, the case would have to wait. Tomorrow, he'd dig further into what Nathan had shared and confront Derek with the information he'd been withholding. Tonight, before the sun set on another day, he needed to spend time with his family.

Barker joined the chatter in the café's kitchen, and

as he stepped in, Olivia's hazel eyes lit up as she squealed and reached out for him from her highchair. He couldn't help but smile, the stress of the evening momentarily forgotten, as he lifted her into his arms.

"Hi, Daddy," she exclaimed, her pudgy fingers gripping his shirt collar. Barker kissed her cheek, the simple joy of the moment a welcome relief.

"Got a picture of the gang earlier," Jessie remarked, flashing her phone. Barker saw two men in dark suits behind what looked like the blocks at Fern Moore. "And don't worry, they didn't see me. Not bad for day one, right?"

Barker bit back another pointless lecture. "Not bad, indeed."

"And Evelyn's coming to our cottage later," Julia said. "She seems ready to discuss what she knows about the Cult of Lunara."

Sue, wiping her hands on a cloth, said, "And I, being the only normal one here, will go home to watch *The Great British Bake-Off* with my husband and daughters. Have you ever tried watching TV, like the rest of us, instead of playing Scooby-Doo every chance you get? I'll finish up in the front."

Sue pushed through the beads, and Barker picked up on a Welsh accent.

"Eton mess," Julia mouthed as an explanation for Anwen. "How'd the interview go?"

"Interviews, and they went okay. I got to know a little more about Anwen. Doesn't seem to have many people in her life."

"Peridale has a way of taking in the strays," Jessie said, digging into her own Eton mess. "Really good, by the way, Mum. Strawberries, cream, and meringue. Simple but effective. What even is an Eton mess, anyway?"

"I did a little research while making it, since it wasn't in Mum's recipe book," Julia said. "They've been serving it at cricket matches at Eton college since the nineteenth century. It's quite the tradition."

"I heard a funny story once," Barker said, recalling hearing something on a police course near Eton. "They say it came about because a dog sat on a picnic basket containing a pavlova. Turned the whole thing into a mess."

"Thanks to that dog." Jessie saluted with her spoon. "But back to more pressing matters, if we are Mystery Inc., which one am I?" She thought too hard about the question as she crammed in a big mouthful. "Probably Shaggy, right? Which makes you two... Daphne and Fred?" She jutted her spoon at them before waving it to Olivia. "And you, small and slightly annoying, are Scrappy-Doo, which just leaves Velma and—"

A loud crash echoed from the front, followed by

Sue's terrified scream. Barker's heart leapt, and he handed Scrappy-Doo back to Julia. Bursting through the beads, he joined Anwen and Sue, twisting to stare through the window.

"You've got to be kidding me," Anwen muttered, grabbing the camera from the chair beside her.

Inching towards the window, Barker's eyes widened at the mysterious figure standing in the village green, swathed in deep black, exactly as the star witness had described. The cloaked stranger stood still in the hazy light. Hood pulled low to conceal every feature, their dark gaze was fixed on the café. They lifted a gloved hand and waved.

"What the…" Jessie muttered.

"Call the station," Julia said. "Barker, don't—"

Barker's instincts had already kicked in. Charging out of the café, he sprinted towards the mysterious figure, who turned and set off at a lightning sprint towards St. Peter's Church.

Without hesitation, Barker chased them, feet pounding over the cobblestone road. The cloaked figure vaulted over the church wall, nearly colliding with Dot and Percy, walking their dogs in the graveyard. Dot screamed, yanking Percy to the ground.

"It's happening again!" she shrieked. "You won't take my Percy, do you hear?"

Distracted by his grandmother-in-law's outburst, Barker tripped over a gravestone, pain searing through his knee. Despite the agony, he pushed himself up and continued his pursuit into Howarth Forest.

The figure was leading him into the dense woods, but as the last rays of light vanished, so did the cloaked stranger. Catching his breath, Barker activated his phone's torch, the beam revealing Howarth House in the distance. Crunching footsteps made him spin around, bracing for a confrontation.

"*Hypocrite!*" Jessie scolded, swatting his arm. "You warned me about throwing myself headfirst into danger *this* morning."

"You're right," Barker said, scanning the forest one last time. "Stupid idea. I just thought if I caught them, it would end everything."

They returned to the safety of the graveyard where DI Moyes and several officers were heading towards the forest edge. Moyes paused, allowing Barker to inform her before resuming her chase.

Back at the café, Julia embraced Barker while Anwen filmed his return, then lowered the camera.

"Sorry," Barker whispered. "The old police training kicked in."

"Cat and mouse, more like," Jessie said. "Or

Scooby after a Scooby Snack. On second thoughts, maybe you're not Fred."

Sue chuckled nervously. "Why were they standing there, staring at the café? It was almost like they wanted to be seen."

Barker agreed, joining Sue's gaze at the green as Dot and Percy scurried back home.

"They know we're investigating."

"It could have been any of them," Jessie added. "Or maybe they're all in on it. A family that cults together…"

Julia sighed. "What do we do now?"

"We keep our wits about us," Barker responded, massaging his swollen knee. "But I won't be scared off. First, let's go home. I need to ice my leg, and you have a meeting with Evelyn. Hopefully, she can shed some light on what's happening."

11

*E*vening descended upon Julia's cottage, the shadowed recesses of the sitting room coming alive with the gentle flicker of the fire roaring in the hearth. Julia had spent most of the night jotting down her thoughts about the case in her notepad, watching the clock for Evelyn's arrival. Evelyn existed in her own world—perhaps she was running on a different timeframe—but it wasn't like her to not follow through. Julia considered calling the B&B to check on her but didn't want to seem pushy, especially as Evelyn was volunteering information that Julia had tried to steal from an unpublished manuscript.

With a bag of frozen carrots, she joined Barker in the dining room, where he was hunched over a map of their village sprawled across the table. Photographs of Arthur and the Knights were laid out, accompanied by snippets of information on yellow sticky notes.

Julia was about to pull up a chair to join him, swapping the carrots for the defrosted peas on his knee, when a soft, hesitant knock interrupted the quiet of the cottage. She opened the door with a smile to Evelyn, whose usually light air now prickled with an unsettling edginess.

"Come in," Julia said, guiding her inside. The sound of the kettle signalling its boil made Evelyn jump, her nerves plain to see. "I'll make us some tea."

Evelyn lingered by the breakfast bar while Julia prepared the cups. Her black kaftan, still unchanged from earlier, struck an uncanny resemblance to the figure Barker had chased into the forest. If Julia's gran were there, she'd have accused Evelyn of being part of the cult, but Julia was more level-headed. She'd known and liked Evelyn for too many years to think such a thing, even if the thought had crossed her mind earlier at the B&B.

With the steaming cups, they made their way down to the bottom of the garden, where the embers in the firepit still glowed from where they'd sat eating their earlier Chinese takeaway. Julia and Evelyn settled on logs and watched the dancing light.

"I can't stay for too long," Evelyn whispered, her voice barely audible over the crackling embers. "I don't want them to worry when they notice I'm missing."

Julia reached out, placing a comforting hand on Evelyn's arm. "What's going on, Evelyn? Is this about Derek and Sophia Knight?"

Evelyn hesitated, then gave a slight nod.

"Are you in any danger?"

Evelyn's silence spoke volumes. Julia studied her troubled expression, the orange flicker from the firepit reflecting in her eyes. The atmosphere grew heavy.

"You own the B&B," Julia reminded her. "If you feel uncomfortable or unsafe with the Knight family there, you have every right to ask them to leave."

Evelyn exhaled up at the starry sky, her shoulders sagging. "They haven't done anything to me or said anything, for that matter. But ever since Arthur's body was found in the forest, there's been this dreadful feeling I can't shake. It's difficult to describe, but there's evil living under my roof."

Julia was used to dealing with Evelyn's vague feelings and mystic predictions, but they rarely carried such weight. As Evelyn reached into her kaftan to clutch at the many crystals around her neck, Julia wished she had one of her own to hold. Evelyn had given her enough over the years to have a fair collection on her bedside table.

"Sophia's book?" Julia prompted. "*The Lost Religions of the Cotswolds*?"

"I met Sophia at a retreat a few years ago—the Crescent Moon Yoga Retreat, would you believe?" Evelyn offered a smile before sipping her tea. "I've met many kindred spirits there, and Sophia is one of them. Our paths crossed several times before we realised how much we shared. I was immediately intrigued when she revealed she was writing a book about the area. I've always known the Cotswolds had a deep and rich history, so I jumped at the chance to read her work. She'd given me snippets to read here and there. She'd been working on it for years, travelling up and down the country, visiting private collections to unearth lost material. I never thought she'd finish it, to be honest, so when she did, I was thrilled to read it. The Cult of Lunara was the one that stuck with me."

"Do you think," Julia began, choosing her words with care, "that the Knight family could be... part of the cult? Maybe descendants or reviving the old practices?"

Evelyn almost dropped her tea at the suggestion, trying to mask her unease with a nervous chuckle.

"Sophia has *assured* me that it's all just an eerie coincidence," Evelyn said, her voice tinged with a rehearsed tone that Julia had heard earlier. "That's why she won't share it with the police. She's trying to protect her family, but I can assure you, they're not part of a cult, Julia. They're nice, normal people who have lost everything. They're not murderers."

"And Sophia knowing so much about this cult and the similarities to how Arthur was found are coincidences to you?"

"Others could have known about the cult."

"But you just admitted the information was considered lost before Sophia compiled it," Julia pointed out. "She doesn't know I've read an extract, and you've read it, so how many others could have known the Moon's Beloved ritual before yesterday?"

"Perhaps you're right, Julia." Evelyn's face grew pale as she stared into her dark tea. "The Cult of Lunara existed in a hidden chapter of our area's history. Much of their lives have been lost to time, but enough survived for Sophia to piece the loose ends together."

"What kinds of threads?"

"They were named after a lesser-known lunar deity, tracing back to the Celtic era. That's the language that was used at the scene. They were a secretive group, seeing the moon as a potent force over Earth's fate." She paused to gaze up at the moon. "They were completely shunned by society, as you can imagine. The Romans and later Christianity tried to erase their beliefs, and they did a fine job. Their ways didn't get passed down through the generations."

"Until now."

"Until now," Evelyn agreed. "The woods we know as Howarth Forest? That place has had many names. The Romans called it Caelumgrove Woods. But before them, the Celts referred to it as Luanach. Forest of the Moon." She finished her tea. "Victorians found artefacts during early archaeological digs. A circle of stones, silver coins, and daggers."

A chill shuddered across Julia's shoulders. "And all of this information is in Sophia's book?"

Evelyn gave a solemn nod.

"So, aside from you, Sophia and her family were the only people who could have known of the ritual before Arthur's murder?"

"It does seem that way."

Julia sensed Evelyn was holding back.

"Evelyn? What else do you know?"

"Before I came to visit you... the reason I was late..." Evelyn inhaled deeply, turning to face Julia. "I was filled with terrible nerves. I had some tea that I imported from Costa Rica. It calmed me right down and blasted open my chakras. I followed the energy to Sam, their eldest son. He was trying to paint in the garden."

"Like he was the night of the sacrifice?"

"Yes," Evelyn said. "I saw his easel out there. He might have been behind there, or he might not have. Though I believe he was there. It's just a feeling. He's been trying to paint most evenings since he's been at the B&B. After the fire destroyed his work, his passion has waned, and tonight, he suffered from a terrible block. I tried uplifting him with positive energy. I even draped my crystals around him, which only irritated him further, so... I offered him a sip of my tea. I should've known better. He wasn't used to it like I was."

"What happened?"

"Sam threw up instantly and started crying as though he'd been holding back tears for most of his life."

Making a mental note to avoid Evelyn's Costa Rican tea, Julia leaned in further as the last embers crackled down, sipping her comforting minty favourite.

"That's when he confessed something to me," Evelyn whispered. "Something he'd never told anyone. Not even his family."

Evelyn jolted off the log, and Julia reached out, her hand grazing Evelyn's before she strode across the grass.

"This could be important, Evelyn," Julia urged. "There was a sighting of a cloaked figure earlier.

Don't hold it in if you know something that might help us."

Understanding dawned on Evelyn's face, and under the muted silver glow of a waning moon, she stepped back towards the fire and Julia, though she remained standing.

"Sam was desperate for recognition in the art world," she began. "He was beyond frustrated that his years of painting hadn't led him anywhere. His sister is a successful accountant, his younger brother is excelling in education, and Sam feels the weight of his father's expectations pushing him into the ground. Sophia's respect for his artistic passion conflicts with her disdain for the profit-driven art world."

Another contradiction, Julia thought, especially considering Sophia's aspirations with her book.

"From what I could gather from his confession," Evelyn continued, frowning, "there was a time when they thought Arthur was just Faith's latest 'project.' Sam revealed his dreams to Arthur. He'd asked his parents for money for his exhibitions, but they always refused. Arthur said he'd get him the money, and he did."

"How much?"

"One hundred thousand."

Julia choked at the sum. "And I'm assuming you don't mean pennies?"

"*Pounds*," Evelyn confirmed. "And worse still, he doesn't know where Arthur got it, and he never got to use it. The money was in cash, and it either burned in the fire or Arthur reclaimed it before setting the place alight."

"That's why Arthur set fire to the house?"

"That's what Sam seems to think. He blames himself for the ordeal. Before he could confess more, Derek pulled him away. Derek can be so dismissive."

"He has a habit of not letting his children speak for themselves."

"Yes," Evelyn sighed. "I've noticed that too. I should go. It's been a long day, and Sophia becomes upset if we miss our evening meditations. She claims they're keeping her sane."

Or Sophia wanted to keep Evelyn, a keeper of her secrets, close, but Julia kept that thought to herself. After promising they'd both stay safe, Evelyn called a taxi to avoid any lurking cloaked figures. Julia waved the car off, leaving her with more questions and unease.

She joined Barker in the dining room, where he was picking at leftover special fried rice. He'd transferred the contents of his notetaking to the wall, creating an investigation board. The map remained on the table.

"What did Evelyn have to say?"

"Quite a bit."

Julia recounted Evelyn's 'special tea' confessions and the history of Lunara and the forest. Each new piece of information was added to the wall. Once finished, they stepped back, absorbing the investigation's enormity. From Julia's perspective, the puzzle had more pieces than she could fit together, though she had an inkling about where the Cotswold Crew might fit in.

"They dress sharply and drive expensive cars," Julia said, tapping the picture Jessie had snapped that afternoon. "If Arthur was working with them, he could have got the money for Sam from them?"

"And that's why the crew wanted to get their revenge?" Barker mused, tapping a finger on his chin. "It would make sense for where Arthur got the money. He was a low-stakes criminal who wasn't flush with cash before the fire. But why target the family, too?"

"Extreme over-correction?" Julia proposed. "Nathan said that Arthur didn't harbour true feelings for Faith, but perhaps something was there? Derek and Sophia strike me as the types of parents who would stand in their way?"

"And then there's Nathan," Barker continued, his tone reflective. "A victim of cyberbullying and a lost collection of his beloved beetles. He was in the village before the figure appeared, young enough to sprint like the cloaked stranger. He could have changed into that cloak in the alley between the café and the post office while I was in the kitchen with you. However, I keep returning to the parents," he said, gesturing at the pictures of Derek and Sophia. Derek, the image of educational excellence, and Sophia posed in a staged yoga stance. "The overprotective, secretive father, and the mother, well-versed in the ritual."

Sophia was the one Julia had her eye on.

"Do you think either of them could have outrun you?"

Barker considered, then shrugged. "Perhaps, but it's not beyond reason that they might all be in on it. Despite Faith and Evelyn's insistence that they're not a cult, I'm not convinced."

"And the map?" Julia leaned in, focusing on the field outlined by Barker in green pen right behind her café, which he'd circled. "What does my café have to do with this?"

"Just a reference point," he said. "I've been looking into public records. This entire stretch behind your café belongs to the council. Used to be market hall there. But these two tiny plots belong to the Knight family. After the road was put in, they were left with these slivers of land. The land behind your café has been left alone, and the other side of the road is part of St. Peter's Primary School's sports fields."

"What does this have to do with the case?"

"Possibly nothing," Barker admitted, scratching his stubble. "But Nathan mentioned his parents' fixation on this land, and he came to me only after Derek shut the conversation down."

"Just like he did with Sam and Faith," Julia pointed out. "What's so special about these two pieces of land?"

A silence settled between them, the room filled with potential leads and suspects, a complicated web with no apparent connections.

The Knight family.

The Cult of Lunara.

Arthur the Arsonist.

The Cotswold Crew.

The farmland.

Julia felt overwhelmed by the puzzle before her. She was at a loss for what they could create if they were ingredients to a recipe.

Feeling exhaustion creep in, she gave the wall one last scan, unsure they would get closer tonight. After finishing the leftover special fried rice with Barker, she checked on Olivia one final time in her cot, tested all the locks, and crawled into bed, hoping fears of a cloaked figure wouldn't disturb her sleep.

12

In the office above Katie's Salon on Mulberry Lane, the late morning sunlight filtered through the windows across the desks cluttered with papers. Jessie sat at one desk, fixated on her laptop screen, while Veronica typed away at another desk near the window, the salon's neon giving her a pink halo glow. The distant hum of Katie's nail drill provided a soothing background noise as they immersed themselves in their tasks.

Veronica's fingers danced across the keyboard, her yellow-framed glasses perched on the bridge of her nose. She was crafting a follow-up article on Arthur's death, detailing the intriguing sighting of the cloaked figure. The sighting had sent a ripple of unease through the village if the comments on Peridale Chat and *The Peridale Post*'s app were to be believed. Veronica was determined to provide the readers with more insight into the mysterious occurrence despite having little to work on outside of the information Evelyn had shared with Jessie's mum the night before.

Meanwhile, Jessie scrolled through a list of cases Veronica had highlighted as potential ties to the Cotswold Crew. She had compiled records of fires, robberies, and other criminal activities that might have links to the elusive gang. Yet, as Jessie meticulously combed through the details, there was no mention of Arthur Foster in any of the cases. She frowned, feeling a growing frustration as the puzzle pieces continued to elude her.

Veronica finally broke the silence, her fingers dancing across the keyboard. "How's the research going? Any leads on the Crew's involvement in any of those cases?"

Jessie sighed. "I've gone through all these cases, and there's no mention of Arthur Foster outside of a few small-scale fires he started for 'fun.' Shouldn't I be out there trying to find this crew so we can point the police at them?"

"It's frustrating, I know." Veronica paused her typing and looked at Jessie with a sympathetic expression. "But remember, there's more to investigative journalism than running around outside.

These things can take time. You can achieve just as much behind a desk as you can in the field. Keep digging."

Jessie wasn't so sure. Veronica had flipped as much as Billy had when Jessie sent her the picture of the members hanging around Fern Moore. The longer she spent in the office, the more she felt like she'd been grounded, and Veronica was her babysitter. Jessie continued to reluctantly scroll through the articles, her mind wandering to where she wanted to go for lunch.

"Email!" Veronica announced. "My police contact has confirmed Nathan Knight's alibi for the time of Arthur's death."

"So, he was in Riverswick like he said?"

Veronica's glasses caught the light as she looked up from her screen. "Officers found witnesses during a door-to-door search putting him where he said he was at the time of Arthur's death."

"They'd never have achieved that stuck at a desk."

"Point made." Veronica's pursed lips tickled into a reluctant smile. "A couple were walking along the river when they saw a redheaded young man on the riverbank. They said he looked 'lost in his thoughts', which explains why he didn't think anybody saw him. Rules him out as a suspect in Arthur's murder."

"But not the cloaked sighting yesterday."

"I'm not convinced by your theory that this cult is a family affair," Veronica said as her fingers nimbly danced over the keys. "Or that it's a cult at all, for that matter. 'Fair is foul, and foul is fair.'" She glanced over the screen and rolled her eyes at Jessie's shoulder shrug. "Macbeth, Act One, Scene Three? Three witches?"

"You can turn the English tutor into a newspaper editor, but you can't stop her cryptically quoting Mr William Shakespeare."

"That's because there's a Shakespeare quote for every occasion." That reluctant smile again. "That line speaks to the idea that things might look one way, but underneath, they're completely different."

Jessie leaned back, pondering. "So, what we see with this so-called 'cult' might be the surface? That there's something deeper we're not catching?"

"We all wear masks."

"Right now, my mask is pretending I'm okay being stuck behind this desk."

"You don't wear it well." Veronica winked. "But we should consider that what we're seeing might be misleading. Just because it walks and quacks like a cult doesn't mean it is a cult, especially not one from 400 BC. There could be layers we've yet to uncover."

Jessie sighed. "This is about as complicated as Shakespeare coursework, but I think I see your point.

We shouldn't jump to conclusions based on appearances."

"Top of the class. Always question, and always dig deeper. And if a bit of Shakespeare helps along the way, all the—"

A knock interrupted them. Jessie glanced towards the door, expecting to see Katie. She didn't usually wait to be called in, despite how often Veronica tried hinting that she shouldn't interrupt their important work.

"Come in, Katie," Veronica called. "If this is about the wax again, I've already—"

The door creaked open, but the figure stepping into the room wasn't Katie. It was Billy. Jessie's heart skipped a beat, which she immediately put down to the confusion of seeing him at the office.

"Nice setup you have here," Billy remarked, eyes scanning the office with genuine interest. "It's impressive."

Veronica, raising an eyebrow and pushing up her glasses, pointed to the office's white walls. "A little too much of a white box for my liking, but Jessie wasn't too taken by my wallpaper choices. Jessie, are you going to introduce me?"

"Veronica, Billy. Billy, Veronica. Billy's quite the dab hand with a can of spray paint. He could fix our white wall problem?"

Veronica's expression shifted to one of sudden understanding. "I'm not sure graffiti is what I had in mind, but it's nice to meet you, Billy. I've heard all about you. I can give you two some privacy—"

"I'm only passing through," Billy cut her off, scratching at the large lion tattoo on his neck. "I'm picking up donations from the butchers down the street." There was a pause, during which Billy seemed to gather his thoughts. "Jessie, I... I wanted to apologise for how things ended yesterday. I shouldn't have snapped at you. I want you to be safe."

"You and me both," Veronica muttered.

"It's fine, Billy. Reading through all this, I'm beginning to realise just how serious the Crew is. We've decided not to print the picture I took. Don't want to poke the hornet's nest without any hard evidence to back it up."

"Then I might have something else for you," he said, pulling out his phone. "I was in the café over on the estate getting a bacon bap for breakfast, and I swear one of the crew members was in there."

"Oh?" Veronica stopped typing and wheeled over. "Overhear anything?"

"Nothing specific, but the tone of the guy he was with was odd." Billy held out his phone, displaying a grainy image of two men hunched over a table. One was in a black suit like the men Jessie had snapped, the other in a hoodie with a baseball cap. "The guy in the hat was running the conversation. Talking down to the Crew guy like he had the upper hand. I thought he might have been someone off the estate being paid to do a job, but it seemed to be the other way around."

"You've seen him before?" Jessie asked, to which Billy shook his head. She squinted at the man. He was older, given the jowls hanging from his jaw. The cap concealed much of his face, but something about his posture felt familiar. "Could it be Derek Knight?"

Veronica leaned in closer, scrutinising the image. The colour drained from her cheeks, her eyes widening just a fraction. Jessie's instincts tingled.

"Veronica? Do you recognise him?"

With a shake of her head, Veronica returned to her desk.

"Do you know him from around the estate, Billy?"

Billy glanced at the photo again. "Can't say I do." His phone buzzed, pulling him out of his contemplation. "It's Hilda. Wondering what's taking me so long. Things must be getting busy at the food bank. I should go."

"You could've just sent the picture, you know."

Billy's face reddened, his hand scratching at his neck again. "I wanted to apologise, mostly. Hate the idea of us being at odds, and after how I was yesterday, I was worried you hated me now."

"Impossible." Jessie pushed forward a smile. "Billy, I—"

"How about a drink at Richie's sometime?" he blurted out. "I think we deserve a re-do after what happened last time."

"Anytime."

He grinned, looking relieved. "Great. I'll catch you later then."

Billy made his way to the door, throwing a parting nod at Veronica, and once the door clicked shut, Veronica wheeled over to Jessie, a mischievous glint in her eyes.

"He seems like a sweet boy," she commented. "Any chance of you two…"

"He has a girlfriend."

Veronica arched an eyebrow. "That's not what I asked."

Sidestepping Veronica's probing, Jessie said, "Did you recognise the man in the photo?"

Veronica's expression turned serious. "No, I didn't. But Billy's right. This gang isn't to be messed with. It might be best if you stepped away from the Cotswold Crew case."

"What? Why? *You* put me on the case."

Veronica sighed. "This is getting a little too close to home, Jessie. I wanted you to gather information, but we might be delving into dangerous territory here, and it might not even be connected to the Knight family. Like you said, there's no point poking the hornet's nest for nothing."

"I can handle it, Veronica. This case—"

But Veronica held up a hand, cutting her off. "'Discretion is the better part of valour.' Henry IV, Part One. Act Five, Scene Four."

"William liked to waffle on."

"It means cautious inaction over potentially reckless bravery." She reached into her handbag and pulled out a twenty-pound note. "Now, grab us lunch from the chippy up the street, and tell them not to scrimp on the vinegar this time."

Jessie moved for the money, but Veronica yanked it back.

"Hurry back because I've got another assignment for you," Veronica said before handing over the note. "The Knight murder isn't the only story around here. Greg Morgan will be at the library for that press conference later this afternoon. I was going to dodge it and nick the highlights from the *Riverswick Chronicle*, but it will be good work experience for you."

"You want me to interview a dodgy politician?"

"Exactly."

"How do I even do that?"

"Massage his ego, and I'm sure he'll give you some quotes for us to print."

"So, you're admitting to taking me off the interesting case to put me on filler?" Jessie said as she walked to the door. "What happened to me only taking the stories I was interested in?"

Jessie left through the back door, her mind buzzing.

Cautious inaction over potentially reckless bravery?

It sounded too much like standing by and doing nothing.

Despite Veronica's orders, Jessie wasn't sure she could leave the Cotswold Crew case alone, especially after Billy's picture. The guy in the cap could have been talking to a Crew member for a million reasons. Given what was going on, there was a possibility that one of those reasons was that he was the puppet master behind the fire.

Find the puppet master, solve the case.

Easy.

But first, chips.

13

The lunch rush in the café had come and gone, leaving behind a peaceful lull. While enjoying the break, Julia and Sue stood behind the counter watching Anwen's attempt to interview Dot. Rupert wasn't present, apparently too hungover, but Ava was behind the camera, with Anwen clenching the microphone on a stick between her knees.

"Now, Dot," began Anwen, her voice clear and professional, "you've gone over your theories about this cult, including the dozens of villagers you're certain are part of it, *several* times now. So, let's pull the lens out a little further, shall we?" She consulted her binder. "Tell us what you love most about living in a village like Peridale."

Before Dot could open her mouth, Ethel interjected from across the café. "Why, the thrill of keeping a keen eye on your neighbours from your window, isn't that right, Dorothy?"

Dot shot her a withering look, adjusting her brooch. "It's called being vigilant, Ethel. Some of us like to make sure the community is safe."

"You're just waiting for someone to trip over a loose cobblestone so you can make a note of it."

"I would not waste my time with such nonsense," Dot told the camera. "When I ran my very successful neighbourhood watch group—"

"So successful you split up."

"As did yours, Ethel." Dot maintained her camera-ready smile. "Peridale's Ears oversaw many interesting cases. We played a vital role in raising awareness to save our local library from the evil clutches of redevelopment at the hands of James Jacobson. If not for our drone, this very café might have been burned to the ground by that madman who electrocuted that singer at last year's festival. What did your group ever do, Ethel, aside from fixing holes in the church roof?"

"Lest you forget all the trouble you caused, too?" Ethel fired back after a sharp sip of tea. "Like when you insisted Malcolm Johnson, president of the Peridale Green Thumbs gardening society, was growing suspicious plants at the allotment. Turned out to be tomatoes, didn't it?"

"Well, they looked very suspicious at first glance." Dot fluffed up her curls at the back. "What about when you spent an afternoon tailing the milkman, thinking he was involved in some grand conspiracy because he delivered early? Don't think word doesn't get around this village, Ethel."

Ethel's eyes widened. "He was always too punctual! Anyone would've been sceptical."

"And wasn't it your group that once raised the alarm over a 'gathering of spies' in the field behind this café?"

"How was I supposed to know they were bird watchers?"

"Spies, Ethel? Sent by whom?"

"Which is precisely why I investigated them."

"And now," Dot said, leaning into the camera, "you can see why the Peridale Eyes group disbanded."

"And why did your group end, Dot?" Ethel stood, casting a hand towards Shilpa and Amy, who had yet to say a word as they sank into their chairs. "What was it I heard?"

"Leave us out of it," Shilpa muttered, finishing her latte.

"I need to get to choir rehearsal," Amy said, pushing away her tea.

Leaning into the camera's view, Ethel said, "They quit because Dot ran the group like a tyrant. This woman has a Napoleon complex."

"Says you, with the stature of a resident of Middle-earth?" Dot retorted, standing to tower over Ethel while Shilpa and Amy snuck out the front door. "And I bet you have the hairy toes to match. You have your complexes mixed up, dear. Dementia must be setting in."

"You're at least a decade my senior!"

"Five years." Dot extended a finger. "Six, at the most."

"Ladies…" Anwen interjected, standing with her palms spread. "Why don't we all just breathe and calm down?"

Dot and Ethel both settled back into their chairs. Julia was relieved that Anwen had been able to defuse the situation. Another minute more, and chairs might have started flying.

"This is being left on the cutting room floor," Sue whispered.

"Oh, definitely," Julia replied, sipping her tea. "Something for the bloopers reel."

"Where were we?" Anwen said with a sigh, consulting her binder. "Perhaps we can steer this back to the charm of Peridale? Paint a picture for the viewers at home to help them understand why Peridale is such a special place to you?"

"Well, aside from the *delightful* company," Dot said, sending a sarcastic smile Ethel's way, "I adore the history of Peridale. Every stone has a story to tell. Like this cult, for example. As terrifying as it is to think any one of us could be next, it is fascinating to learn about what the people of this village were up to thousands of years ago."

"Weren't you there to see it first-hand?" Ethel muttered.

Dot cast her a sideways glance but didn't rise to the bait this time.

"Enough about the cult," Anwen pressed, the pen sinking deeper into her bun. "The charm, Dot? Why do you feel so protective over this village?"

"Yes, I indeed enjoy keeping an eye out for my fellow villagers. There's a strong sense of community spirit here. Living in such a small place, you experience the rhythms of life together. Villages like ours need people to look out for them. Cults, developers, murderers, busybodies who accuse bird watchers of being spies." She paused, clearing her throat. "If not for the people who value Peridale doing their duty, things can go awry in the blink of an eye. *Oh*! That rhymed."

"Yes, it did," Anwen said, scratching her bun with her pen. "So, I think that wraps up my—"

"Without my spy from up high, Peridale would surely sigh," Dot continued, her posture dramatic and her voice taking on a transatlantic tone again. "And maybe even cry! For every tie, lie, or mischievous guy, there's Dot, the ever-watchful eye. And perhaps someday, when I'm up in the sky after I die, they'll remember me, oh so spry. And if you eat food that is Thai, you might—"

"Is there an off switch?" Ethel interrupted.

Anwen blinked, taken aback by the sudden theatrical performance, while the remaining customers sat in dumbfounded silence. Sue offered a slow clap.

"I think we got everything we need," Anwen finally managed, nodding at Ava to turn off the camera. "Well done, Dot. That was very... intense."

Dot took a theatrical bow, casting a pleased-with-herself look at Ethel, who was busy checking her nails. Julia wondered if her gran had stopped by Evelyn's for some Costa Rican tea on her way to the café.

"Forget a documentary," Sue said, "those two need a sitcom."

The gentle clink of cups and saucers and the familiar hum of low-level bickering from Dot and

Ethel served as the café's soundtrack. Anwen, with strands of hair falling from her bun and a drained expression, walked over to the counter. Ava began packing the camera equipment.

"Your grandmother is quite a character. I'm not sure any of that will make the final cut."

Giving her a consoling smile, Julia said, "Thanks for entertaining her. It might just give the rest of us a bit of peace."

As Sue excused herself to attend to the empty table left behind by Shilpa and Amy, a slight hesitance clung to Anwen. Her eyes darted to the floor, then returned to meet Julia's. Julia retrieved a delicate glass dish filled with an Eton mess's swirled peaks and valleys. Setting it before Anwen, she pushed a spoon alongside, urging her to dig in.

"On the house. Now, what's bothering you?"

"You can read people like a book, Julia."

"Comes with the job. Is it about the cloaked figure we saw yesterday?"

"I don't want to speak out of turn, but it might be." Anwen stabbed the spoon in, but it didn't make it any further. "Sam and Sophia were arguing intensely in the garden at the B&B late last night. I wasn't trying to eavesdrop, but they didn't notice me. I was out there getting some fresh air and reviewing some of the footage we've captured on my laptop. Sophia said something like, 'How would it look if people found out it was you?' I thought she could have been talking about the cloaked figure. Should I inform the police?"

Julia frowned. "You could, but perhaps it could have meant something else altogether? Evelyn mentioned that Sam borrowed money from Arthur before his death. A considerable amount that hasn't been seen since the fire."

"Now, that does paint a clear motive for Sam." Anwen sighed and scooped in a mouthful of strawberries and cream. "And then there's Sophia, who wrote the book on it. Just something to think about."

Julia's footsteps whispered against the kitchen floor. She paused, her gaze fixing on the delicate dance of Sue's hands scrubbing the cups.

"You look miles away," Sue said, turning off the tap before grabbing the dish towel. "I'd say you're due your lunch break."

Julia hesitated. "It's Sophia Knight. Something about her doesn't sit right with me."

"The woman who wrote the book you found at the B&B?"

Julia nodded, leaning against the island. "There were pages upon pages about the Cult of Lunara, so why's she acting like she knows nothing now?"

"You think she's hiding something?"

"All signs point to that cult," Julia said, staring through the window. Grey clouds had swallowed the morning blue. "Whether she's a member or not, she should have been the first person to step forward when Arthur was found. Not lurking in the shadows, pretending she's never heard of a thing. Why all the secrecy?"

"People have their reasons. Maybe she's scared. Maybe she has shadows. Maybe she knows things don't look good for her."

"Or maybe she's guilty." Julia's gaze hardened, a determined fire burning within. "I think I need to confront her at the B&B. She seemed too caught up in watching Faith's words the only time I spoke with her. If I can get her alone, she might be more honest with me."

"Just be careful. I'm still freaked out after what happened on the green last night."

As Julia nodded, the distant jingle of the café door yanked them back to reality. Julia pushed through the beads as they swung inwards with a gust of wind, revealing Percy with Lady and Bruce. The dogs bounded ahead of him, their tails wagging as they performed a weaving lap of the café.

"Anwen, get a shot of the dogs," Dot instructed, clicking her fingers at the director. "Everybody loves dogs. You could put them on the poster."

Ethel recoiled as Bruce, the tiny French bulldog, bounced on his back legs to lick at her leftover Victoria sponge cake. Julia let out a small laugh, but it cut off when she noticed how Percy was panting for breath like he'd just sprinted a marathon.

"Percy, my love?" Dot said, wrapping an arm around him. "What is it?"

"It's... It's happened again."

Through the windows, people from the village green were drawn to the alley between the café and the post office. Anwen pulled her phone from her pocket and was already filming before she sprinted outside.

"What's happened again?" Julia could barely get the words out.

Percy finally managed to steady his breath, but his voice still quivered. "I was walking the dogs behind the café. The crows, there were so many. They were all pecking. Oh, it was awful!"

The weight of his words enveloped the café in an eerie silence. Without a comment, Julia and Sue dashed through the back door. Julia hammered her knuckles on the door to Barker's office as she passed through the yard. As they emerged onto the path, the shrill sirens of police cars echoed in the distance. Above, crows scattered against the milky grey canvas, their sharp caws speckling the tense atmosphere.

Ahead, a cluster of villagers had gathered around something in the field's centre.

"Can you believe this?" Barker cried, holding up his phone. "People are discussing my new book on Peridale Chat. It's been bootlegged!"

Julia, already overwhelmed with the situation, shot him a sharp glance. "Barker, that's terrible, but it'll have to wait."

Barker opened his mouth to respond when his gaze fixed on Detective Inspector Moyes, cutting through the crowd purposefully.

"Oi, Laura!" he called, waving to get her attention. "What are you playing at? I trusted you."

But Moyes didn't stop or look his way, her focus entirely on the unfolding scene before her. Realisation dawned on his face.

"Julia?"

"I think there's been another killing," Julia said, her throat as dry as a sand.

The cluster of whispering villagers parted as Julia and Barker made their way towards the epicentre of the disorder. There, nestled among the green grass blowing in the wind, a woman with crystal necklaces draped across her bloody chest was surrounded by stones inscribed with moon symbols. Two gleaming silver coins rested atop her closed eyes, and the burnt-down candles hinted she'd been there for hours.

Taking in the scene, Julia felt her heart race. Beyond the cluster of officers and villagers lay the open field, with the back of her café visible in the distance. While she'd been inside, laughing at her gran's banter with Ethel, Sophia Knight had been outside—alone with only the crows, waiting for a dog walker to stumble upon her.

Murdered, just like Arthur Foster.

Just like the story in her book.

∾

Barker sat behind his cluttered desk, the weight of the day's revelations pushing him deep into his chair. Opposite him, Anwen tried her best to maintain an air of professionalism. The camera in her hands was steady, but her eyes betrayed the worry she felt.

"Barker, the documentary needs your perspective. What do you make of the latest murder?"

His gaze seemed distant, caught between the grim events outside and the whirlwind of thoughts inside his head. He rubbed at the lines on his forehead, wishing he could wake up from the surreal dream he'd slipped into since Anwen and her cameras arrived.

"Are you even listening?" Anwen's dwindling patience was evident in her voice. "The sooner we get through this, the sooner we can leave. But it's better to capture this stuff raw and fresh. So, tell me, what do you think about the latest murder?"

Barker sighed, running a hand through his dishevelled hair. "I can't wrap my head around all this, Anwen. Everything feels so... surreal."

"We're all trying to process it. But the village needs clarity, and who better than you to provide some?"

After a moment's pause, he leaned forward, elbows on the desk, and looked Anwen in the eye. "I need to go and talk to the Knights. Find out what's going on from the inside."

"You think they'll talk to you?"

"There are things that are more important than filming right now. I have to get to the bottom of this."

Before Anwen could respond, Barker was already halfway out the door.

Every visit to the B&B felt like he was delving deeper into an enigma, and tonight was no different. After Arthur's reappearance, he'd visited the Knight family in the garden, having no idea it would be the final time he'd see the family together. And then again after Arthur's death, when he'd left with more questions than answers. But tonight, the atmosphere held a weight of expectation.

Perched on the old sign of the B&B was a crow, its dark eyes studying Barker intently. It let out a raspy caw before flying off towards the forest. The memory of the crows fleeing the field when he'd joined Julia came flooding back, making him feel uneasy. He had been too upset about his bootlegged book to notice the murder scene right in front of him.

Barker knew he had to solve this. There was no telling how many more bodies would turn up around Peridale in rings of candles and symbols of the moon.

He hurried up the garden path through the wildflowers, a distant wind chime playing a haunting melody from somewhere in the garden. Uniformed police officers stepped out, trading hushed conversations. DI Moyes emerged, her expression sour as she glanced back at the B&B before letting Evelyn close the door behind her.

"Laura?" Barker called out, his voice dripping with anger. "I gave you my book because I wanted to know your thoughts, not the thoughts of half the village. What were you thinking by leaking it?"

Moyes arched a brow. "Come on, Brown. Do you think I'd do that to you?"

"You're the only other person with a copy. So where is it?"

With a sigh, she took a moment to puff electronic clouds towards the night sky. "I didn't leak it, Barker. I lent it to someone."

"You *lent* it to someone?" Barker's laugh was one of

disbelief. "I know I didn't explicitly say, 'don't pass this around', but I thought it was implied, given that it's an *unpublished* manuscript?"

"I gave it to PC Puglisi," she admitted with a sigh, raising her hands in a gesture of surrender. "And I'm sorry. I messed up. But the second he knew I had it, he was desperate to read it. You know he's a fan of your first book. With this case keeping me so busy, I thought, 'Who better to read it and give me the highlights?' I intended to get to it when I had the time."

Barker shook his head in disbelief. "Thanks to you and Puglisi, all my summer efforts were for nothing."

"It was only the other day you weren't even sure you were going to publish it," Laura snapped back, her nostrils flaring. "Look, I've apologised. I can't undo giving it to Puglisi, but I will reprimand him for putting it online. Right now, it's not the most important thing. I have another body on my hands, and last I checked, you're still employed by the Knights. I hope you have better luck finding Derek."

Moyes slammed the gate and followed the officers back to the station across the road. Barker yanked on the musical chain, wondering if he could have handled things better as Anwen hurried up the road from his office.

Barker expected Evelyn to answer, but Mark met

him, no happier to see Barker than during their previous two meetings.

"Gran's devastated," Mark stated, narrowing his eyes at Barker. "Great job solving things, PI. Can't wait to read about how you're the hero of the hour in the next one."

"Mark, I—"

Mark shut himself in the private room behind the check-in desk. As much as Barker wanted to end the growing tension between himself and the son of his first book's victim, that wasn't why he was there. Steadying himself with a deep inhale, he set off searching for Sam. He found Nathan slumped in a chair in the sitting room. Before Barker needed to ask, Nathan nodded towards the back window before heading upstairs.

Barker stepped onto the soft grass of the garden behind the B&B, his gaze falling upon Sam, who sat on a garden stool in front of a large easel. The sorrowful moonlight illuminated his slumped form. Tears streaked his face, making the half-finished painting of the moon he was stabbing at appear even more haunting. The paintbrush trembled in his hand, more a weapon of rage than a tool of creativity.

Approaching cautiously, Barker cleared his throat, trying to announce his presence. "Sam?"

Sam initially didn't acknowledge him, the brush

stabbing into the palette. "It's not right. The moon isn't right."

"Sam," Barker pressed, a little more firmly this time. "We need to talk."

Sam's grip on his brush tightened, and he turned to face Barker, fury evident in his eyes. "Talk? About what? My mother's death? Or how my world is falling apart?"

Barker hesitated for a moment, but his determination pushed him forward. "About Arthur Foster and the £100,000 you borrowed from him."

Sam scoffed, wiping away his tears. "So that's what this is about? Money? Is that what our lives come down to?"

"This isn't just about the money, Sam. It's about connections, motives, and the truth. Arthur Foster lent you a considerable sum, and then he died."

"So, you're suggesting I killed him?" He sloshed paint across the canvas. "And then killed my mother?"

Barker wasn't sure what he was suggesting, but Sam had taken it there. Not wanting to aggravate him to the point of storming off, Barker leaned against the shed door behind him, observing the painting in silence. The moon, even in its unfinished state, seemed to mock him. He wasn't clear where the celestial body fit into the mystery's bigger picture.

"Do you know where Arthur got that kind of

money? I know he wasn't exactly a rich man," Barker broke the silence when Sam's brushstrokes slowed. He already knew the answer to his next question but wanted to hear it from Sam. "Why did you borrow it?"

Taking a shaky breath, Sam's defiance crumbled. "I confided in Arthur. Told him about my dreams and my aspirations for my art. He seemed so clueless, naive... When he said he could get me the money, I laughed it off. I said, 'Sure, get me the money'. I never believed he could or even would. It was just what two blokes say after too many beers—all bravado, like my sister's previous pets. But the next day, he turned up at our house with a bag full of cash. I thought he was nuts. Said I didn't have to hurry to pay him back, either."

Barker's eyes narrowed. "And did he mention where he got it from?"

Sam hesitated, his gaze dropping to the ground. "Not a word."

"Any chance it was from a gang?" Barker pushed. "Ever heard of the Cotswold Crew?"

Sam nodded, his shoulders slumping. "Dad's been trying to keep them at bay for months despite what he says. Do you know he's not even honest with us? His kids? And now look what's happened. Look at all we've lost."

Barker felt a twinge of guilt. Behind his direct

questions was a genuine desire to help, to console, and to bring clarity to the chaos swirling around the village.

"Sam, do you know where your father is?"

"Vanished after hearing about Mum. He's scared. We all are. But do you want to know the worst part?" Sam clenched the brush like a dagger and thrust it through the canvas's middle, ripping the moon to shreds. "I can't say confidently that he isn't behind all this. I don't know what to think anymore. Nothing has made sense since the fire."

Sam's legs gave way, and he collapsed into a ball on the grass. Barker, acting on instinct, reached out to support him. He remembered the night he'd lost his mother, only days after the picture on his desk had been taken. The grief had been intense, and the raw emotion felt all too familiar, though Barker had been sobbing on his older brother's shoulder back then.

Holding the young, tormented artist, Barker hated himself for wondering if he was holding a murderer, a master manipulator, or a grief-stricken son.

14

Jessie climbed out of her car outside the refurbished library, illuminated against the deepening indigo of the night sky. She hadn't visited the place since before her travels, and she barely recognised it as she approached the propped-open double doors with the evening wind whipping around her.

The inside of the library had seriously levelled up. Last she remembered, the place reeked of stale air and ageing pages. But this? It looked straight out of a hipster's dream. The walls were painted in a slick shade of teal she wouldn't have minded in her bedroom. Dark wooden bookshelves stretched out in every direction, grand and imposing, filled with books lined up like soldiers on parade.

Between those shelves were chill-out spots with plush seats that begged someone to curl up with a good book and a corner with a coffee shop that rivalled the café, with prices more like those in Fern Moore. High above, the ceiling was crowned with a new glass dome that would have bathed the place in bright, natural light during the day. If not for the glow of the strip lights, Jessie might have been able to see the stars. She had never been much of a reader, but she felt a strange sense of pride seeing the place. She'd heard all about the campaign to save the library when she'd been travelling with her brother, and here was the old dump: saved and thriving.

"Good to see you, Jessie," Neil, Sue's husband, exclaimed, a bright smile lighting up his face behind the sleek counter. "I heard about your recent GCSE exam success. Congrats."

"Just an A and two Cs," she said with a shrug, taking in the surroundings. "Look at you, though, the king of this castle."

"All thanks to Mr Jacobson's investment. It's changed everything. Hard to believe, but people want to come here now." He laughed, closing his book *A Tree Grows in Brooklyn* by Betty Smith. He nodded at the ID badge around her neck. "I assume you're here for the press conference. You're a tad late, but I suppose the whole thing is after being pushed back, given what happened earlier. Sue was in bits on the phone telling me. Are you going to be fine sleeping in your flat tonight, so close? Our sofa's always free if you need it."

Jessie thanked him. She hadn't considered that she lived so close to the crime scene. She'd been in the office when Veronica got the call to rush to the scene, but the police hadn't let them get close enough to do anything more than stand on the sidelines with the other spectators.

The children's section felt oddly tense and formal, with half a dozen reporters crowding around their local politician. Greg Morgan, a man Jessie had only seen in photographs in the paper, looked rather comical in a chair designed for someone a fraction of his age. He was a stout man of around sixty and his hair, or what remained of it, was wispy and receding, giving more prominence to his broad, tanned forehead. His dark eyes, oddly familiar in person, hardly blinked as he scanned the gathered press. That unnaturally wide grin he had in every picture she'd seen of him was plastered across his face, revealing teeth that were surprisingly white for a man of his age and appearance.

Jessie tagged onto the back of the gathering, snapping pictures of him on her phone. She was scribbling a few initial notes, trying to blend in with the rest of the reporters, when a reporter from the *Riverswick Chronicle*, the closest to her in age, took the lead with the questioning.

"So, Mr Morgan," he asked in a deep voice, "is there any truth to the whispers about your involvement with the Henderson Place housing development? Rumour has it there might've been some financial incentives thrown your way to speed up the process to have those houses thrown up in record time. We have locals writing in weekly complaining about the issues with their 'new build' homes."

Greg's hearty and resonant laugh filled the room as he leaned back in his chair and adjusted his tie. Jessie was surprised they were diving right in with the hard-hitting questions. Her gaze landed on a reporter from the *Riverswick Chronicle* while Greg let his answer stew. He had a confident stance, standing out from the older reporters. His skin had a rich, warm hue, and his hair was styled in neat twists on top of his head. He was stylish, too. He wore a slightly unbuttoned crisp cream shirt, brown fitted trousers, and a gold chain glittering around his neck.

"Oh, those silly rumours!" Greg wafted his hand. "They do have a life of their own, don't they? Let me tell you, Henderson Place was a brilliant initiative to transform an underutilised piece of land, and all buildings require maintenance."

Jessie's pen paused on her notepad. That wasn't the whole truth, and she knew it. That 'underutilised piece of land' used to be a forest beyond the allotment, teeming with life, now replaced by rows of identical red brick houses – one of which was inhabited by Sue and Neil.

"Henderson Place is a feather in my cap," he continued, his smile unwavering, "and if you ask me, and one of my proudest achievements before I left the council to put myself to use in the Houses of Parliament, for the people of this fine village and the surrounding areas."

"Any comment on if you were involved in your predecessor, Hugo Scott's, untimely death that triggered the by-election you went onto win?"

"By a *landslide*, might I point out," Greg said, peering at their pads as though making sure they were writing it down. "And those rumours are not only incredibly upsetting to me but also Mr Scott's widow. The brakes on his car malfunctioning like that were a tragic accident, and I refute any conspiracy theory that I was somehow involved."

Jessie's pen couldn't keep up. She'd expected to be there to write a fluff piece, but Greg Morgan seemed to have more skeletons in his closet than she'd read in her Greg Morgan folder, left to her by Johnny before he'd handed the paper over to Veronica. She might have understood what it was supposed to mean if he'd filled it with these rumours instead of leaked accounts and schedules.

"Mr Morgan—"

"And speaking of redevelopment," Greg carried on, cutting off Jessie's first attempt at a question. "Another of my proudest moments was saving this very library. A place of knowledge, of community. For the people."

Jessie frowned. She'd been in India during the library drama, but even she knew that was a stretch of the truth. Veronica had told Jessie to massage Greg's ego, but right now, she felt more inclined to follow the path of her fellow reporters.

"Mr Morgan," Jessie began, hearing the unsure wobble in her voice. She cleared her throat. "Wouldn't it have made more sense to fund this library *before* it needed saving instead of trying to sell it off to the highest bidder? If it weren't for James Jacobson's change of heart after you sold him this place, we'd be sitting in a restaurant now."

A ripple of murmurs surged through the crowd. Initially taken aback, Greg's eyes darted to meet hers, though the smile remained stuck as he adjusted his tie. "And who might you be, child? I don't think we've met."

The *Riverswick Chronicle* reporter shot her an appreciative glance, a hint of a grin touching his lips. Jessie returned the gesture with a slight nod before announcing, "Jessie South-Brown, *The Peridale Post*."

"Ah, *The Post*," Greg said, adjusting his posture. "As you can see, Ms South-Brown, the result is a testament to what can be achieved when the public and private sectors collaborate."

"But that doesn't answer my question," Jessie said, undeterred. "The locals signed petitions, protested, and still you went ahead with the sale."

From the side, the *Riverswick Chronicle* reporter leaned in towards Jessie, whispering, "Good luck getting a straight answer from this guy."

"As I said," Greg replied, his gaze fixed firmly on her. "This library is a testament to what can be achieved from collaboration. Next question?"

"What about this 'redevelopment of left behind areas' you alluded to in your last press release?"

Greg's gaze lingered on Jessie briefly before moving along like nothing had happened. "As an MP, I've been actively liaising with the local councils in the area. Given my extensive history serving as a councillor, I still have many contacts and am privy to numerous exciting developmental initiatives currently underway."

"Any specifics?" pressed the reporter.

"All in good time," Greg responded smoothly, but the practised veneer couldn't mask the defensiveness in his voice.

It was the *Riverswick Chronicle* reporter's turn to probe further. "Why convene this press conference if there's nothing substantial to share? Are you attempting to divert attention from the Henderson Place bribery story set to break?"

Jessie couldn't help but admire the reporter's audacity. The game was on – and everyone was watching Greg Morgan's next move. Every reporter leaned forward, waiting to pounce on Greg's response. When he claimed there was no such story and moved on to talking about the redevelopment of Wellington Manor into Wellington Heights, Jessie almost chuckled. And then, he dared to play the library card again.

But Jessie was done letting him wriggle away.

"Mr Morgan," she started, her voice firm this time. "Any comments on the recent murders that have sent shockwaves through Peridale?"

The room went silent, and the hum of the air conditioning seemed deafening. Reporters turned to her, eyes wide, while Greg's mask of composure cracked as he flapped his tie three times. He appeared at a loss for words for the first time that evening.

Continuing her momentum, Jessie pressed on, "Are you aware of the gang called the Cotswold Crew? As our local MP, surely you must be working on a strategy or initiative to address this growing threat to the people. Or are you only bothered about property and redevelopment?"

Greg's jaw flapped, his usual eloquent self replaced by a man scrambling for words. "This... this isn't the platform to discuss such matters. I won't involve myself in ongoing police investigations. The local constabulary has everything under control. And now, I thank you all for coming, but I have a train to catch. Tomorrow, I'll be in The House of Parliament, in Westminster, championing causes that truly matter to our community, like funding for a brand new neonatal unit at our local hospital and advocating for agricultural rights."

Without another word, Greg Morgan, MP, made a swift exit, leaving behind a room buzzing with whispers and speculation. As reporters began packing their gear, the assertive reporter from the *Riverswick Chronicle* approached Jessie with an outstretched hand.

"Dante Clarke," he introduced himself. "You

certainly know how to press his buttons, Jessie. Well done. You must be working under Veronica Hilt?"

"I am." Jessie shook his hand, feeling a rush she hadn't expected. "And thank you. It's my first time at a press conference."

"Then I commend you for having the guts to take it there," Dante said. "And how is my old English tutor? Still wearing those whacky glasses?"

"Yours too?" Jessie said, still shaking his hand. "And it's a different colour every time I see her. What's the story with the bribery rumours? And the brake cutting?"

"He might be right about the brake cutting being a conspiracy, but the bribery? Without a doubt. You throw money at Greg Morgan, and he'll catch it. He's just too good at covering his tracks."

"When can I expect to read the story?"

"No story, yet. I wanted to test the waters to see if he'd slip up," Dante admitted in a whisper. "But Greg knows when to duck and cover, but you had him on the ropes there for a minute." With a playful wink, he handed her a business card, and said, "I'll see you around, Jessie."

As the last reporters left the library, Jessie pulled out here phone to send a message to Veronica.

JESSIE

> We're not the only paper on Morgan's trail. The Chronicle is digging. Got some good stuff. Also, Morgan acted super weird when I mentioned the recent murders. Might be onto something there. P.S. Dante says hi.

Jessie stowed her phone in her pocket, catching sight of Dante as he strutted to his car. As he was about to slip into the driver's seat, Jessie raised a hand in farewell. To her surprise, he paused, looked back, and returned the gesture with a smile and a casual wave.

With a sudden surge of confusing feelings, she ducked into her car. Hands resting on the steering wheel, she took a deep breath. Thoughts rushed through her mind: the press conference, the revelations, the adrenaline of confronting Morgan, and the unexpected camaraderie with Dante. She wondered where this winding road of journalism was leading her. She hadn't wanted to attend the conference after being ripped off the gang case, but she was glad she had.

VERONICA

> Good job. I'm still at the office. I'll put the kettle on if you've got nothing better to do.

> **JESSIE**
> On my way. Make mine a double shot. Gonna need it.

>> *Going to need it.

> -_-

Phone still in hand, she pulled up the picture Billy had sent her at the office that afternoon. She stared at the photo for a moment, adjusting the brightness of her screen. It was taken from a distance, a little grainy, but it was clear enough. A man in a baseball cap, which didn't completely hide his features, with a Cotswold Crew gang member in a sharp suit.

There was a familiarity she couldn't shake off.

She zoomed into the face of the man in the cap. The sagging jawline, the distinctive arch of the eyebrow, and that ever-so-slight curve of the lips in a smile. Without thinking, she quickly swapped to the photos she had snapped at the press conference. She flicked back and forth between her recent pictures and the one Billy had sent.

Could it be?

15

The strong scent of nail varnish and hot wax hung in the air in Katie's Salon. With her vivacious energy, Katie swished around, her peroxide curls bouncing with each step. She brought in bowls filled with rose petal-infused water and neatly folded warm towels.

"Now, this," she began, showing off a golden bottle of face serum, "will work *wonders* for those pesky little lines, Julia."

"You don't have pesky little lines," Sue said with an amused laugh, with her twins, Pearl and Dottie, playing with clips in each other's hair by her feet. "Compared to Katie's smooth face, I think we all have lines."

Not much older than his niece, Olivia, Vinnie

played peek-a-boo with her, making her giggle. Every time Olivia's round face lit up with joy, Julia tried to share in that joy. She laughed at the right moments and felt grateful for the thought behind the pampering session. But she couldn't shake off what had happened behind the café no matter how hard Sue and Katie tried.

The cawing of the crows.

The crowds around the body.

The glint of the coins on the eyes.

"Now, then," Katie said, dragging Julia's hands across the table after slathering her face in the gold serum. "We'll do paws and claws, and then it's onto your eyebrow *situation*. I can't believe you haven't had them threaded since your birthday, and that's just around the corner again."

"Oh, yeah," Sue said. "What are you doing for your birthday?"

"I can barely think about that right now."

Upstairs, the sound of wheels rolled across the office floor above.

"That'll be Veronica," Katie said with a slight roll of her eyes. "She's up there before I got here and long after I leave. Barely leaves that desk most days. Bless her. You know, I might ask her to join us. Make it a real girl's night. Stay here, and I'll be back in two swipes of a nail varnish brush."

As Katie's heels clicked towards the stairs, Julia felt more restless than she had all night. She looked around, her gaze settling on the salon's entrance.

"Go," Sue said with a sigh. "Don't say I didn't try."

"What are you going to tell her?"

"That a man in a black cloak dragged you away," she said with a wink. "I'll think of something. Consider your eyebrows spared."

As Julia left the warmth of the salon, the night's cool breeze hit her, ruffling her hair. Julia's pace quickened as she hurried around the corner of Mulberry Lane, determined to talk to any member of the Knight family. After Barker had filled her in on his conversation with Sam and gone off in search of Derek, Julia knew there was more to be uncovered. As much as she wanted to leave the grieving family alone, as Barker had pointed out over the phone, not only were they suspects in the murder investigation, they were now potential targets for the cloaked killer's dagger.

The B&B beckoned her, and after being let in by Evelyn's grandson, Julia found Faith in her familiar spot by the windowsill, the room dimly lit by the moonlight. Shimmering crystal necklaces lay around Faith's neck, dancing with an ethereal shimmer. Julia approached cautiously, settling beside the young woman, who barely reacted to her presence.

"Your mother's necklaces?"

"Always thought she was silly for wearing them," Faith said as she caressed a black stone. "For such an intellectual woman, falling for this spiritual stuff never made sense to me." She gave a wry smile, her lips trembling. "But it was just her way. Her path. Over now."

Julia understood loss and the pain of losing a mother, though she'd already lived for twenty years without hers by Faith's age. Saving her words, Julia reached out and rested a hand on Faith's knee.

"I'm sorry you're going through this," she began cautiously, looking for a reaction, still unsure of Faith's guilt or innocence. "Faith, about Arthur. Last time I was here, you didn't deny that the two of you were an item?"

"We met one evening at a train station," Faith said, her honesty a surprise. "It was random, or fate... I don't know." She swallowed hard. "He was hurt. Someone had beaten him up. I saw him rolled out of a car, left there like he was nothing."

"And you helped him?"

Faith nodded. "How could I not? I took him home and patched him up. He was so different that night. Vulnerable. Not the Arthur people keep talking about."

"And the people who did that to him, they were the gang, weren't they?"

Faith looked away, a tear escaping her eye. "*Why* would he burn our house down? He loved me. We had our differences, but he told me he *loved* me." The anguish in her voice sent a dagger into Julia's chest. "He told me he just needed some time to sort himself out. To straighten his ways. Time to get away from those suited idiots, to find himself."

Julia observed the young woman in front of her: heartbroken, shattered, lost in the vortex of emotions. For a fleeting moment, Julia was transported back in time, seeing her younger self reflected in Faith's pain, a mirror of shared grief. Julia had waited far too long for her first husband to change in all the ways he'd promised her he would.

"You believe he was innocent?" Julia asked. "That he didn't start the fire?"

"He was *misunderstood*," Faith stated firmly, her eyes meeting Julia's. "He wasn't out to get us. It's just a big, terrible, tragic misunderstanding, and now he's dead, and my mother..."

Julia placed a comforting hand on Faith's as tears swallowed up her words. Though Julia could see how love had clouded the younger woman's judgment, she couldn't ignore that her pain was genuine.

"Who would want to kill your mother, Faith?"

"I don't know," Faith stated, staring down at the garden below. "None of this makes any sense to me. The cult, the rituals, it was just a book."

Faith crossed the room and pulled out the bound copy of *The Lost Religions of the Cotswolds* by Sophia Knight. She handed the book to Julia, and the weight of it took on a whole new meaning now that the author was dead with the story unpublished.

"There might be something in there," Faith said, perching back on the windowsill. "Find whoever is behind this. I've already lost too much."

"I promise, Faith, I'll try," Julia whispered, clinging to the book.

As she clutched the weighty book, Julia thought about the chapters of Sophia Knight's life that would never be written. Three children now without their mother, a husband without his wife, and her life's work still unpublished. Was the book a treasure map to something more sinister? With those questions bubbling in her mind, Julia walked out, more determined than ever to read between the lines.

∽

Amidst the remnants of charred wooden beams and blackened walls, the faint outline of Derek seemed to meld with the remnants. He was the picture of despair, hunched in the rubble of his former family home.

Clutched in Derek's hand was the photograph he'd shown Barker the last time they'd been at the ruins together. The edges were slightly singed, but the image was intact. Like the family picture Barker had on his desk, it was a Christmas memento of happier times, never to be repeated with all family members again.

Barker stopped a few paces away, taking in the sight. In the aftermath of all that had transpired, Derek's presence amidst the ruins was unsettling.

A grieving husband?

A guilty man?

Both?

The crackling of scorched wood underfoot gave away Barker's arrival long before he settled next to Derek on a foundation stone missing its floorboards.

"Derek, I'm truly sorry," Barker started, no words worthy of the moment. "I wish I could have intervened earlier, caught Arthur Foster before all this spiralled out of control."

Derek remained silent for a while, just the occasional shuffle of the photograph in his hands, but eventually, he found his voice, albeit strained and raspy. "Are the police searching for me?"

Barker nodded. "They've been looking

everywhere. I was at home, getting ready for bed when I remembered you said you came here after Arthur was sighted. I'm surprised the police haven't checked here."

Derek's hollow eyes glanced around. "Where is 'here' anymore? We're sitting in what used to be my study." A painful smile touched his lips as he gestured to the emptiness surrounding them. "You wouldn't believe it, but these walls, which barely stand, once were lined with books. History, literature, my memories. All reduced to ash. And now, this mess has taken my wife." He stared at the picture, adding a tear to the glossy surface. "We weren't perfect. We certainly had our moments and many differences. But, Barker, we *were* a happy family. Until Arthur came into our lives, I don't think I would have changed a thing. Not my daughter's bad taste in men, my teenage son's strange ways, my eldest's 'tortured artist' cliched way, or even my wife's belief in worlds I didn't believe in. Not a thing. I loved our chaos. It was *normal*."

Barker inhaled deeply, feeling the urgency of the moment. "I've pieced together a bit of what happened, Derek. It doesn't seem that Arthur stumbled upon your family by chance. My wife spoke with your daughter earlier, and Faith mentioned that Arthur appeared in her life being rolled out of a car, promising he'd change for her."

"At the train station, yes."

"And how often did your daughter catch that train?"

"Every weekday."

"Same times?"

"I dropped her off every morning before I drove to Oxford."

"Then I believe that moment may have been manufactured," Barker said. "I believe that was the Cotswold Crew's way of infiltrating your life. Your son, Sam, accepted money from Arthur that could have come from the Crew, but I strongly feel that's not the real reason Arthur targeted your family. You've been keeping something from me since our first meeting, right?"

Derek looked away, avoiding Barker's eyes. The night's chill seemed to seep deeper into the bones at the tension between the two men.

Barker pressed on, his eyes narrowing. "It has something to do with that land, doesn't it, Derek? Those two strips of land on either side of that road once belonged to your father's farm. Right by where your wife was found. What's so significant about them?"

Derek's face contorted as though he wanted to be

anywhere else, thinking about anything else, and Barker still tried to help him on that journey. But first, they needed to go through the fire, and Barker wished it didn't have to be so soon after another tragedy, but until the truth was aired, he wasn't sure how much further he'd be willing to go.

"How did you come to know about my father's land?" Derek asked.

Barker hesitated, briefly toying with telling him the truth about Nathan's confession. Instead, he chose his words carefully. "While trying to make sense of Sophia's death, I went through public records, hoping to find a connection to the location she was found. The strips of land owned by you caught my attention."

Derek's facade crumbled as his shoulders slumped. He buried his face in his hands, releasing guttural sobs that echoed the anguish of a broken man. "It's all my fault, Barker. My *foolish* pride. I should have sold the land when they asked the first time, and none of this would have happened."

"Sold the land to whom?" Barker pressed.

"I don't know their real names. If I did, I'd reveal them to you." He wiped away his tears. "Men from that gang started approaching me months before Arthur entered our lives. Always different, always in suits. They wanted the land and kept increasing their offers with each refusal. But that land is part of my history, my legacy, Barker. I promised my father on his deathbed."

Barker's brow furrowed, piecing the story together. "So, when you declined, the gang started to target your family?

Derek nodded. "I was warned they would do *anything* to get what they wanted. But I never imagined they'd go to *these* lengths. Not my home, not my Sophia. Everything's unravelling. My life will never be the same because of this."

Both men sat silently for a moment, lost in their thoughts.

"The question is, Derek, why that specific land?" Barker asked with a sigh. "What makes those strips of land, which wrap around that road, so valuable?"

Derek sighed deeply, wiping his tears away, "I've been wracking my brain but can't find an answer. Perhaps there's something buried there? All I know is that they're determined to get their hands on it, and the price now seems to be the lives of those I love. I shouldn't have been such a coward in coming here. I should be with my children, protecting them."

Barker placed a comforting hand on Derek's shoulder. "It's not cowardice, Derek. You're in shock, and it's only human to seek solace in familiar surroundings. But now we have to act before another body shows up."

Derek nodded slowly, lifting his gaze to meet Barker's. "What do you propose?"

"Maybe we can get the land surveyed and see if there's anything worth all this chaos. Meanwhile, you need to get to a safe location. They believe you're their key to the land. Your hiding will buy us time to uncover their motives."

"But my children…"

"Once we tell the police everything you've just told me, they'll arrange for their immediate protection. I'm sure of it."

"Do you think the gang is behind these deaths?"

Barker paused, connecting the dots in his mind. "I've been thinking, Derek. Your wife's research, the land, the gang. Could there be a link to that cult?"

"If they infiltrated our life with Arthur, there's no way to be certain they didn't read my wife's manuscript. I wish I'd never given my wife those academic papers that sparked her interest all those years ago. My family, we're not part of a cult, Barker." He laughed off the suggestion, looking down at the picture. "Like I said, in our dysfunction, we were *normal*. My wife had abnormal interests, but like yourself, she just wanted to share her interests with the rest of the world in the written word. And I encouraged her every step of the way. That was the first domino that started this, but regret is a fool's game. I've made far too many mistakes up until this point." He traced the edges of the photograph. "I saw that spark in her eyes every paper she read, every theory she discussed. That passion, Barker, made me fall in love with her even more. We were like chalk and cheese. The professor and the hippie, but somehow, we worked. She was my world."

"There's a world waiting for you beyond this," Barker said, helping Derek up from the stone. "You still have three children to live for."

"And let's make sure to keep it that way." Derek took a shaky breath, releasing it as he glanced again at the ruined remnants of his life. "Because when this is over, and that gang is behind bars, I'm going to rebuild our lives. Right here."

Barker nodded, his gaze distant as if seeing a storm on the horizon. "And I'll do everything in my power to help. But we should prepare, Derek. This isn't over just yet."

As he walked Derek away from the ruins, the beams of a torches sliced through the dark, landing squarely on both men. Derek looked on, petrified, as several uniformed officers rushed out of the dark.

"Don't panic," Barker whispered. "It's only because you went missing when you did."

"But surely they don't suspect—"

"*Police*! Stay where you are!"

The hiding was over, but questions loomed larger than ever. Barker hoped Derek would be as forthright across the interview desk, but given everything he'd hidden so far, Barker wouldn't be surprised if they kept him for as long as they could for the sake of having someone to arrest.

Maybe he'd just been duped.

His instincts told him otherwise.

If the Cotswold Crew was behind everything, Barker had to find a way to prove it while convincing Moyes to get the Knight children under surveillance.

16

Rain danced on the window of the kitchen in the cottage the following morning. Julia sat hunched at the breakfast bar, her fingers wrapped tightly around a mug of steaming black coffee. She needed the caffeine to help unstick what felt like another dead-end as she reviewed her notepad after filling it with hers, Barker's, and Jessie's new findings.

Beside her, Jessie was engrossed in *The Peridale Post*, but the usual spark in her eyes was missing. "'Darkness Falls Over Peridale After Second Sacrifice Slaying: Who Will Shine the Light?' It's so... grim." She took a deep breath and set the paper aside. "All this new information, and we're still missing *how* we put it together."

Scratching at his stubble as he consulted his phone, Barker said, "They're still holding Derek."

"Do you think they'll charge him?" Julia asked, stirring up her porridge.

"Unless they have something we don't, I don't know how they could," he said, fingers firing out a reply. "Sam's confirmation about Arthur Foster's loan and the implication that the money came from the Cotswold Crew lends credibility to them being behind the fire. It's a clear motive. The land, on the other hand, complicates things, and Derek admitted that was going on before Arthur showed up."

"And Faith still thinks Arthur could be innocent of the arson," Julia added. "Maybe she's blinded by love, but it's something to investigate."

"Definitely blinded," Jessie muttered.

"I need to read more of Sophia's book today, too. There might be more information that could lead us to figure this out."

"Or hint at who the next victim could be," Jessie said. "Did you convince Moyes to put a watch on the B&B, Dad?"

"Took a bit of twisting, but she doesn't want another body on her hands if Derek is a dead-end."

"Peridale's local police not putting up a fight?" Jessie laughed. "This must be serious."

"When it comes to this gang, it always was,"

Barker stated, washing his finished coffee cup at the sink. "I still don't want you going looking for them, Jessie. Veronica should never have put you on their scent in the first place, but at least she's done the right thing in taking you off it. The Crew, the cult, the land, it's all interwoven somehow, we have to figure out how."

"And then the unravelling can begin," Jessie said. "But if the Crew is as dangerous as they seem, they'll have eyes and ears everywhere already. The police, the politicians, the businesses. How do we prove they're behind this and bring them down?"

"*We* don't," Barker said. "We figure out whatever we can, hand it over to the police so they can get on with their jobs. Anything else?"

Julia hesitated in bringing it up, but the cameras would turn up again eventually.

"The documentary?"

"Right," Barker said with a sigh. "Leave Anwen to me. She can't have much more footage to get, though something tells me she won't be satisfied until she has an ending, so the sooner we put this case to bed, the sooner the shoot can wrap."

"I thought *we* weren't putting this to bed?" Jessie pointed out. "Or does staying out of danger only apply to *me*, the only one with an official badge? Speaking of which, I have a brunch meeting with a new contact, so you two go and play good cop, bad cop, and the *real* investigator will get on with her job." She crammed in the last of her toast and kissed Olivia on the head. "Stay away from cloaks, even if they have fistfuls of sweets."

Jessie left, and Julia and Barker both exhaled sighs simultaneously.

"She'll be fine," Julia said with a firm nod. "I'm sure she'll be fine."

"Are you sure because I'm—"

The landline phone rang by the fridge, so loud and unexpected that Olivia burst into immediate tears. It rang infrequently, and only one person ever bothered to use it rather than call their mobiles.

"Hi, Gran."

"*Julia*!" Dot cried. "Get down here *right now*. You've been *marked*!"

The abrupt end of Dot's urgent message sent a cold chill down Julia's spine. Hastily packing Olivia up for the day and grabbing their coats, they rushed down the lane in Barker's car. They arrived at the village green where a small gathering had collected outside the café. The crowd parted, and a jarring sight greeted them.

Julia's Café was defaced with bold red initials 'CC.'

The café's window, once pristine, was now tainted with the undeniable evidence of a threat. The meaning of the letters was immediately up for debate, though it was apparent to Julia who had left them.

"It has to mean *Cult Corpse*," Dot announced. "They're coming for you next, Julia. You must be close to figuring all of this out."

Ethel, who never passed up an opportunity to counter Dot's theories, clicked her tongue. "I'd say it means *Café Cult*. It's not a warning *to* Julia but to all of *us*. Don't you all think it's *strange* how this one family seems to be at the centre of every murder?"

"*Every* murder?" Dot rolled her eyes. "You were a suspect when your former Eyes leader met her end."

"Mark my words," Ethel continued. "You want to find a cult? Look no further than the South-Brown-Wellington-Croppers and whatever other names they'll tack on when they *lure* in their next member. It's not too late to divorce, Percy. *Divorce!*"

"How absurd!" Percy remarked, pulling the dogs closer. "Right, my love?"

The feeling of being directly threatened by the Cotswold Crew made Julia's blood run cold more than the ludicrous suggestion that she was a cult member, though she now joined the list of the other hundred or so villagers accused over the past few days. Her heart raced as she took in the crowd of onlookers, their whispers morphing into a dull roar in her ears.

Barker and Olivia took a protective step closer to

Julia, his phone in his hand. "I've just reported it to the station."

But Julia, showcasing a strength she wasn't sure she had believed she had, lifted her chin high. "It's just some spray paint. Whoever did this wants to scare me. To scare us all. I won't let them." Her voice betrayed her with a wobble. "I'll get a bucket and a brush, and anyone who wants to help get rid of this mess, step forward."

Murmurs of approval spread among the gathering, and Julia saw a bright camera light and a hovering microphone racing towards them.

Once inside the café, the confidence drained from Julia, replaced by the real fear she felt. Another day, another warning, and the threats were inching closer to home. As she filled the bucket at the sink, her fearful reflection in the tap water stared back. But she didn't know what else to do besides what she'd always done in her sanctuary.

She put on a brave face and pushed through the beads, and when the spray paint was gone, and the cabinets were filled with cakes for the day, she'd sit down with Sophia's book along with her notepad and keep digging.

With a sore back from spending the first hour of his morning helping scrub the graffiti off, Barker took a moment to stretch out before approaching the B&B. He was pleased to see the marked police car sitting outside, and he recognised officers mingling with the guests in their civilian clothes in the dining room.

Among them was PC Jake Puglisi, who was helping himself to croissants at the breakfast buffet. Barker wasted no time making a beeline for Jake, and he must have looked as angry as he felt because Puglisi tripped over a chair in his rush to cross the room, spilling orange juice down his shirt. Barker grabbed his collar, guiding him away from the food-laden table and into the hallway.

"I swear, Mr Brown, I didn't—"

Still holding onto the collar, Barker interrupted, "Didn't what? I haven't even told you why I'm mad yet."

Puglisi's face flushed crimson, and Barker, showing a hint of mercy, let go of his collar, then straightened it out for him.

Taking a deep breath, Barker asked, "Jake, why did you leak my new book online after DI Moyes gave it to you?"

"*I* d-didn't, I swear," Puglisi stammered. "Look, I was reading the first few chapters at the station. They're fantastic, by the way, but then I was sent here last night to take a statement from Sam to review his alibi again. I left the manuscript for just a moment." He pointed to the sideboard with Evelyn's framed pictures from her exotic travels. "When I got back, it was gone."

Barker's eyes narrowed. "So, you're saying a guest took it and uploaded chapters to the Peridale Chat group?"

Puglisi nodded. "I swear, Mr Brown, it wasn't me."

"Okay, Jake. I believe you," Barker said, handing him a napkin for the spilt orange juice. "Ask around and see if you can track down the thief while you're here, okay?"

"Absolutely, and if you've got another copy, I'd love to finish—"

"Don't push it, Puglisi."

Looking around the busy B&B, Barker's mind raced. Could it have been one of the Knights? After conversing with Sam and Derek, he'd subconsciously discounted them as suspects, but perhaps he'd been closer to the truth than he realised. The complex case now had another layer, and there was no putting his book back in the drawer.

Thoughts of his book were interrupted when he spotted DI Moyes making her way down the staircase. Her eyes locked onto Barker's, and she didn't try to hide her little sigh at the sight of him.

"Barker," she greeted him, exhaling a vapour plume from her e-cig. "I'd say it was a pleasant surprise, but it's neither pleasant nor a surprise that you're here right now."

He raised an eyebrow, a smile curving his lips. "Just here to check in on the family."

"Until this is put to bed, they've been instructed to stay in their rooms. No one goes in or out, and that includes you."

"Their welfare is my concern too, Moyes, and I don't need to remind you that Derek has hired me to prove their innocence in this case. Have you released him yet?"

"We have." She held his gaze for a moment. "The last thing I need is you muddying the waters. It's great that you found Derek last night and finally got him to open up about why the Cotswold Crew targeted him, but—"

"So, you're officially linking Arthur to the crew?

Gritting her jaw, she looked around before sitting on the bottom step. "Derek believes someone from the Crew must have got their hands on Sophia's manuscript. That's how they knew about the cult angle. Of all the crazy things I've heard this week, that makes the most sense. Maybe that's why Arthur was at the B&B the day he died. He might have known about it, brought it up to the Crew, and they had him sneak in to find out more information, which they then used to kill him?" Sighing, she rubbed at her temples. "Or maybe he read some of it earlier and came to the B&B for different reasons. I don't know. It's still all making my head spin. My gut has told me these deaths have nothing to do with an actual cult."

Just then, the soft rustle of fabric alerted them to Evelyn's presence, seemingly having appeared behind the check-in desk from thin air. Clothed in mourning black, she exuded melancholic energy that could have wilted her wildflowers. Even a cynic like Barker would've described her aura as dark and stormy.

"I apologise for prying," Evelyn whispered, her voice hoarse. "But I think you're right about this being a ruse. At first, I genuinely thought that perhaps the long-forgotten cult wasn't so forgotten by everyone. There are layers to our existence that most people refuse to see, but sometimes, the logical, Earthbound explanation is the answer. I spent most of the night meditating, consulting leaves, cards, and crystals. I called upon my spirit guides, ancestors, even Astrid, and I kept returning to one explanation."

Moyes and Barker shared a look.

"Which is?" Moyes prompted.

"Sophia's book," Evelyn said, her far-off gaze snapping onto the detective. "The very presence of the book itself. I should be able to count on one hand the people Sophia claimed to have had access to the book, but it wasn't like she had the manuscript under lock and key."

"Now, there's an idea," Barker muttered, glancing at Moyes.

"Your wife almost walked out of here with it," Evelyn continued, gesturing to Barker. "So yes, the Cotswold Crew, or anyone for that matter, could have read the section about the Moon's Beloved ritual and replicated it. And there's something else. Not just the presence of the book but the content. The first death coincided with a full moon, just as the Moon's Beloved ritual stated in the manuscript. But the timing of Sophia's tragic transcendence had *nothing* to do with the moon's cycle. If this was a real cult, as we're supposed to believe, given the effort the murderer has gone to, why stray from a pattern set in stone thousands of years ago?"

"Smoke and mirrors," Moyes said.

"That's what I feel to be true," Evelyn sighed. "For a moment, I began to believe that Sophia might have had something to do with all of this, but why would she pull from her work in such an obvious way? Only someone who wanted to frame her would be so obvious, which begs *why* Sophia was killed when she was and not at the next full moon."

Evelyn paused, prompting Moyes to take a step forward. "Do you have a theory, Evelyn?"

"My dear friend was an intelligent woman, and even though she might have been trying to keep herself out of the frame by concealing what she knew, she would have been trying to figure out what was going on as much as anyone else. Perhaps Sophia brought about her death because she put the pieces together and figured out who read her book."

Moyes vaped silently for a moment before giving one last nod, then headed for the door without sharing her thoughts. Barker almost followed, but she'd said she didn't want him muddying the waters.

"Do you have any idea who that person could be?" Barker asked.

"I can vouch for Derek when Sophia disappeared," Evelyn said, her eyes clouded with sadness. "I heard they're placing her death somewhere around 3 a.m., and with everything going on, I couldn't sleep. I came down around 2 a.m. to make some warm almond milk, and Derek was in the sitting room just over there," she said, pointing a finger at one of the armchairs. "I stayed with him for a few hours, offering him spiritual counsel. We heard some people coming and going, but that's not unusual for a B&B. It was a warm night, so I assumed others couldn't sleep. Perhaps Sophia went out for a walk, or perhaps that's when she was taken..."

Evelyn's words transformed into tears, and Barker wished he had one of those handkerchiefs Julia was always carrying with her. Mark appeared through the door of the staff quarters.

"Nan?" he wrapped an arm around her. "What did you say to her?"

"Mark, it's not Barker's fault," Evelyn insisted. "Please, find it within your heart to forgive him for the wrongs you think he's done. Barker is not a bad man. You must try to see that."

"Must I?" Mark sneered. "If you'd done your job properly and found Arthur when you should have, we might not be here right now." Shaking his head, he pushed past Barker and went to the door. "Good luck figuring all of this out. Maybe if you do, you'll have another book to write. I'm going to the graveyard."

Mark slammed the door, silencing those still finishing breakfast in the dining room. Puglisi and the rest of the undercover officers sprung up.

"Sorry, please forgive my grandson. Today is..."

"Astrid's birthday?"

Evelyn nodded, dabbing at her eyes with the corner of her kaftan. "Mark is forgetting that if you and Julia hadn't figured out the truth behind what happened to Astrid, he would never have known she was his real mother, and I'd never have known I had a grandson."

"It's the book he's upset at," Barker said, sighing. "And I'm starting to wonder if he might have a point. Maybe I should have left that case alone. If I hadn't written it, I wouldn't be here now with my latest book floating around on a local gossip group."

"Do not regret a single step on your journey, Barker Brown," Evelyn said with a sudden firmness and strength. "Once this day has passed, he'll return to his senses. This occasion is usually one of celebration for us, honouring Astrid's memory. But now, with this dark cloud hanging over the B&B since the discovery in the forest, I fear it's reminding him too much of the horror humanity has to offer. Focus on the task at hand. You have the skills to put an end to this. I believe in you, Barker."

Barker sighed, running a hand through his hair. "I promise, Evelyn, I'll do everything possible to help lift that cloud."

"Figure out who read Sophia's manuscript," Evelyn stated. "That's where your answers lie."

17

Sipping a coffee in a takeaway cup from the café, Jessie stood on the edge of the field and stared off. The police, like ants in the distance, were combing the area where Sophia Knight had been found. The image from Billy's message burned in her mind, and she pulled out her phone, glancing at the photo once more. Could that man be Greg Morgan?

Jessie didn't have evidence or a clear connection. It was just a gut feeling, made more potent by Veronica's elusive behaviour from the previous night, paired with their shallow article on what went down at the library conference. It was maddening how the higher-ups insisted they play it safe, unwilling to take the heat for what could happen if they printed false allegations about a sitting MP.

Lost in her thoughts, a gentle tap on her shoulder caused her to jump out of her skin. Swirling around, she met Dante's eyes. Too focused on watching the police, she'd almost forgotten about their planned brunch meeting at Richie's Bar.

"I should have cleared my throat or something," Dante said, his eyes twinkling with mischief. "Thought I was the cloaked killer trying to catch you off guard?"

Jessie let out a breathy laugh. "After the twelve hours I've had, I should be so lucky. Did you read our Greg Morgan article?"

"I did."

"After all the editing and censoring, it almost sounds in favour of him, doesn't it?"

"It does." Dante rocked back on his heels. "That's Cotswold Media Group for you. They own *The Chronicle,* too, and they're terrified of being sued for printing anything defamatory without hard evidence to back it up. There's not enough money in village papers to stand up to someone with as many rich friends as Greg Morgan. But more about that over brunch. My treat."

They stepped into Richie's Bar, an instant contrast

to the rural surroundings of Peridale. Owned by Richie and paid for by his wealthy father. The midtempo tropical house music, filament light bulbs, and faux brick walls might have seemed dated compared to some of the places Jessie saw during her travels, but in Peridale, it was practically space age.

"Surprised to see you here in the middle of a weekday, Jessie," Richie said, wiping down the counter as they approached, his twinkling eyes giving Dante the once over. "Though I'll take any customers I can get right now. All these rumours of cults seem to have everyone spooked. Even your mum's café seems unusually quiet."

"Maybe everyone is at home sewing their cloaks to join the cause?"

Richie let out a laugh. "You might be onto something there. Stranger things have happened. So, what can I get you and your new friend?"

After placing their order—a plate of burger sliders and two steaming mugs of coffee—they settled into a booth, and Jessie couldn't help but glance across the table as Dante stirred brown sugar into his coffee. The Edison bulb lighting accentuated the sharpness of his jawline and the depth of his eyes. He glanced up with a smile, and realising she was openly staring at him, Jessie hesitated before pulling up the photograph on her phone. She handed it to Dante, whose brow furrowed in concentration as he studied the image. The ambient noise of Richie's Bar seemed to fade into the background.

Rather than dive into why they were there, Jessie was surprised when Dante opened with a personal question.

"So, I've never seen you around before," he said. "You from these parts?"

"I am now." Lifting her coffee cup, she considered which version of the story she'd give him. She opted for the truth, short version. "I was adopted by this couple. Mum's a baker, Dad's a PI. They're great."

"Adopted?" His brows shot up. "And before that?"

"Straight in with the deep questions."

"We're journalists, aren't we?" He winked. "Sorry, you don't have to tell me."

Jessie almost didn't, but she felt a little thrill from being lumped in as a 'journalist' by a journalist.

"Parents died when I was just a baby. I was raised in the system."

Dante's eyes widened a fraction, as though he'd expected something else. "I'm sorry, Jessie, that sounds really tough."

She shrugged. "It is what it is. You can't change where you came from, only where you're going."

"Very true," Dante said, nodding in agreement.

"What about you?"

"Raised by my mum and dad in Riverswick," Dante said, shifting in his seat. "I still live with them, actually. Grandad too. Pretty normal compared to..."

Dante's words quietened and he reached for his coffee, wincing at his words.

"I was homeless for a bit, too, just to really spice it up." Jessie laughed. "I know my upbringing wasn't normal."

"Look at where you are now though," he said, a little too brightly. "Where'd you study then?"

"You mean uni?"

"Oxford," he admitted, holding up his hands. "I know, I know. So, you?"

Jessie couldn't help but notice the stark differences between their worlds as he talked. Not just because of how they'd grown up, but how sure he was she must have been to university despite what she'd just told him. Those Riverswick houses were much nicer...

"I did my GCSEs this year," she said bluntly. "Uni isn't on the cards."

Again, Dante looked taken aback, but only for a split second. His eyes softened, and he grinned. "Like you said, can't change where you came from, right? Coffee's good here, isn't it?"

Jessie laughed with a nod. As surprised as he seemed—maybe that they were in the same career from different backgrounds—he didn't seem to be judging her. She knew that feeling *all* too well.

They sat in a slightly awkward silence, and Jessie remembered why she'd used the business card he'd sent her to meet with him. She pulled up the photograph on her phone and handed it over to Dante, whose brow furrowed as he studied the blurry face on the screen.

"Do you recognise him?" Jessie asked, to which he shook his head. "Any chance it's Greg Morgan?"

"It could be?" he said. "But it could be anyone. There is something familiar about the face, but it's so blurry."

"And what do you know about the Cotswold Crew?"

He took a deep breath as he slid her phone back. "They're bad news. Real bad. They've got their fingers in all sorts of nasty business around here. We get random tip-offs about them, but my editor won't touch that stuff. Doesn't want to make us a target."

"Know where they're based?"

"No," he said, his eyes narrowing on her, his lips pricking into a smile. "You're not trying to *find* them, are you? That's not a good idea, Jessie."

Tired of hearing that, Jessie didn't answer and instead asked, "Think Greg could be working with them?"

"That's a stretch."

"Yesterday, you accused him of accepting bribes for Henderson Place, and another reporter accused him of cutting his predecessor's brakes."

"But working with a gang like them would be a full deep dive into the underworld. The repercussions of that would be... quite frankly, a little insane. Would certainly be enough to bring him down if you could prove it." Sipping his coffee, he stared off into the empty bar. "He *has* become more obviously power-hungry since he crossed over from being a councillor to an MP, though."

"Where did this guy even come from, anyway? I didn't even know there was an election recently."

"A by-election in the dead of January will do that," Dante said before leaning in and whispering. "Record low turnout. It barely made a splash. It's almost like he snuck in through the backdoor. Greg grew up not far from here, you know? Small farm, outskirts of Peridale. It's a pretty standard upbringing if the version of the story on his website is to be believed. He studied politics at Cambridge, and when he returned, he climbed the local political ladder and hopped around a few parish councils. Settled in planning before he snagged himself a seat in Parliament. Sells himself as the sort of bloke you could chat with down the pub, but he only cares about one thing, in my eyes."

"Which is?"

Dante rubbed his thumb and forefingers together.

"Money," Jessie echoed.

"Exactly." A small shadow of regret flitted across Dante's face. "Before your previous editor, Johnny, left, we were trying to expose his corruption. He thought if the local papers all worked together, we'd stand a better chance of nailing something to him that might stick, but Cotswold Media Group always stood in our way. I can't say I blame Veronica for wanting to take a different route. She made herself quite clear when she moved out of the main building. I still can't believe she pulled that off, to be honest. Is it true you're snuck above some tacky salon?"

"My step-grandmother's salon," Jessie said, holding back a laugh. "I got us a discount."

"Ah, Jessie, I'm sorry, I—"

"I didn't disagree with you about it being tacky." Jessie winked as she reached into her bag, her fingers wrapping around a familiar folder. The papers were slightly worn, filled with scribbles, notes, and newspaper clippings. "Johnny gave me this before he left. Everything he'd collected on Greg."

He reached into his bag, and with the movement, Jessie caught a whiff of his aftershave—a woodsy, invigorating scent that somehow fit his personality. He produced a similar folder, laying it on the table next to Jessie's.

"Snap."

"I can't make heads or tails of any of it," Jessie said, pulling out some of the accounting spreadsheet pages. "Numbers have never been my thing."

Dante leaned in, his fingers brushing the pages, zeroing in on a sequence of digits. "See these transactions? Large sums were transferred to Greg quickly, right around the time the library was sold. You were right to push that line of questioning yesterday. You had him on the ropes."

"So, they're proof of the alleged bribes?"

Dante wavered. "On paper, no. They're labelled as fees for public speaking arrangements. Greg's been making a killing from these appearances for years. Some clips end up online occasionally, but they're mostly for private functions. That's not too unusual for people in his line of work. But the amounts? It's absurd for someone of his status to charge the sort of fee you'd expect from a former prime minister."

Jessie scanned the large transactions again. The names of the senders had been blanked out. "So, it's safe to assume *these* bribes—or should I say, public speaking payments—were sent from James Jacobson?"

"The timeline fits," he said, putting his folder in his bag. "Listen, I have to go. As much as I'd love to dig deeper with you, I've got a puff piece about a nursing home charity event waiting for me."

"Our food hasn't even come yet."

"I'm sorry," he said, edging out of the booth. "When you called to meet, I was hoping you'd have some new info to share with me about Greg. My editor doesn't like me digging into this Greg story as it is. He thinks it's a waste of time."

"Oh," Jessie said, sipping her coffee. "I'm sorry for wasting your time then."

"I didn't mean it like that," he said, looping his bag over his shoulder. "They're stretching me thin, and I'm on the clock right now. I'll see you around?"

"I hope so."

As he left the bar, Jessie watched him go, wondering if her background has scared him off. She wasn't sure it had, but she didn't enjoy leading with that story, especially the further those years were behind her. She placed her forehead on the table, cursing herself. *I hope so.* She should have said 'sure' and left it at that.

"He was cute," Richie remarked, nodding toward the door as he placed the plate of sliders down. "Got a charm about him."

"You noticed?"

"New boyfriend material?"

"Don't be daft."

"One of us should be so lucky."

"You seeing anyone?"

"*Was*, and that's the barman's question to ask, not answer." Richie cast an eye over the paperwork still on the table. "What's all this then?"

"Proof your dad might have bribed the council to sell him the library," Jessie said, watching him closely. "Know anything about that?"

Richie shrugged, the accusation not phasing him. "Even if he did, you think he keeps me that much in the loop?"

Jessie believed him. From what she knew about the father and son duo, James was the type to throw money at his close family, not time and the sharing of secrets. "Seen him recently?"

"To my surprise, he dropped by this place last weekend. Just a quick visit. Passing through on business. Still claiming he's moving into that new place he built up the lane any day now, but I stopped believing that one about six months ago." Richie folded the rag and looked off to the green. "Can I get you another coffee?"

"I'm good," she said, plucking up a slider and cramming it in her mouth. "I have a tacky office to get to."

After finishing the sliders to herself, Jessie walked to Mulberry Lane and climbed the narrow staircase leading up to the newspaper office. Inside, Veronica was hunched over her desk, where Jessie dumped the file. Veronica shot up, cramming on her glasses before they slid off. She scowled up at Jessie for disturbing her before reaching into her desk drawer to pull out a much thicker file, thudding it next to Jessie's.

"What?" Veronica exclaimed. "You didn't think I'd just stop where Johnny left things, did you? And nice of you to finally admit that he gave you a copy, too. I was wondering when you'd whip it out."

"Because I didn't understand much of it until this afternoon. I had a meeting with a contact who—"

"What contact?"

Jessie's cheeks flushed. "Because you *always* tell me who your contacts are."

"Editor." Veronica pointed at herself before pointing at Jessie. "Rookie."

"Not important." Jessie flicked open the folder and pulled out the spreadsheet. "What is important are these transactions. Large sums around the time the library was sold. Could be the evidence we need to print about Greg to prove he's no good."

Veronica glanced at the figures, but she didn't look impressed.

"You said we need evidence, so here is—"

"Don't you think I've already gone over those figures?" Veronica said, producing a satsuma from her drawer. She began peeling it with one hand. "They're payments for speaking engagements and won't do much. Greg's always found a way to mask his tracks, and it's all technically legal. It's frustrating, but we need more. And besides, it's old news. Ironically, this might be enough if the original restaurant plan had gone ahead, but we need something current. He'll get what's coming to him."

"So, are you going to tell me who is Greg to you?"

Veronica busied herself, separating the satsuma into segments.

"You have something against him beyond all of this stuff," Jessie continued. "I asked you that same question when you hired me, and you didn't answer me then either. I need to know where you stand. If this is just some petty vendetta—"

Veronica shot up from her chair. "You think this is a *petty* vendetta?"

"I just want to understand."

"Regardless of any connection I might have to Greg Morgan, Johnny was the one who started connecting the dots before he left. Before I was thrust into this position." She glared at Jessie as though daring her to interrupt. "This isn't about me. It's about knowing that a man like Greg Morgan will trample over anyone to get what he wants. If you knew the things I've been hearing from my contacts..." She sighed, closing her eyes. "You need to trust me."

"What things?"

"Just trust me, okay?"

"*How* can I trust you if you're keeping secrets from me? Why should I care about what Greg Morgan is up to? Johnny cared. *You* care. But me?" Jessie pushed the folder across the table. "I never asked to be part of this."

Their eyes locked, a storm of emotions brewing between them. The air felt thicker, the salon below too silent, and she could imagine Katie and her clients on hooks waiting for the next raised voice. Taking a steadying breath, Jessie pulled out her phone and showed the picture to Veronica again.

"You recognised him the moment Billy showed you this picture."

Veronica's eyes flickered across the photograph. A few days ago, she'd denied any recognition. Now, she merely remained silent.

"I know you do," Jessie pressed. "I think it is Greg. And not just because I recognise him, but because of *your* sudden change as soon as you saw this picture. You yanked me from the gang story and threw me straight onto Greg's trail. You made that connection, sent me to do the legwork, and now you're backing off. Why?"

Veronica's face had a forced calmness as she finished her last satsuma segment. "Because if it's true if he is working with the Crew, and that's a depth I never thought he'd sink to."

Jessie saw something she hadn't seen before in Veronica: vulnerability, fear, and a flicker of hope that she was wrong about Greg Morgan.

"Tell me who he is."

"Jessie..."

Jessie's patience had ended, the frustration simmering throughout their conversation now bubbling over. She stuffed the folder from Veronica's desk into her bag.

"I'm not playing your games, Veronica," Jessie snapped, her voice quivering. "I'm not content to sit around waiting for answers to come to us."

Veronica opened her mouth to speak, but Jessie was already moving, her footsteps heavy as she approached the door.

"Where are you going?"

Jessie paused in the doorway, turning back to look at Veronica, her eyes hard. "I'm going to do what you pay me to do. Investigative journalism. Some things can be solved from behind a desk, but this isn't one of them."

Veronica's mouth hung open like she had more to say, but nothing came out. She simply stared at Jessie. Jessie's jaw tightened, and without another word, she turned and left, the door slamming behind her with a resounding thud.

18

"Aren't you terrified for your life?" Dot asked as Julia locked up the café later that day. "You should pack a bag and leave Peridale until all this blows over. We *all* should."

"My Dorothy might be right," Percy agreed, holding steady as Bruce tried to yank his arm off, the French Bulldog preoccupied with a cat. Lady politely waited by Dot's feet next to Olivia's pram. "Just seeing the moon every night is giving me the heebie-jeebies."

"A *cult*, Julia." Dot's voice trembled as she pointed at the window, her face pale. "CC!"

Julia's mind raced. Would telling Dot about the gang make things better or worse? Her heart pounded as she considered the villagers' terror, knowing there was yet another dangerous group lurking in the shadows.

"The cult is called Lunara," Julia pointed out instead, dropping the café keys into her bag. "And they're more a religious sect than anything. They existed thousands of years ago."

"Those two murders didn't happen thousands of years ago, did they?" Ethel called as she passed the café. "But it's been noted that you were just discussing the cult again."

"*Get a hobby*, Ethel!" Dot cried after her as she made her way to the church. "And I hate to agree with Ethel, but she's right. Those murders happened this week. The first two of who knows how many? I don't know why you're not taking this seriously."

Julia had done nothing but pore over Sophia's book all day, making notes, spinning around in circles, doing little but taking things seriously. She was relieved to see Barker heading towards them from the direction of the B&B.

"We have some filming to do," Julia said, kissing her gran on the cheek before dipping to brush Olivia's curls away from her face in the pram. "I'll pick you up in about an hour, okay? And Gran, make sure to lock the doors."

"So, you *are* scared." Dot pursed her lips. "And we'll protect her with our lives. Won't we, Percy?"

"We've developed quite the system. We always have eyes on every door and window. Nobody is snatching us in the night, though I must say," Percy paused to let out a rip-roaring yawn, "the night watches are becoming quite tiring. I can't believe we missed the graffiti artist."

"Yes, well, as you said, it's been quite tiring," Dot said, her gaze avoidant. "I may or may not have nodded off for a split second. You can imagine my shock when my eyes opened to see the red markings." She looked as though she might try to convince Julia to hide again, but she wafted her hand in defeat. "There's a cottage pie in the oven that'll stretch if you're hungry when your filming is finished. Feel free to bring the crew over to capture some more footage. I'm sure Anwen will be itching to expand my part after yesterday."

Dot and Percy headed across the green with Olivia and the dogs, and Julia joined Barker, who'd been lingering by the alley's opening. After a quick hug, Barker dove straight into asking Julia if she'd found anything interesting in Sophia's manuscript. As they walked down the alley, Julia pulled out the book and flipped to the page she'd marked:

The Cult of Lunara's selection process, especially concerning identifying the Moon's Beloved, has been a subject of extensive research and fascination. The method by which members were chosen for the ultimate honour of sacrifice is emblematic of the complex interplay between myth, symbolism, and community within the cult—the initial stage of the selection involved scrutiny of family lineage, personal attributes, and omens. A potential candidate was identified through a combination of divination, individual assessment, and sometimes voluntary nomination. Once the candidate was selected, marking them and their household began. This was a highly ritualistic affair, carried out by the high priest or priestess, often accompanied by a select group of the cult's inner circle. The chosen one's dwelling would be marked with symbols of the moon, sacred to the Cult of Lunara. These symbols, intricate crescents and full moons were carved or painted on the doors.

"Family lineage could explain why Sophia was chosen if one of the Knights is behind this?" Julia suggested once Barker had read the extract. "But it seems like they had a rather broad catchment. The part about the doors... do you think..."

"It was on your window, not your door," Barker pointed out, wrapping a hand around hers. "Nor do you live at the café, and it wasn't symbols. How have you been holding up today?"

Julia took a deep breath. "Uneasy. Given how close everything happened, I half expected the café to be busy, but it was deserted. People must be genuinely frightened, or Ethel's gossiping about us being cult members kept everyone away."

"The whole village feels different at the moment," he said, looking around the empty field. "And given the Crew's usual style, some graffiti is a light warning."

A shiver ran down Julia's spine as she considered what else awaited them. As they continued into the field where the fading sun painted the sky with oranges and purples, they reached the spot where Sophia Knight's body had been found. The grass was trampled and scattered with left-behind evidence markers. Even the early evening dog walkers had chosen to avoid this grim spot.

"Evelyn made a good point earlier," Barker said, breaking the silence as they stared at the spot. "Even if someone is using the selection process in the book, they're not exactly following it to the letter. Was there anything in there about killings happening on days outside the full moon?"

Julia scanned her memories of the long Lunara chapter. "I think the full moon seemed to be the only day."

"Then why break thousands of years of tradition?" Barker said, shielding his eyes from the setting sun as he stared back towards the café. "Here she comes. I'll be glad when this documentary business is done and dusted. I want to get back to our normal lives."

Julia nodded, tucking a stray hair behind her ear. However, she couldn't remember what normal felt like anymore as she watched Anwen hurry across the field with Ava, the camerawoman, in tow. Both seemed out of breath, their faces flushed as if they'd sprinted from the B&B.

"We're losing the light!" Anwen exclaimed, her voice teetering on the edge of panic.

"No Rupert?" Barker asked.

Anwen, not bothering to hide her exasperation, shot back, "That's film graduates for you. Can't trust them to be reliable for a minute." She started fiddling with the camera, much to Ava's annoyance. "Must have been given a better job. Haven't seen him all day."

Julia could see a flicker of something in Barker's eyes—recognition, perhaps, or surprise. She remembered how, just a few days ago in the café kitchen, Anwen had been gushing about how great recent graduates were. Barker's raised eyebrow and the slight tilt of his head communicated that he'd also picked up on the inconsistency.

"Aren't you a little worried about him being missing?" Julia asked. "Given what's going on?"

"He's not missing, just unprofessional," Anwen said as she positioned Julia and Barker on either side of the crime scene. "He's been sending Ava Snapchat pictures all day. Right, we are losing the light, so *action!*"

∼

"Let's pick up where we left off," Anwen began, her tone soft, almost compassionate. "Your mother, Barker. She was the initial inspiration for you wanting to write, right?"

Barker tensed, the opening question throwing him off. In the comfort of his office yesterday, he'd probably shared more than he'd wanted to, even if there had been a camera pointed at his face. Today, in the vast openness of the field, he felt the most uncomfortable he had with the light blinding him.

"Yes, she was."

"Her death must have been a profound experience for you," Anwen pressed on as Ava moved closer. "Do you think your writings, especially the dark elements, are a way of coping with her loss?"

Barker found himself grappling for words. "I'm sure every writer puts a part of their experience into their work. Darkness and light."

Anwen, with a tilt of her head, continued

prodding, "Some critics say your work exploits tragedies, real human pain. How do you respond to that?"

From the corner of his eye, Barker saw Julia stiffen. Anwen's insistent gaze held him.

"I write to make sense of the world, not to exploit it." In a lower voice, ducking out of the camera's way, he asked, "Where did you hear that?"

"Just something I overheard at the B&B."

"I thought we were here to discuss what happened to Sophia?" Julia interjected. "Or even the graffiti sprayed on the front of my café?"

"We'll get there, but the heart of this documentary, Barker, is you. The case is the background, but you are the protagonist. This emotional journey you're on amid all this turmoil is what people want to see. How do these events impact you? How do they dredge up old memories, old wounds?"

Barker blinked, thrown by the pivot, and he was glad for Julia's presence as her hand grabbed his.

"These murders affect the entire community," Julia said. "There are so many threads we're pulling at, so many connections we're trying to—"

"Of course, Julia," Anwen cut her off smoothly, "but the human angle, the personal narrative, resonates with viewers. And Barker, as a writer, is a conduit of emotions. This story, his story, is the beating heart of the documentary."

Barker could feel the weight of Anwen's intense focus, the pressure building like a vice around his chest. Yet, Julia's frustration and the subtle battle of wills between the two women concerned him most. Her fierce protectiveness was evident, and he appreciated her efforts. But Anwen was a master of her craft, a maestro conducting the narrative to fit her vision, and she wouldn't let Barker dodge her questions.

"Maybe my work is exploitative," Barker said, staring down the camera's lens rather than at Anwen. "Much like a documentary could be considered exploitative. Yes, my relationship with my mother inspired those first seeds of me wanting to write crime fiction, but I write here and now because it helps me make sense of the world. I must write about something, just as you must have a subject for a documentary. I wrote about what was happening in my life then, and I was part of those cases. Not as much as the victims' families, but I tried to be as sensitive as possible. And I must point out that the person you overheard those comments from permitted me when I first wrote my book. I would have written about something else if Mark had voiced his concerns back then."

"We'll cut there," Anwen announced, pushing forward a smile like nothing had happened. "I think we have something we can use there. Thank you for your candour, Barker."

"What was that about?" Julia asked, her arms folding. "Is it naturalistic to prod like that?"

Anwen considered her response as Ava glanced between the two women. "As a director, I employ many tactics to get the footage the story needs. I'm sorry if that doesn't make much sense to you now, but I assure you, it'll all make sense when you see the finished..." Anwen squinted off in the distance, her head creeping forward. "What's that? Ava, get rolling again!"

Barker turned as the last vestiges of light flickered across the horizon. His heart raced as his eyes fixed on the cloaked figure in the distance. It was an unwelcome shadow against the approaching night.

"Wait here," he told Julia.

Julia called after him, but her voice sounded distant, drowned out by the pounding of his heartbeat in his ears. As he neared the shadow on the edge of the field close to the strips owned by Derek, the figure became more apparent. The cloaked stranger was motionless, its form stiff and unnatural. It took Barker a few more steps to realise it wasn't a person but a scarecrow.

"Good one," he muttered under his breath.

Leaving Anwen and Ava to capture footage of the scarecrow, Barker returned to meet Julia, who'd been trying to catch up.

"Just a prank," Barker said. "Or another warning."

"It's been a long day. Let's pick up Olivia and head home."

As the pair moved away from the scene, Barker couldn't help but glance back again at the scarecrow. Prank or not, the unsettling feeling remained, gnawing at the back of his mind. The game of cat and mouse was far from over.

"*There* you are!" DI Moyes cut him off, appearing from the direction of the café. "I was starting to think I was too late."

"Too late for what?"

Moyes had a manilla envelope clutched in her hands. She looked as though she was considering if she should hand it over, but the worry on her face had Barker snatching it from her grip. He reached inside and pulled out three glossy photographs.

"I should have brought this up earlier," she admitted, her voice laced with guilt. "It's my first major case at my new station, and I didn't want to seem inept."

Barker stared down at the first of three pictures. It was a shot of Arthur Foster, taken somewhere in the village, squinting off into the distance, unaware. Symbols, like those found around his body, had been scratched into the glossy surface around him. Two red lines had been crossed over his eyes. Barker flipped to the second, a similar shot of Sophia meditating in the garden at the B&B. Symbols and scratches.

The third picture was of Barker, looking over his shoulder as he scrubbed the graffiti from the café's window. His face was marred by the same haunting symbols and the vicious red scratches over his eyes.

"The picture of Arthur arrived the evening he was killed, and nobody noticed it until the morning after. The second was delivered not too long before Sophia was killed. The third was mixed in with our post."

Julia's face had gone ashen, and she grabbed his hand.

"We're going to put you under witness protection."

"No," Barker said, surprising even himself with the firmness in his voice. "No, I refuse."

"Barker, don't be foolish," Julia protested.

"If I've been marked, they'll have to come out of the shadows to get me. Maybe this is how we catch them."

"You're not bait," Moyes insisted.

"I won't run. I won't hide. This is my village, my home, and I will not be driven away by fear. If Evelyn's suspicions about Sophia dying because she figured it out, then why me?"

Moyes sighed, her shoulders slumping in defeat.

"I'm onto them," he said.

"Very well," Moyes said, her voice thick. "But I'm putting a pair of officers on your tail. And just for the record, I don't think this is bravery. It's stupidity."

Barker tapped the picture up and down in his palm as he stared at the first hint of the moon in the darkening sky. Stupid or not, he knew he must be getting close.

19

Jessie arrived at Fern Moore as the last of the day's light faded. Music pounded from several of the flats, gangs cluttered the wooden park, and a familiar black electric scooter was parked outside the barbers.

The hum of clippers and rhythmic snipping of scissors echoed through the night. Pulling her black hood over her hair against the chilly night air, Jessie approached. Billy was in one of the chairs while a barber gave him a fresh fade. From the looks of it, his cast had been taken off.

She was about to make her presence known, but a glimpse of vibrant red hair caught her attention. Paige was in another chair, flipping through a magazine, a sleeping baby in her arms. Her toddler was waiting by

Billy's chair. The young family brought an unexpected lump to Jessie's throat. She wouldn't disturb them.

Ducking her head, Jessie turned away from the barber and focused on the mission. She remembered the maze of tunnels Billy had taken her down; her pulse quickened as she contemplated navigating them alone. Taking a deep breath to gather her courage, Jessie set off.

"I must be crazy," she whispered to herself.

In the settling darkness of Fern Moore, Jessie's silhouette darted between the shadows. The buildings seemed more foreboding, taller somehow as if they'd risen with the night. She rounded the back of the flats, pausing to stare at where she'd seen the two suited men laying into the poor sucker they'd had pinned against the wall on her last visit. She wasn't going to get lucky twice. A couple of teenagers were drinking from cans, but no black cars or men in suits. Rather than retracing her steps back to the courtyard, she set off in the opposite direction around the back of the flats.

Jessie's mind was ablaze with Veronica's words, her pulse still racing from the confrontation. She'd repeatedly replayed the conversation on the drive over, wondering how it had ended with Jessie slamming a door.

Navigating her way through shadowy walkways

around Fern Moore, questions swirled around her. What was Veronica hiding? What was the nature of her connection to Greg Morgan? Jessie's investigative instincts screamed that there was more to the story than confusing transaction records and a trail of bribes and money.

She recalled the photograph, the one that had triggered the flicker of recognition that had seemed to strike fear into Veronica. If Veronica wouldn't provide answers, she'd have to find them herself. With a deep breath, she cast aside doubts and focused.

Her ears caught the faint hum of an engine. She spotted headlights off in the distance, the car's colour dark enough to blend into the night as it cut across the field. There was no road, but that wasn't stopping whomever the driver was behind the tinted windows.

As if drawn by an unseen force, Jessie trailed the car from afar until they reached the empty car park outside Platts Social Club. In the lone glow of a lamppost, a teenager waited, shifting his weight nervously from foot to foot. The car pulled up smoothly beside him. There was a brief exchange, which Jessie couldn't decipher from her distance, and then the teen was gone, swallowed by the night.

It struck Jessie then, in a lightning-bolt moment of clarity: she could follow the car, tail them to their hiding place, find the Cotswold Crew, hopefully with

Greg Morgan too, and have it all wrapped up before midnight.

Without giving herself a chance to think it through, Jessie acted. Yanking her hood up further over her face, she ran back to the barbers, glancing at her yellow Mini. Far too bright. Billy's scooter still waited outside as if for her. She'd ridden similar scooters while travelling with Alfie; how different could this one be?

Twisting the handle, she jerked forward, narrowly missing the wooden structure of the playpark. A gasp escaped her as the scooter veered dangerously close to the swings, its wheels skidding on woodchips. The gangs called out, some laughing, and a can filled with beer trailed after her as she righted her path and shot off into the night.

All she'd need to do was mark the spot on a map for the police.

They would take care of the rest.

Easy.

∼

The wooden sign of The Plough creaked in the breeze as Barker sat at a table outside. The sharpness in the air made the warmth of the pint in his hand more welcoming. The low hum of chatter from inside the pub, disturbed occasionally by a burst of laughter, filled the otherwise quiet evening. To Barker's side, DI Moyes was halfway through her pint. Across the road, outside the police station, two undercover officers chatted on a bench, their eyes darting up and down the road in an obvious manner.

"You know, it's funny," Moyes said, putting her glass on the wooden table. "You reacted worse to your book leaking than that picture."

Barker laughed. "One hurt a little more than the other."

"There was a brief moment earlier when I couldn't find you where I was so wracked with guilt, I thought I was going to throw up. One of the last things I did was foolishly trust PC Puglisi with your book, thinking he wouldn't lose it," Moyes revealed. "The boy can just about tie his shoes."

They both laughed.

"He seems harmless," Barker said. "Sweet, almost."

"If you say so. And I wasn't joking about the shoes." She winked. "I managed to read some of the chapters, by the way. I have to say, I was enjoying them before the mods of Peridale Chat took them down."

"They did? That's something of a relief, at least."

"I may have pulled a few strings. It's amazing what

a flash of a DI badge and talk of copyright infringement can get done."

"Cheers, pal. I appreciate that."

"It's the least I could do," she said, drawing in a deep breath from her device before puffing out a cloud into the night. "DI *Boyes* is quite a character. Stern-faced, husky-voiced, and perpetually humourless. I'm assuming she's inspired by someone we both know?"

"For legal reasons, I must remind you that any resemblance to real people is purely coincidental. But if she were to be inspired by a real person, I hope that person doesn't take offence to how I chose to portray her. All came from a place of respect."

"None taken. You can send ten percent of the profit my way, and I won't get my lawyer onto you." She raised her pint and said, "To DI Boyes and all the stern-faced detectives trying their best out there. I'm sure the world will love her when you get a new publishing deal."

"I wouldn't hold your breath for that one," he said, shifting in his seat. "Those few chapters uploaded to Peridale Chat might be all the light this book sees. Probably wasn't that good, anyway."

"Did you even read the comments?" Barker shook his head, drawing more of his pint. "People were enjoying it," Moyes said with a shrug. "I think the villagers like the fact you're writing about things that happen on their doorstep."

"No talk of exploitation?"

"Not that I saw. You'd better find a way to get that book out there when it's finished."

"Or else what?"

"I'll..." Moyes sipped her pint, considering her threat. "I'll stitch you up for my next unsolved case." They both laughed, but her gaze cast down to the cobbled road. "After how this case has gone, I might just be shunted back to cold cases. There are too many false leads and puzzles, and the superintendent doesn't have enough patience for me right now. Here's to my first and last case as the official DI here."

Moyes raised her pint again, but Barker didn't join her.

"Who are your prime suspects?" Barker asked instead. "I'm leaning towards the gang being behind all of this, but I'm still unconvinced by the Knight kids."

"We've got as much chance of finding the gang as we have a needle in a haystack. My money's on Faith," Moyes revealed in an instant. "She claims to have loved Arthur, but what if that's a cover-up for him breaking her heart with the fire? And her parents were standing in their way before that, so maybe that's why she chose her mum? Would have had access to the manuscript too."

"It's an angle," Barker agreed, though not convinced. "And what about Sam and Nathan? Either have alibis for the time of their mother's murder?"

"They're sharing a room at the B&B, and both claimed to have been asleep, neither noticing the other leaving. Faith said she was up all night catching up on work. Derek has Evelyn's alibi, but I don't trust her either." Moyes glanced back at the B&B next door. Most of the lights lit up from soft lamps. "I'm not sure I buy her hippie-dippy persona."

"Evelyn's been consistently Evelyn since the day I met her," Barker said. "I don't think she's involved in this at all. Her grandson, on the other hand..."

Barker's gaze landed on Mark, who was observing them from the top circular window of the B&B. The room used to belong to Astrid. Moyes joined him in staring up before the young man backed away, ripping across a black curtain.

"He seems to really hate me," Barker whispered. "I'm not saying he did it, but he ticks some boxes. Would have been in the B&B to read the manuscript."

"The goth grandson?" Moyes arched an unsure brow. "But what motive does he have to kill Arthur and Sophia? You're not suggesting he's doing all this to get back at you for some perceived slight?"

"When you put it like that, it does sound far-fetched."

"A very Barker-centric view."

"You're right," Barker agreed, frustration peeking through in his tone. "It's just, every time we interact, he keeps making these sideways remarks at me. Like I'm the antagonist in his story. Evelyn thinks it's just the timing of his mother's birthday, but what if that's been bubbling for a while, and he's decided to pour that hurt onto me?"

"With crackpot theories like that, maybe you weren't as good a DI as they say."

Glancing across the road, Barker sipped his pint. "They say that?"

"For one, you didn't get fired like DI Christie and probably me by the end of the week," she said, leaning in and lowering her voice. "In their eyes, your downfall was falling in love with Julia. She became too interested in fighting the good fight, and you were too happy to step aside and let her muddy your investigations."

"Believe me, I tried," he said, smiling at the memories of those early days. "We were always butting heads. Believe it or not, she was even more stubborn back then. We both were. Evelyn said I shouldn't regret my past, and I don't regret anything I did during that time. That police life felt like a cage to me. When I dared dream that I could leave to become a writer, Julia encouraged me, and she was there every step of the way. And again, when I changed direction to become a PI, she was right there. And again, writing this book. I love her too much to let my old colleagues think she was my downfall, so set them straight for me, okay?"

"Understood." Moyes drained her pint and slammed it down. "I should get home. I don't want to keep Roxy up all night waiting for me. You get home to that wife you love and try to ignore your two new shadows." She jerked her head at the officers standing up as Barker and Moyes did. To Barker's surprise, Moyes pulled him into a brief hug, patting him on the back. "If you still trust me, print me off another copy of your book, and I'll read it. Properly this time. Don't give up."

He smiled, touched by the unexpected gesture. "And you don't give up on this case. Tomorrow's a new day, and who knows what will happen."

Moyes nodded, shooting him one last determined look before heading off. Now alone with only his trailing officers waiting for his next move, Barker glanced up to the B&B once more. Maybe it had been the pint talking, but he still couldn't shake the feeling about Mark.

There was something there.

He knew it.

Barker noticed a silhouette in one of the windows of the B&B as he prepared to leave. It was the softer and unmistakably distinct profile of Faith. A sense of intuition tugged at him, urging him towards the B&B.

After a brief exchange with Evelyn at the entrance, who was in slightly better spirits though still heavy with grief, he found Faith in her room, staring out of the same window he'd seen her from.

He took a tentative seat on the edge of her bed.

"You here to check up on my alibi?" Faith asked without turning around. "I was here. Working. I had a deadline for some demanding clients. I was up all night trying to make sure I met it. Police took my laptop to check the logs to prove it."

Barker nodded, looping his fingers together as he leaned forward on his knee. "I'm more interested in your relationship with Arthur. Why are you so sure he didn't burn down your home?"

Faith hesitated, her shoulders slumping. "He came to see me the day he died."

"Did he threaten you?"

"No, he didn't. I just wanted answers. I wanted to know why he did what he did."

"And?"

Faith paused, her fingers tracing patterns on the windowsill. "I think my parents were right about him.

I've been seeing what I wanted to see in Arthur. Love has a strange way of mixing everything up, and I've always fallen too fast and hard for the wrong guys. I asked him to come to the B&B that morning to get some answers from him, and when he was scared away, I wobbled. I thought he was scared because he was being framed, but why wouldn't he stick around to explain that? Why wouldn't he defend himself? I sent him a message to come back later."

"And did he?"

"I saw him around 4:45 p.m. but didn't get to talk to him. My mother confronted him at the back door. She wouldn't let him inside."

Barker ran a frustrated hand through his hair. "And did you tell anyone about this until now?"

She shook her head. "He came here because *I* told him to. I heard what the police said. He was stabbed not long after that. He would never have been in this village if not for me."

Barker processed the information for a moment. If Sophia had intercepted Arthur at the back door, could she have committed the murder, influenced by her writing? Faith had told Julia before that she was obsessed with her research. So obsessed that she'd want to test out the ritual for herself? But it didn't fit. If that were the case, the only apparent suspect for

Sophia's murder would then be Faith, out of revenge for her lost love.

The fact Faith was in front of him and not in a cell meant they'd probably confirmed her alibi with her laptop.

But his thoughts kept racing. If Arthur had returned to the B&B around the time of his death and was prevented from entering by Faith's mother, it was highly probable that the next person he bumped into was his killer.

Leaving Faith to continue her window-watching, Barker decided to test this theory further. On his way out, he stopped to speak to Evelyn, shuffling through a deck of tarot cards in an armchair alone in the sitting room.

"Evelyn, have you noticed anything out of place in your garden? Anything missing?"

"Draw a card," Evelyn said instead, offering the deck.

"Evelyn, anything missing?"

"I'm thinking," she said, pushing the cards closer and beckoning him into the room. "Draw a card, and don't overthink it."

Barker sighed in frustration and plucked out a deep purple card from the middle of the pack. It depicted a lone figure carrying a lantern illuminating a path. He offered it back to Evelyn, and she drew it into the lamp's light with a squint.

"Ah, *The Hermit*!" she said, as though relieved. "An introspective soul seeking wisdom, always searching for truth. It is a sign of solitary exploration and personal discovery." She paused with a wagging of her finger. "Now that you mention it, I am a garden gnome short. They tend to have minds of their own, wandering around the garden as they please, but he hasn't turned up yet."

"Was it in the back garden, by any chance?"

"*He* was," she said, her smile widening as she sunk deeper into the chair. "I always knew you had a touch of the sight about you, Barker. Why don't you grab a chair and pour yourself some tea?"

"Another night, Evelyn," he said, reaching for his phone. "And maybe enough tea for tonight?"

Leaving Evelyn to return to shuffling her cards, Barker pulled out his phone.

BARKER

Sorry to take up any more of your night, but did forensics determine what struck Arthur over the head? And was it made of ceramic?

MOYES

How did you know and why do you ask?

> You may want to check Evelyn's B&B garden. I suspect there might be traces of Arthur's blood there. Follow the missing gnome...

Taking a moment to breathe in the cool evening air on the doorstep, he gazed back up at the B&B's windows. If Arthur was killed there, it didn't prove much about who was behind the murders, but unless the Crew had been lingering around the place on the off-chance Arthur showed his face, the suspects had just narrowed to people present in the B&B on the day of the first killing.

∾

Julia felt trapped in her cottage. Olivia's soft breathing from her cot was the only sound anchoring Julia to the present moment. She wanted nothing more than to bolt out the door, search every nook and cranny of the village, and find Barker and Jessie, but she couldn't leave her daughter behind.

She took out her phone again, dialling Barker's number for what felt like the hundredth time. No answer. Then Jessie's. Still, no response. She called her gran again, but Jessie's flat lights weren't on.

"We checked Richie's, too, and she's not in there,"

Dot said. "Maybe she's gone to see Billy? Or that handsome man she was spotted with earlier?"

"So why not answer her phone?" Julia replied. "Or her texts? You were right, Gran. We should have packed our bags and left when we had the chance. This whole case is too big a mess for me to figure out."

Hanging up, Julia thought back to the threatening image of Barker that had been sent earlier that day. He'd promised he'd be home after a quick drink with Moyes to go over some details, but he'd been hours. She pulled back the curtain; the police car was still parked outside. Across the lane, the lights were on in Veronica's cottage. There was a chance Jessie was there, but Julia couldn't leave Olivia to go and check.

She collapsed onto the sofa, burying her face in her hands. Thoughts raced through her mind. What if she had done things differently and put something together sooner? She'd wanted to support Barker with the documentary, but even that had soured, and now, with the graffiti, a threat against his life and him not answering his phone, she had no way of knowing if the officers were doing their job trailing him.

And poor Sophia. Julia felt guilty about how their only conversation had gone. The woman had been holding her cards close to her chest, but if only Julia had pushed further and asked the right questions, she might have seen what was coming.

Julia reached for her notepad to go back over everything again when the familiar sound of the key sliding into the lock echoed through the cottage, making her jump up and run into the hallway.

Barker walked in, looking more tired and rugged than usual. The relief that washed over Julia was so overwhelming her hands moved around him almost instantly, pulling him into a tight embrace.

"Do you even know how worried I was? The picture they sent to the—"

"Mind games, Julia," he said, squeezing her tight. "I'm fine. After my drink, I went to the B&B to talk to Faith again. She revealed that she saw Arthur at the B&B soon before he was killed, which means he could have been killed there. Police are searching the place as we speak."

But calm was the last thing Julia felt. "Have you seen Jessie?"

"No?" Barker shook his head. "She's probably at home."

"She's not," Julia said, pulling away from his embrace. "She was last seen at Richie's earlier in the afternoon. She's not answering her phone. I wanted her to come here so we could all be together to stop me worrying about her all night, but what if something has happened?"

"I'll go looking for her."

"No," Julia said, snatching her keys, "Stay here. Watch Olivia. I'll go and see if Veronica has seen her."

The wind nipped at Julia's face as she swiftly crossed the lane to Veronica's cottage. Despite the darkness that enveloped the surroundings, a faint light flickered from the back of the house. With increasing anxiety, Julia knocked on the door.

A few seconds later, the door opened, revealing Veronica. Without her characteristic large glasses, her eyes seemed unusually small, almost lost in the tiredness that marked her face.

"What's wrong?" she whispered, her voice laced with concern. "Come in."

"It's Jessie," Julia began, struggling to hold back tears. "She's not answering her phone, and with everything going on, I'm worried sick. I haven't seen her since this morning, and she hasn't been seen since she met some guy at Richie's, and—"

"She came to the office after that meeting, where she met with a fellow journalist who wouldn't harm a hair on her head," Veronica interrupted. Her eyes darted to the side, a weariness in her gaze. "No, I haven't seen her since then. We had a disagreement, and she didn't leave on the best terms."

Julia's heart sank. "Did she say where she was going?"

Veronica paused, biting her lower lip. "She was

upset and said she would find undeniable evidence on Greg Morgan. She's convinced he's connected to the Cotswold Crew."

Julia's eyes widened, her breath catching in her throat. "Why would she think that?"

"Because I'm afraid she might be right," Veronica admitted, her voice breaking. "And I pointed her right at it. I thought she'd be home by now. I'm sure she's fine, Julia. She's a smart, street-wise..."

Julia's mind reeled, the information knotting her stomach. The implications were enormous, and the fear for her daughter now had a shape and a name.

The Cotswold Crew.

The very gang they'd tried their best to warn her away from.

They hadn't tried hard enough.

Pulling out her phone and heading for the front door, Julia redialled Jessie's number, each ring amplifying her panic. The vastness of the village felt like a daunting maze, and Julia had no idea where to begin looking for her daughter.

20

A ringing phone pulled Jessie from her groggy state. She'd had her fair share of hangovers, but this had to be one for the books. What had she been drinking for her head to pound like it was? She wanted to reach out and slap her phone to shut it up, but her hands didn't move, and the sound was coming at her, all distorted as if echoing down a long tunnel. She felt cold, her back pressed firmly against something rigid.

As the haze of unconsciousness retreated, and clarity sharpened, panic gripped Jessie. She wasn't in her warm bed or the comfort of her flat above the post office. Her hands were bound, her wrists protesting the tight grip of the ropes as she tried to pull free. The musty scent of dampness filled the air, and water dripped from somewhere behind her. Blinking hard, she tried to adjust to the stark brightness pointed at her, the silhouette of her surroundings coming into focus.

Her first thought was the documentary camera, but the lights were scattered, like those her brother would use back when he'd lived in the village and worked as a builder. They cast creeping shadows that played tricks on the eye as men in black suits moved about like ghosts. Their hushed conversations barely reached her ears, amplifying her unease.

The faint sound of something being sharpened punctured the silence, the rhythmic grinding setting her already frazzled nerves further on edge. Trying to decipher where she was, she took in the cavernous space around her. The high ceilings, wooden beams, and the lingering scent of hay and aged wood led her to conclude that she was in a barn.

She hoped she was at Peridale Farm, just up the lane from her parents. Given how silent everything was beyond the stone walls, she doubted it.

One of the figures paused and caught her eye before clearing his throat. Four men turned to regard her with a chilling, calculated calmness.

She'd wanted to find the Cotswold Crew, and she'd done that all too well.

Easy?

Idiot.

Her dad's warnings. Her mum's. Billy. Veronica. Dante. Why hadn't she listened to any of them?

"Quite the setup you have here," Jessie began, hearing the wobble in her forced lightness. "Very rustic. You could rent it out for weddings."

One of the men stepped closer. Jessie straightened her spine, gulping down her fear like a mouthful of dry meringue. She searched the faces of her captors for any trace of amusement but was met with an unwavering, inscrutable stare from each man. The tension in the room could have been cut with a knife —quite literally, she thought, hearing the persistent sharpening sound.

Trying to ground herself, she harkened back to her last memory. Racing through Fern Moore, the thrilling chase, the sudden blinding brake lights, the desperate swerve... And then, there was a sensation of weightlessness before the world went dark. Pain pulsed through her body now, but it was a dull, throbbing sort rather than the sharp sting of a fracture.

No broken bones, the guy performing her autopsy would say. Small mercies, she supposed.

The men remained unresponsive, their collective silence amplifying the metallic grinding from the corner of the barn. Jessie squinted, peering beyond the encroaching shadows. A lone figure was methodically sharpening a sizable knife, its blade glinting in the hanging lights.

No broken bones, but we think the three-hundred-and-two stab wounds might have had something to do with her death.

"With a knife that size, you must be making me a giant steak," she said, managing a laugh this time. "Hope it's medium rare. I wouldn't want to waste good beef. I don't know anything about steaks, but you always hear that, don't you? 'I'll have mine medium rare.' How do you guys like your steaks cooked?"

Jessie's question hung unanswered in the air.

The men before her were like statues, but Jessie had always been the sort to take the bull by the horns, and this wasn't going to be an exception.

"Not very chatty, are you?" she began, adopting a casual and challenging voice. "Seeing as we're all here, having this lovely little mother's meeting, fancy giving me a clue as to what's going on?"

She leaned forward as much as the restraints would allow, meeting the gaze of everyone in turn. A suit closer to her, with slightly greying hair at the temples, cleared his throat.

"You're a fearless one, aren't you?" he remarked, voice dripping with amusement and annoyance.

"Fearless or reckless, depending on who you ask,"

Jessie replied. "So, you guys just wanted some company and figured I'd make for some cracking conversation?"

The man allowed a small, begrudging smile. "You've got spirit, I'll give you that. But sometimes, spirit can get you into trouble."

"Evidently. So, now that we've established my impressive spirit and the fact that I can crash a scooter just as well as my ex, how about letting me in on why I'm here?"

The rhythmic sharpening had ceased. The man with the knife moved out of the shadows, placing the blade on a table. He looked at the older man, who nodded slightly.

"You've been nosy, Jessie," the knife-wielder spoke in a deep, gravelly voice. "Poking around where you shouldn't be. The Cotswold Crew doesn't take kindly to prying eyes."

She smirked, though internally, her heart rate was skyrocketing. "Well, maybe if you lot weren't so secretive, I wouldn't have had to do any poking around. Ever think of that? What happened to an informative website? Or maybe a flyer or two? Ever thought of holding a little fête? People around here love fêtes, especially the old—"

The knife went into the wood with a silencing thud.

"You wanted answers, and you'll get some," the older man said. "But maybe not the ones you're hoping for."

The almost eerie quiet outside made it all the more apparent to Jessie: they were isolated. Isolation, in her current mess, wasn't exactly comforting. She let out a short laugh, trying to keep the atmosphere light – for her own sake as much as anything.

"You lot are skilled at the old disappearing act. The police can't pin a thing on you." She paused, taking a deep breath, and tilted her head, studying the men. "Aren't you all going to introduce yourselves? You know my name. Hardly seems fair."

A tall figure, whom she hadn't noticed, stepped forward. "Names are a liability. We don't use them. Just numbers."

Jessie raised an eyebrow, bemused. "Like... One, Two, Three, Four?"

He nodded. "Precisely. I'm Three. It's an efficient system. Can't be a rat if you don't know who to point the finger at."

"And the rest of you?" Jessie eyed up the guy with the greying hair. "I'd say you're the leader, so you're One?"

"Yes, I'm One. And we don't have a leader. We're a cooperative. All decisions are made based on a group vote."

"How civilised. What happens if there's a tie? Because I couldn't help but notice you're lacking a female on the team, and I'd like to put myself forward. Shake things up a little. Do I need to fill out an application?"

"You're entertaining, I'll give you that," One said. "And, yes, there's a test of sorts."

"Arthur," Jessie blurted out. "Was he one of you?"

A momentary flicker of reluctance danced across their eyes. The man sharpening the knife said, "Arthur didn't pass our test."

"And which one are you?"

"Six."

"So, there's more than four of you? How many?"

"Enough," Number One replied.

"If there's an entry exam, maybe I won't get in then," she said, "unless it's in English. I was pretty good at that in the end. If I get some help from my old tutor, maybe?"

The room remained tense, but she could tell she had them on their toes. But the mention of English, of literature, stirred deep within her. Veronica's voice floated back to her, and a lump rose in her throat. Veronica would forever think she'd sent Jessie to her death, and to make matters worse, Six returned to sharpening his knife.

"To be or not to be in a gang, that is the question,"

she said in her best Shakespearian delivery. "Arthur didn't meet your measure, but you still found a way to use him?"

Number One sighed, "We had a job to do. Intimidate the Knights. Get them to sell their land."

"Those two strips on either side of that road?" Jessie ventured. "So, you got Arthur to do your dirty work. He was already close to the Knights because of the daughter, wasn't he? Or did you set that up?"

No answer.

"And your employer, Greg Morgan, what's his game with that land?"

The man in the corner halted the rhythmic sharpening of his knife. All Jessie could see of him was a towering silhouette against the dimly lit room. For a fleeting moment, she imagined it to be Greg Morgan, the puppet master finally revealing himself. But the height was all wrong, and they still didn't answer her question.

"You've seen too much," Number Three began, his voice cold. "And you know too much."

"I'm great at keeping secrets. Honestly, I don't even know your names. You guys, you all look...similar ish. If you let me go now, I'll get on that death trap of a scooter and ride like I've seen a ghost. And you'll be just that, a nightmare I can't wait to forget."

A short, mocking laugh echoed from the back, but

Number One silenced him with a raised hand. The shadowy figure with the knife took deliberate steps towards Jessie. Her heart raced; every instinct screamed at her to fight or flee, but she was trapped.

The distance between them closed, and as the blade glinted in the dim light, Jessie braced herself for what might come next.

As the sharp blade sliced through the ropes binding her, Jessie's relief was cut short when she was briskly pulled to her feet. Jessie's heart stopped as her captors turned her around, her eyes falling on what awaited her. There was a well in the middle of the old barn. Its grey stone, worn and eroded by time, seemed to absorb the room's dim light, casting an eerie shadow across the cracked wooden floor.

The well's mouth gaped open like a dark abyss, the blackness within hiding its unfathomable depth. Moss clung to its jagged edges, and a rickety wooden bucket hung beside it, frayed rope coiled around a rusted pulley. Forgotten for years, perhaps decades, suddenly awakened to serve a purpose.

"Of course," she muttered, her voice laced with sarcasm. "No mess, no evidence."

Number One tilted his head and smiled. "You catch on quick. Everyone will think it's a tragedy – a young woman, disappointed by not being able to get the answers she craved, coming to this forsaken farmhouse in the middle of nowhere. And by the time you're found, we'll be but distant memories."

Feeling the tightening grip on her arm, Jessie hesitated but moved closer to her impending doom. With nothing left to lose, her mind raced with questions she still needed answers to.

"So," she started, her voice shaking but insistent, "was Arthur about to rat you out? Is that why you took care of him? What about Sophia? Did you use her manuscript as a cover-up, making it look like a ritual from the cult?"

The man she'd not heard from cleared his throat, his voice devoid of emotion. "We didn't kill Arthur. Or Sophia."

"So you're saying they just... stabbed themselves with daggers? Took their own lives?"

A hint of annoyance crossed Number One's face. "We had nothing to do with that. We have our methods, but that was not us."

For a moment, she believed them. Their voices were sincere, but the looming well made it hard to focus on anything else. Jessie had one final thought as she felt the cold chill of the damp stone against her back.

Jessie never should have slammed that door.

She hoped Veronica wouldn't blame herself.

The dark abyss of the well seemed to call to her,

and her mind screamed out in desperate hopelessness. As she mentally braced herself for the end, the distant wail of sirens pierced the stillness. The rhythmic beat of their approach grew louder and more insistent, causing panic to ripple through the room.

"I thought you said we were in the middle of nowhere!"

"We are!"

A flicker of hope ignited in Jessie's chest. Had someone traced her phone?

As her captors moved to flee, tugging her along with them, adrenaline coursed through her veins like electric fire. Jessie seized the chair she'd been strapped to and swung with all her might. The chair collided with the knife-wielding man's arm; the surprise registered on his face just as he staggered backward, crashing into a stack of discarded wooden crates.

But before she could celebrate her minor victory, another suited figure lunged at her from the side, his fists clenched. Thinking fast, Jessie grabbed the bucket by the well and launched it towards him. It hit him square in the shins, causing him to stumble and clutch his leg in pain.

Two more figures were closing in on her. She had to act quickly. Remembering the knife Six had dropped, she snatched it off the ground and brandished it in front of her.

"I swear I'll use this," she growled.

"You wouldn't dare."

"You want to test that theory?"

The mere threat made them pause, and that moment of hesitation was all she needed. Turning on her heel, Jessie darted toward a gap in the barn's crumbling walls. Hands reached out, clawing the air to grab her, but Jessie was the only one small enough to slip through. She hurtled through the opening and found herself outside, where she quickly hid behind the cold brick of a chimney, nestled next to a rusted old tractor.

Taking a moment to catch her breath, her ears picked up the sound of revving engines. Vehicles sped away in a rush, leaving behind a thick cloud of dust and the scent of burnt rubber.

Her heart still pounded, but it was a rhythm of victory now. Jessie knew she had fought against the odds and won this round. But the night was far from over, and she had to move.

The distorted blare of sirens drew Jessie out from her place of concealment. Squinting through the dark, her heart sank as she failed to spot any blue lights. Instead, a figure on a squeaky pedal bike wobbled towards her, holding a handheld speaker in the air.

"Billy?" she whispered in disbelief as he clumsily crashed the bike into the side of the building. He looked up, face reddened from the exertion.

"I'm gonna kill you!" he rasped, rushing over.

Pulling back, she looked up into his face, eyes shining with relieved tears.

"The crew almost beat you to it."

"I *told* you not to mess with them."

"And you were right," she sighed, nudging him lightly. "But how did you even find me?"

"Think you're the first person to 'borrow' my scooter off the estate?" He flipped the wrecked scooter to reveal a tiny white device blinking softly in the dark. "Just in case. I called the police, too, but it'll be ages before they find this place." He pulled out his phone and paused a video titled '12 hours of police siren noises.' "Had to think on my feet, didn't I?"

"Never change, Billy Matthews. Though I was right about that scooter being a death trap. The thing almost killed me before the Crew had their chance." Glancing at the desolate surroundings, she asked, "Where exactly are we?"

"About fifteen miles deep in the sticks. Middle of nowhere."

"You can see the stars," Jessie pointed out. "No light pollution."

"Forget the stars," Billy said as he propped the bike upright. "Hop on. I'm taking you home."

"My phone, I heard it ringing," Jessie said, already returning to the barn. "Give it a call, will you?"

Jessie stared into the well while waiting for her phone to light up in the barn—almost her final resting place, but not today. The knife was still on the floor, the smashed chair left where she'd destroyed it. She'd been a hair's breadth away from death, yet all she could do was laugh.

Her phone lit up on a wooden table on the other side of the barn.

"Got it!" she called back, her voice echoing around the abandoned building. "Oh, hello. What's this?"

21

If Derek had been upfront about the significance of the land around the road, Barker might have pieced together the puzzle earlier. But with the recent revelations from Jessie's evening, the motive behind the fire was coming into focus.

The early hours stillness was only disturbed by the rhythmic tapping of Barker's fingers as he sat in the cottage's dining room, engrossed in the historical data of the land behind the café. The land he'd previously uncovered had been the location of the long-forgotten market hall and had been snapped up by the council in 1969.

An old article in *The Peridale Post*'s archives had revealed to him that the council at the time had justified buying the land in the light of the destruction of the market hall to 'protect an area of outstanding beauty from future development.'

They'd paid £3,000 for fifteen acres.

Barker had then researched how much the land would sell for on the current market, but he hadn't needed to guess. The land had been on the market for an entire year, and for those same fifteen acres, they now wanted £225,000.

Or at least, they had when it had first been listed.

The price has dropped almost every month since, with £165,000 being the current asking price.

The subtle creak of a door drew him from the screen. Julia entered in her pyjamas with her tousled hair and sleep-deprived eyes.

"Can't sleep either?" she asked.

"Too many thoughts are running through my head," he said, twisting the laptop to her. "Did you know that field behind your café has been up for sale for the past year? Almost from the moment the festival packed up and left."

"There's no 'FOR SALE' sign." Moving closer, Julia's voice grew troubled. "Barker, I can't shake the feeling that Jessie wasn't honest with us about what happened with the Crew tonight."

Barker sighed, pulling the laptop lid shut slightly. "She's safe. That's what matters right now. And she did manage to get some valuable information from them."

Leaning against the edge of the dining table, Julia's fingers traced the wood grain. "If we're going to believe the Crew had nothing to do with Arthur and Sophia's deaths, then who did? Because the longer this goes on, the less I suspect the Knights ever had anything to do with this."

"We're narrowing down the suspects. Moyes just messaged me. They found traces of Arthur's blood at the B&B, so I was right about that. Who knows, maybe they'll find the killer's DNA too?"

"I just can't shake this feeling."

"Now you're sounding like Evelyn."

"There's something bigger going on here. Something we're missing."

Closing his laptop, Barker crossed the table and looped his fingers through Julia's. "We'll figure this out tomorrow. I know it."

∽

Julia's eyes snapped open at an unexpected noise echoing through the cottage. She bolted upright and blinked into the darkness. Next to her, Mowgli nestled against Barker, both undisturbed by the sound that had awoken her.

Throwing the covers aside, Julia padded into the kitchen. The pre-dawn light revealed Jessie standing by the cupboard, rigid as a board with a cup in her hand.

"Sorry, I was trying to be quiet," Jessie whispered as she closed the cupboard. "Can't sleep. Thought I'd make some hot chocolate."

"Let me help."

Together, they worked silently, preparing mugs of rich hot chocolate and adding squirty cream and marshmallows. The mother and daughter pair shared a quiet moment as they each held their warm cups.

Taking a deep breath, Jessie began, "I don't doubt it now. Greg hired the Crew. They were honest when I asked them about Arthur and denied killing him and Sophia, but when I mentioned Greg, nothing. Complete silence. And then they said I knew too much."

"And you think Greg is after the road access to that field behind my café?"

"If not that, then what else? He wants it for something."

Julia gently placed a comforting hand over Jessie's. "Right now, I don't care about any of that. I want to know you're okay. What happened to you there, Jessie?"

"I'm fine, Mum. Honest." Jessie took a deep slurp of her hot chocolate and added, "They had a knife, okay? But Billy got there in the nick of time, and I survived. You and Dad were right. I shouldn't have gone looking for them, but I never would have got this."

Jessie looked around the kitchen before reaching into her clothes, draped over a stool. Julia had folded them when Jessie headed for a shower after her nonchalant return, brought home on the back of a bike by Billy. She pulled out a map and spread it across the breakfast bar, and in the hazy morning light, it took Julia a moment to recognise it as a map of the Cotswolds. Their slice of it, at least. Tons of locations had been circled.

"Moyes told Dad they weren't digital, and what's more non-digital than a map? Fool proof if you don't leave it behind in your hurry to flee." Jessie jabbed a circled point in the middle of nowhere. "I think this is the barn I ended up. Which means all these other places could be their other hideouts. No wonder they never get caught. Who knows how many abandoned buildings are around here? Enough stakeouts, and they'll turn up at one of them."

"Jessie, promise me you'll never go looking for them again."

Jessie held up her little finger, and Julia wrapped

hers around it. Sharing a smile, they held them there for a minute.

"Lesson learned, good cop."

∽

The soft hues of the dawn sky washed over the village, casting the patchwork of fields rolling off as far as the eye could see in the prettiest pink light. Birds chirped their early morning tunes, and Veronica's battered roses swayed gently in the morning breeze.

Jessie and Veronica were sat on the bench under Veronica's sitting room window, each holding a mug of coffee. The air between them was heavy with questions, yet a truce seemed to have been silently declared.

"You were right about Greg," Veronica said, breaking the silence that had settled since she texted Jessie to come over if she was awake; she'd barely had a wink. "I did recognise him in that picture when Billy showed it to us."

"I won't say I told you so, but..."

"Please, gloat." Veronica's lips pricked into a strained smile. "I deserve it. All my years of teaching, I should have known that telling you not to do something would only spur you on. Your tenacity is one of the reasons I wanted you on my team before anyone." She tapped Jessie's knee. "But Jessie, next time, remember to follow the rules. I can't afford any rogue actions from you."

"I promise."

Veronica's stern look didn't waver. "I mean it. If you ever do something like that again, I'll take your badge away without a second thought. I can't... I won't have your death on my conscience." Her voice broke on the last word, betraying the depth of her concern. "So, are you going to tell me what happened? Because I spoke to your mum last night when you finally came home, and she seems to think you've told her about a quarter of the truth."

"About a third, but close enough."

"And the other two-thirds?"

The hot coffee burned, a friendly reminder that she was alive.

"Wasn't sure I'd get to see another sunset."

"Oh, Jessie." Veronica's eyes clenched. "I should never have mentioned that tip-off to you. I don't know what I thought you'd do with that information, but I should have known this was the inevitable outcome."

"They had me tied up, Veronica," Jessie continued, staring at the swaying roses. "This guy came at me with this giant knife, and I thought that was it. And then he untied me and spun me round, and there was a long drop into a well waiting for me to frame my suicide."

"Jessie, I—"

"If I had died there," Jessie interrupted, "you'd have been one of my final thoughts. I didn't want you to go the rest of your life thinking you caused that, so I didn't blame you even then. More than anything, I felt bad for storming out like I did. Old Jessie rears her head from time to time."

Veronica hung her head as though she couldn't stand the weight of knowing. Jessie nudged her arm with her elbow and nodded at the roses.

"You have no idea how to garden, do you?" Jessie asked. "They look proper rubbish."

Veronica laughed, shaking her head.

"I'd appreciate it if you kept those details to yourself," Jessie whispered. "Nobody else knows, and I'd rather not cause more panic than I already did. You should have seen my mum's face when I walked through the door. Somehow, she had a worse night than me."

"You have my word."

"Good," Jessie said. "So, I've shared mine. Your turn. Who is Greg Morgan to you?"

Veronica's gaze turned distant as she hugged her coffee. She took her time blowing on the surface like she hoped it would swallow her. She stood up, and

Jessie thought she would return to her cottage with the question ignored again, but she walked to the garden's edge. She stared far into the distance, shielding her eyes from the rising sun.

"There's a little dairy farm just on the other side of those rolling hills," Veronica said, pausing as a large white van trundled down the lane. "It's this cute little place these days. They have this indoor play area in the barn with zip lines and hay bales to climb, and there's a little shop where you can buy ice cream."

"How lovely?"

"It was a very different place when I was a little girl," she said with a tight smile, hugging her coffee close. "I didn't have much of a childhood. My parents didn't believe in it like most do. They worked us hard, morning till night, day in, day out. Always something to be doing on a farm, and if you weren't doing it right, there was always a belt or a cane not too far away to set you straight." Despite her stern words, Veronica smiled. "They saw reading as a waste of time, so I had to do it secretly. Can you imagine that? Discouraging a child from reading? But the more they told me not to, the more I wanted to." She winked at her, but her smile immediately turned sour. "Greg and I, we'd run over those hills and come into the village every chance we had. We never had much money, but he'd always slip books into his jacket. He got me all the

Narnia books one by one and then as many Enid Blyton's as he could. They were my escapes from our life, giving me big ideas about what the world could be."

Jessie, eyebrows furrowing in confusion, asked, "You were neighbours?"

"No." Veronica took a deep breath, her eyes never leaving the distant hills. "I once told you I kept my married name even after my husband divorced me."

Jessie's heart raced, her eyes widening. "No way..."

Veronica nodded. "There were three of us. Sebastian was the eldest. Then there's me in the middle and Gregory... Gregory is the youngest. My maiden name is Morgan, and our local ruthless MP is, unfortunately, my little brother."

Jessie's breath caught in her throat, her mug of coffee suddenly feeling twice as heavy.

"Shocked?"

"Very."

"Scared away?"

"Don't be daft," Jessie said, wrapping an arm around her. "Can't change where you came from, only where you're going. What does this mean?"

"It means I know what he's capable of." Veronica's blank stare fixed on Jessie's. "The library isn't the only thing about my brother that is old news. He's done terrible, terrible things, Jessie. The fact that he's climbed to the position he's in is terrifying but not surprising. He always said he was destined for greater things and was right. There's nothing he wouldn't do to get what he wants."

"So, what has he done?"

Veronica stared at her and then through her. The corners of her mouth curled down, and Jessie saw the walls build right back up as Veronica lost herself in her memories. She shook her thoughts away as fast as they'd taken over and looked across to the cottage across the lane as someone tugged open the curtains.

"Ah, I hope that's your dad," Veronica said, setting her coffee cup on her doorstep. "As shocking a revelation as I'm sure that was, I'm not quite finished yet. Remember when I told you about Johnny's attempt to have a documentary filmed before I took over the paper? I should have double-checked those old emails sooner."

22

Julia emerged from the bathroom, steam trailing behind her, still feeling the warmth of her hot shower. Surprisingly, she saw Veronica on her way out of the cottage while Jessie leaned against the back of the sofa, chewing her lip in apparent anxiety. With a look of deep contemplation, Barker hung in the dining room doorway. His expression was one of concern, and he seemed lost in thought.

Barker followed Julia as she walked into their bedroom. She dug jeans and a jumper out of the washing basket; the weather was becoming unruly outside. She glanced at Barker, expecting some revelation, but his face remained impassive. He perched on the edge of the bed with Mowgli, their cat, who curled onto his back, purring at the gentle dance of Barker's fingers across his tummy.

"What did I miss?" Julia asked.

"Could be nothing," he replied. "Probably isn't. Are you in the café today?"

"Sue's in for the morning, and I'm taking over for the afternoon."

"Good," he said, tugging off his pyjama shirt before reaching around her as she wriggled into her jeans to grab his deodorant. "We need to get to Evelyn's B&B. I think you were right last night."

"About what?"

"About us missing something," he said, pulling on a shirt that needed ironing. "There is something bigger going on, and we've been directed to focus on all the wrong things."

After dropping Olivia off with Dot and Percy for the morning, Julia, Barker, and Jessie made their way to the B&B. None the wiser about what Veronica had said to Barker to put that look in his eye.

Upon entering, they were greeted by the whirlwind of chaos that had erupted overnight. Police and forensic officers had taken over the back garden, their presence a grim reminder that the case was still wide open to solve. Barker found Moyes, their faces tense as they talked in lowered whispers. Jessie pulled out her Cotswold Crew map, gesturing wildly as she pointed to different spots, showing PC Puglisi and other uniformed officers. Feeling like a spare part, Julia lingered by the front desk with Evelyn.

Donned in a bright red kaftan and matching turban, Evelyn wore a strained smile that made her seem out of place in her home, her usually vibrant personality clashing with the surrounding turmoil.

"Good morning, Julia!" Evelyn said, a little too cheery, pinned against the door to the private area. "Quite the scene here today. They've found blood in the garden. It seems that Arthur and Sophia were attacked right under my nose. Turns out I was right about evil happening right under my—"

Evelyn lurched forward, the door behind her shaking. With her hands behind her back, she seemed to be stopping someone—or something—from getting out.

"Evelyn...?"

"It's nothing, dear." Evelyn's grin widened as she lurched again, jamming a foot against the desk to push back into the door. "Just a little... situation. It's all under control, and it's best the police don't see."

"What situation?" Julia arched a brow. "Are you holding someone hostage?"

"It's for her own good, I assure—"

With a sudden, jarring rip, the door swung outwards, knocking Evelyn off balance. She caught herself on a coat rack, revealing Ava, the usually demure camerawoman. Standing in the doorway, she looked around as though for the first time, her eyes as wide as saucers dancing with an inner light that Julia had never seen before. Pushing past Evelyn, she approached Julia and she took a step back as Ava's outstretched hands came at her. She gently grabbed at pieces of Julia's hair, lifting them as though she'd never seen anything so fascinating. Her fingers moved to Julia's cheeks, prodding and poking like she was moulding something out of clay. DI Moyes passed by, glancing quizzically at the odd spectacle, but continued up the stairs without question.

With Evelyn's assistance, Julia guided Ava back into the room behind the counter. As Julia stepped into Evelyn's private living room, the scent of burning incense hit her like a thick wall. Earthy tapestries draped the walls, glowing from the salt lamps of all different sizes dotted around the room. A low table surrounded by plush cushions seemed to invite meditation, and they managed to get Ava to settle into a soft cushion before Evelyn locked them inside.

Ava was busy dancing her fingers in front of her face.

"I can see colours," Ava announced, her voice filled with childlike wonder.

Julia blinked, her mouth agape as she tried to

make sense of Ava's words. She looked at Evelyn, hoping for some rational explanation, but found only a shared perplexity.

"Evelyn, you need to throw away that Costa Rican tea."

"I promise, after Sam, I didn't offer it to her," Evelyn replied, her hand clasped against her forehead. "She just helped herself. I really should label my private tea collection better."

"How long has she been like this?" Julia asked as Ava climbed atop the coffee table. She reached for the light fitting, batting at the dangling fringe like Mowgli would with the edge of the bedding. "Shouldn't we take her to the hospital?"

"An hour or two," Evelyn admitted. "And she's quite safe but has been saying the strangest things."

Ava suddenly tumbled backwards, laughing, and Julia and Evelyn had to rush to catch her before she hit the ground. They settled her on a different cushion, and Evelyn handed her a glass of water, and she poured it straight into a potted plant instead.

"He told me he wanted it," she said, tapping her nose conspiratorially. Then, with a smile, she tapped Julia's nose, then Evelyn's. "He's called Jeff and doesn't like that you're staring at him."

Julia exchanged a worried look with Evelyn.

"Have you seen him?" Ava asked.

"Jeff?" Evelyn asked, rubbing the plant's waxy leaf. "He's right here, and I am sorry for all the staring, Jeff. He's been rather quiet about it."

"Of course he's quiet," Ava said, batting Evelyn's hand away. "He's a gentleman. Not like Phil, the fern over there. He never shuts up."

Julia glanced at the innocent-looking fern, then back to Ava. "Does Phil have anything interesting to say about our situation?"

Ava paused, cocking her head as if listening. "He thinks the curtains are a dreadful colour. But then again, he's been complaining about the décor for years. And you still haven't answered me. Have you seen him?"

"Seen who?"

"Rupert," Ava groaned as though it should have been obvious. "Where is he?"

"Rupert?" Julia echoed, crouching by Ava's side. "No, I haven't seen him. He left to go on another job, didn't he?"

"He's gone. Gone. Gone. *Gone.*"

With a sudden movement, she launched herself across the room as though she were about to dive through the glass window and into the back garden. Instead, she yanked at the dark velvet purple curtains, ripping them from their railings. She wrapped them around herself like a cloak and swished to face them. Ava pointed a trembling finger at Julia.

"You fell for it."

"Fell for what?" Julia asked, her voice catching in her throat, the uncertainty and confusion growing.

Ava's only response was to twirl, the curtain billowing around her like the gown of a fairy-tale princess as she danced about the room. Julia was sure she was picking up what Ava was putting out.

"Was Rupert the person in the cloak seen on the village green?" Julia pressed.

But Ava was lost in her dance. Her movements were graceful one moment, clumsy the next, a mesmerising and disturbing spectacle. Without warning, her dance ended, and she collapsed into a wicker chair, her body slumping, her energy spent.

"I'm tired," she declared.

"Finally," Evelyn said with a breathy laugh. "I was hoping that would be the last gasp of energy."

"What did I fall for?" Julia asked, crouching by the chair. "What do you mean, Ava?"

"All of it," Ava replied, her voice a whisper behind a yawn. "But so did I. Should have believed the blind items."

"Blind items?" Julia repeated, her confusion growing. "What are blind items?"

Ava's laughter erupted again, but this time, it was

different, more genuine, and she looked at Julia with an expression of almost pity. "Oh, you're so old." She sprung up and pretended to hobble around the room, using an imaginary cane. "Come now, dear, let's get you some knitting and a nice warm blanket."

Julia rolled her eyes but couldn't suppress a chuckle. "Hilarious, Ava. Care to share with this old woman what a 'blind item' is?"

"Anonymous confessions online about people. I should have believed them."

"Blind items about who?" Julia pressed, her mind racing. "Rupert? Is he behind all of this?"

Ava's laughter turned to tears, her face scrunching up as though in deep pain. "He's dead too, isn't he?"

"I... I don't know. Wasn't he sending you pictures? Snapchats?"

"Grass," Ava said, yawning. "Sky."

"So, anyone could have sent them?"

Ava shrugged. "Never really knew the guy. I think he fancied me. We all met for the first time the day we checked in. I should never have answered the ad. Who cares about awards anyway?"

Ava's words trailed off, and her eyelids began to droop. She slumped further in her chair, exhaustion overtaking her.

"Ah, I've been waiting for this part to happen all night," Evelyn said softly. "Quite the ball of energy when she gets going. You're lucky you missed the whackiest of it."

"It got whackier than Jeff and Phil?" Julia asked.

"Oh, yes," Evelyn said, brushing Ava's hair from her face. "At one point, she became convinced she was Taylor Swift and performed a two-hour private concert for my pleasure." Leaning in, she added, "She could have been making the words up, for all I knew, but it kept her entertained. It was nice to see her expressing herself. She's barely said boo to a goose since she arrived. She'll wake up like none of this happened, and I promise, the tea will go straight into the bin." Clasping Julia's hand, she added, "No harm done, eh? And please, keep this between us?"

Julia's mind was spinning, the puzzle pieces shifting and rearranging themselves. Ava's words, the blind items, Rupert's disappearance – it was all connected, but how?

"I won't tell the police about your tea collection," Julia promised, her voice firm, "but if what Ava is saying means what I think, I need to talk to them."

Julia's mind was a whirlwind of questions and possibilities, each leading her further into a mystery growing darker and more tangled by the moment.

The Knights had been framed.

And everything else had been a distraction.

With the young camerawoman snoring like a contented cat under a velvet curtain, Jessie sank deep into one of the cushions scattered across the floor, her phone in her hand as she scrolled through the search results. Evelyn and Julia were huddled around an old computer that hummed like it was on its last legs at a desk in the corner.

"I think I've found it," Jessie announced.

The forum she had uncovered, 'Behind the Lens', was a digital labyrinth filled with dark alleys and hidden corners, an entire section dedicated to blind items about dodgy directors. One mysterious entry spoke of a 'famous fracking woman' who'd pushed boundaries far beyond ethical limits, staging protests and intimidating locals for her documentary's success.

"This one might be even worse," Jessie whispered. "Someone is alleging they witnessed her reverse over the star fox from *Secrets of the Urban Fox* in her hurry to get the little guy on camera, and instead of reporting it, just threw him into a bin and started following another fox like it was the same one. This woman is nuts."

"Hardly the naturalistic style Anwen claimed to embrace," Julia remarked.

Evelyn, twisting in her computer chair, said, "She's worked with a different crew on every film. And her latest have awful reviews. A documentary about toilet wipes, a ghost who haunts graveyards, and another about Princess Diana, an exhausting topic, if ever there was one. This woman's been staying here. I knew evil was under my roof, but she masked it so well."

Jessie couldn't help but reflect on earlier wisdom, "'Fair is foul, and foul is fair,'" she recited, her voice rich. She looked up at Julia and Evelyn, who stared back, their faces reflecting Jessie's confusion when Veronica first quoted the line. "Hamlet, Act something, Scene whatever. We all wear masks, don't we? So, what foul mask has Anwen been sporting since she arrived, and more to the point, what's she so desperate to hide? She's as nutty as a squirrel's breakfast."

Julia's voice, barely above a whisper, cut through the tension like a knife. "Evelyn, tell me she's in her room."

The silence that followed was as chilling as the wind outside.

"She *might* be, but she went for a walk last night when the police turned up. I don't think she's been back since."

This was darker than any cult or gang.

At least Jessie had known where she'd stood with the Crew.

∽

While the police huddled around something at the bottom of the garden with the wind and rain battering them, Barker found himself pacing in Evelyn's backroom, his mind a whirlpool of thoughts and suspicions. He'd just read the blind items, and the information about Rupert potentially being the one in the cloak had set his heart racing.

"The madness started after Anwen turned up," Barker said. "This was supposed to be an arson case with a sprinkling of a gang, so how did we end up in a convoluted web involving a cult and two murders?"

"She covered her tracks well. I'll give her that," Jessie said. "Having Rupert be the one in the cloak while she was sat in the café stuffing her face with Eton mess. Of course, we weren't going to suspect her. Do you think he's in on the murders? Could be why he's done a runner."

"Barker?" Julia rested a hand on his shoulder as he stared out at the police working outside. "What's on your mind?"

"Anwen said she overheard someone calling me exploitative here at the B&B," he said, his voice tight.

"She must have heard that from Mark. So, it begs the question, what else has she overheard while she was here?"

He thought back to Nathan's statement. He'd mentioned that his parents would talk about the land they owned when nobody was around. Anwen could have heard them talking about Arthur the day she checked in, and the possibility sent a chill down his spine.

Julia pulled Sophia's manuscript from her bag. "She must have dug around their rooms and found this?"

Evelyn gasped, her hand going to her mouth.

"Faith gave me the book," Julia explained. "I didn't steal it this time."

"It's not that," Evelyn said, her voice trembling. "The afternoon I checked her in, I was walking upstairs to take Sophia and Derek some lunch, and I saw outside their door. She had her hand on the handle. She said she was lost and couldn't find her room. I didn't think much of it, with her room being in a similar position on the floor above, so I pointed her in the right direction and got on with my day. But Derek and Sophia weren't in their room. They were next door with the kids, chastising them for the scene they caused when you came to see them in the garden, Barker."

"So, she could have been leaving their room?" Barker suggested.

"The door was unlocked."

"But how could she pull all that off the same day?" Jessie asked.

"That first day we met her," Julia said, pulling her hand from Barker's shoulder. "When we talked about the documentary in the kitchen, she told us she wanted to get started that right away. She said she worked fast."

"And she wasn't lying," Barker said, wincing at his memory from that day. "I think I might have pointed her right to the Knight family. When I left to meet them at the B&B, she drove me here, and I told her more than I should have about the case, but I had no reason not to trust her. She said she smelled awards on me."

"All this for some poxy awards?" Jessie laughed. "Bit mental, isn't it?"

"Desperation makes people do strange things," he said, his voice heavy.

Ava stirred from her sleep in the corner, a frown creasing her forehead as she squinted at the curtain draped around her.

"Did I rip this down?" she asked, her voice tinged with confusion.

Julia and Evelyn nodded.

"So, it wasn't a dream then," Ava muttered.

Barker was surprised to hear her talk. She'd been mostly silent behind the camera. But now, there was a presence in her eyes that hadn't been there before.

"Ava, did Anwen set everything up for the documentary?" he asked, his voice gentle, trying not to frighten her. "The murders? The cult?"

Ava's gaze darted away, and she seemed to shrink into herself. "I don't know for certain, but she wasn't against the idea of faking things."

The room fell into silence as they absorbed her words. Barker felt a cold dread settle in his stomach.

"Ava, what do you mean by that?" Julia asked.

She looked as though she was about to cry. Evelyn handed her a fresh glass of water, and she gulped it down.

"The scarecrow," Ava said, wiping her mouth with the back of her hand. "She wanted to get Barker's reaction to seeing a cloaked figure on camera. She said she missed it the first time because you ran off too fast. I told her it wasn't right, but she insisted it was the best thing for the documentary. I didn't do it, but I watched her. Said she got the cloak from a fancy dress shop, but it looked identical to the one I saw on the green when Rupert stood me up for that drink at Richie's. I haven't seen him since, and that's what I thought: if she didn't mind faking a scarecrow, what if she convinced Rupert to do the same?"

The confessions hung heavier than the incense.

Outside in the garden, there was a commotion, and Barker turned to see Moyes, hands on hips, staring off to the bottom of the garden. She glanced back at the B&B, and her eyes met his with a shake of her head. They'd found something. Barker, Julia, and Jessie huddled together by the window.

"We've been watching the wrong film this whole time," Barker said, his voice low and urgent. "We've been distracted by the gang, the cult, the Knights… everything. If the scarecrow was Anwen, and the figure on the green was Rupert, why not the spray paint on the café, too? The pictures with the faces scratched out? The murders? I think this has something to do with her grandparents. Not directly, but she shared something with me. For all I know, it could have been a lie, but looking back, it was one of the few times she was vulnerable with me."

"What about her grandparents?" Jessie pushed. "Were they also crazy killers?"

"Not that she mentioned, but she seemed to love them a lot. She missed their final days because she was away filming. She said she regretted it and hadn't been home since their funerals. She lives on the road, going from film to film."

"Sounds like running away to me," Julia said.

"Running away that was rewarded," Barker said, returning to Ava, who was gulping down more water with Evelyn's assistance. "Those blind items accused her of bad behaviour, and she was awarded for it. That will have only spurred her on, making her think it was the only way to get things done. Ava, do you know anything else about Anwen? Where was she before Peridale?"

"I'm not sure, but I think she was living in her car. A sleeping bag was in the boot when she picked us up from the station. Said it was for night shoots, but Rupert said he didn't believe her."

"Oh, dear," Evelyn said, closing her eyes. "She didn't pay for the rooms upfront. Her card declined, and she said she'd ordered a new one because it kept doing that, and she'd make sure to pay before leaving. Given that she was here shooting a documentary, I didn't suspect she could be lying to me. She seemed so sweet."

The room fell into a heavy silence, and Barker reflected on his first meeting Anwen. She hadn't been the woman he'd expected from their emails—maybe her first sign of deception—but he'd thought she was sweet, too. Her unassuming nature had lowered his walls to rid him of his nerves, and she'd dug deep, pulling out stories about his mother and life in

Peridale. He felt sick, wishing he could take those stories back.

"Veronica..." Barker paused, dropping his head as he exhaled. "Veronica told me that a director reached out to Johnny months before he left to set up a documentary focusing on the deaths in Peridale. The director framed it as promotion for the paper, but Veronica was juggling too much when she first took over, so she fobbed the director off and stopped hearing from her."

"It was Anwen, wasn't it?" Julia asked.

Barker nodded.

"Veronica mentioned something about a documentary when Anwen first showed up," Jessie said. "Why didn't she join the dots then?"

"Because she couldn't remember the director's name," Barker said, recalling their discussion in the dining room that morning. "Only that it was something Welsh sounding. She realised it was the same director when she overheard Anwen trying to interview people in The Plough, but she didn't want to say anything because..." He let out a strained laugh. "She didn't want to steal my thunder, but it was never my thunder to steal. This wasn't about me or my books; this was about Anwen hearing about murders in our area and seeing awards. I was just her way in, and I fell for it."

"Feel sorry for yourself later, Dad. What now? We need to nail her before she continues her rampage."

"We need some concrete evidence," he said, scratching at his stubbly jaw as he looked around the room. "Ava, do you have the camera? We need to go over all the footage. There must be something in there of Anwen slipping up. If she were sloppy enough to include you in her scarecrow ploy, she'd have been sloppy in other areas, too."

"She took it with her when she said she was going for a walk last night," Ava replied. "But there's a hard drive with the footage if that helps. There's just one problem. It's in her car, and I don't have a key."

"Jessie, figure out a way into that car and go through the footage with Ava," Barker instructed. "Find something that will wrap this up in a neat bow, so she can't wriggle out of it and keep pointing her finger at a cult from thousands of years ago. Julia, fill Moyes in."

"And what about you?"

Barker's eyes met Julia's. "I'm going to look for her."

"Barker, don't be an—"

He silenced Julia with a kiss, cupping her face in his hands. "Trained police officer, remember? I won't put myself in harm's way, but I can't just sit around waiting for the official cogs to get moving."

"Mum's right, don't be an idiot," Jessie said, shoving him. "My turn for a lecture. She's clearly got issues and will do anything. Look what happened when I threw myself into a stupid situation last night. She isn't worth it, Dad."

"This... this is personal. I was right that morning before Anwen arrived when I was nervous. I was just some guy to her."

"Look what happened last time you ran after a shadow," Jessie said, not giving up easily. "This could be a set-up."

"She doesn't know we're onto her."

"The picture, Barker," Julia whispered, following him to the door. "She marked you."

"To scare us."

"Consider me scared."

"I love you," Barker kissed Julia. "I know what I'm doing."

With those words, he left the back room and ran straight into PC Puglisi.

"Barker, I think I know who leaked your book! It wasn't a guest."

"Can it wait, Jake?"

"Yes, sir," he said. "Everything okay?"

"It will be soon."

Derek Knight was walking down the stairs in a dressing gown, his face drawn into a weary frown.

Nathan, Sam, and Faith were behind him. Barker almost stopped to explain to them what he'd uncovered, but he couldn't get the words out.

Your wife died because my ego closed my eyes to the killer I invited into this village.

He'd explain later when he had Anwen in hand to throw into the police station. He hurried out of the B&B, back to where it all started.

The Romans had called it Caelumgrove Woods.

Luanach, to the Celts.

To the villagers of Peridale, it was just Howarth Forest, and nothing had been the same since Barker discovered Arthur's body there. The streets were quiet, the green deserted, but not for much longer. The show was ending, and if Anwen had cast him in the starring role, it only felt fitting that he'd be the one to call 'Cut!' on her mad scheme.

23

Barker's steps crunched on the forest floor as he walked deeper into the shadows of Howarth Forest. The trees seemed to leer at him with gnarled branches like twisted arms reaching to ensnare him. Overgrown bushes rustled in the wind, and the faint call of distant crows seemed to mock his search.

Barker paused to look around, his breath misting in the chilly air, his mind reeling from the day's revelations. Even before Jessie and Julia had shared their new findings from Ava, he'd narrowed things down to Anwen, thanks to Veronica's confession in the dining room.

"A director contacted Johnny last year before he left the paper," she had told him. "He thought it would be good press to raise sales and impress the higher-ups. The director wanted to create something about all the strange murders in the village as the angle, but when I took over, I didn't have the time or energy to continue negotiations, so I let it go. I didn't think anything of it again until Anwen tried interviewing me in The Plough, and her accent stuck with me. Welsh. I didn't know why, but her name... Anwen Powell. What sounds more Welsh than that? So, I went back and looked over the emails again, and lo and behold, Anwen Powell was the director trying to use the paper for her documentary."

Barker's heart ached as he recalled the earlier scene at Howarth House, the camaraderie, the shared excitement, and the thrill of uncovering history. How naïve he had been to trust so quickly, to allow himself to be drawn into Anwen's web of deceit.

"Anwen?" Barker cried at the top of his lungs. "If you're out here, I will find you."

In the dining room of the B&B, with DI Moyce sat across from her, Julia couldn't take her mind off the picture of Barker with the scratched-out eyes. An empty threat, he'd said—a symbol to scare them. The soft clinking of cutlery and hushed voices filled the room as the Knight family, the only guests brave enough to leave their rooms, picked at the breakfast spread Evelyn had thrown together.

"Anwen Powell," Julia began. "She's not who we thought she was, Moyes. She's been manipulating us. Barker and I discovered evidence of her involvement in the entire thing."

Moyes studied Julia's face, and the silence lingered for a moment before she finally nodded, her face reflecting the gravity of the decision. "Barker told me about the newspaper documentary. Are you sure?"

"No," Julia sighed. "But after Jessie goes through the hard drive, you might have the evidence to put your first Peridale case to bed."

"So, where is he then?"

Sighing deeply, Julia looked down at her hands, her fingers intertwining in a worried dance. "He's gone to look for Anwen. I tried to stop him, but you know how he is."

"Any idea where he's gone?" PC Puglisi asked through a mouthful of a croissant. "We could put together a unit to search the village?"

Julia shook her head, the echo of her worry from Jessie's disappearance the night before bouncing back at her. How had she found herself in this situation again?

"Jake, do just that," Moyes ordered, standing up.

"You're looking for Barker and Anwen Powell; whatever you do, do not approach. She's already killed three people."

"Three?" Derek Knight asked, standing up. "Who else?"

"We found a body at the bottom of the garden in a shallow grave," Moyes said, her jaw gritting. "We think it's Rupert Jones, her cinematographer."

"Stabbed?" Julia asked, the words barely coming out as she looked around for Ava. She was outside with Jessie near Anwen's beat-up Volvo.

"Strangled," Moyes said, blasting a cloud above her. "I'd say there's doubt that it was the same killer as the first two, given the lack of pattern, but it was never her pattern, was it?"

"It was the Cult of Lunara's," Derek said, sitting heavily back into his chair. "Why did I ever give my wife those research papers?"

∼

As Barker clambered over a fallen tree near Howarth House, the daylight offered a harsh reality that the evening had managed to shroud in mystery. The house was long beyond being on its last legs, but there it waited for him, and just like his previous visit, there was a light on somewhere inside.

Anwen wasn't there to point it out this time.

She'd made their journey to the forest seem so natural.

They'd started at the school, the location of his previous book, and then she'd suggested they film in the graveyard, just by the forest, only for Rupert to point out how cool the moon looked over the forest. Maybe he'd been in on it from the beginning, or perhaps he'd played right into Anwen's hands. Somehow, she'd have found a way to get them into that forest to get the shots she needed. She'd gone to such trouble setting it all up the first time.

He pushed open the broken gate and crept into the house as the memories of his previous discovery played in his mind like flickering film. The dancing candlelight, the strange symbols etched in chalk, the silver coins on the eyes of Arthur Foster. It was a scene that had settled in his soul, one he'd never forget.

Today, as the grey morning light poured in, the room was nothing more than an empty dining hall filled with the first crisp leaves of the oncoming autumn, the ghosts of the past ingrained in the fabric of the building.

Even without murder, the place had stories to tell.

The history of Duncan Howarth, his lost love, and the Cult of Lunara artefacts found nearby would have been worthy topics. If only Barker had pinned down the arsonist before the devious director turned up.

Anwen's creative passion had twisted into something dark and malevolent. From one creative to another, he couldn't shake a sense of empathy for her downward spiral, torn between condemning her actions and somehow understanding the morbid obsession that drove her. He'd never kill to give him something to write about, but he'd been drawn to Astrid's story like Anwen had been drawn to Peridale.

Moths to a morbid flame.

A creak from upstairs snapped him from his contemplation, sending him towards the staircase.

~

"So, saving you from a kidnapping wasn't enough for the week?" Billy said, wriggling the screwdriver in the lock of the boot of the old Volvo. "You're determined to get me into trouble, Jessie."

"Something tells me the police have more pressing matters to deal with. Can you get it open or not, Billy?"

"What sort of question is that?" he grunted, and with one final jab, the boot popped open. "So, who was that guy you were spotted with at Richie's?"

"Seriously?" Jessie frowned at him as Ava climbed

straight over the backseat and through to the passenger seat. "Just a friend from Riverswick. Are you keeping tabs on me?"

Jessie dug around in the boot as Billy thought up what to say. She pulled back the sleeping bag and a shiny tin of red spray paint glistened among food wrappers and plastic bottles. That solved the 'CC' graffiti.

"Word gets around these parts, doesn't it?" Billy said as she pocketed the can. "And last time I checked, if I weren't keeping tabs on you, you'd currently be six feet under, thanks to the Crew. They're still showing up around Fern Moore, by the way. Did you show the police that map?"

"I'm sure they'll do something with it," Jessie said, giving him a quick hug as Ava climbed back, hard drive in hand. "I'll catch you later, and I still can't believe you're driving around on that scooter."

"We can't all afford yellow Minis, can we?"

Neither could Jessie, but she didn't stop to remind him it had been a present from Barker for her eighteenth birthday. She looked out across the village, hoping that the idiot hadn't got himself killed.

Back in Evelyn's private sitting room, Jessie and Ava huddled around the old computer and waited for an age for it to even recognise the device.

"I was present for all filming until the day of the

sighting," Ava explained, scrolling past the first few dozen video clips. "She told us to take the night off to dig deeper with Barker, so this should be the first one she was filming alone."

Ava opened a clip of Barker. He was behind his desk, a slight smile on his face. She scrubbed along a little, moving him at double speed before letting some of the clip play.

"If not for being head over heels in love with Julia, I'm not sure I would have stuck in Peridale after that," Barker admitted, his voice filled with passion and sincerity.

Jessie's finger hovered over the play button, a pang of something unrecognisable twisting in her gut. Julia had kept Jessie in Peridale in those early days, too. She fast-forwarded again, the images blurring into one another, stopping again further along.

The footage continued and changed to an outdoor shot.

"The field behind the café," Jessie muttered.

"Significant?"

"The reason all of this happened," Jessie said, moving closer to the screen as Anwen appeared. She gave the camera one glance before setting off with careful strides. "If you ever want to make a documentary about a dodgy politician, I know a guy who doesn't mind hiring insane gangs to intimidate families."

Anwen reached the middle of the field. She held up a hand and waved.

Just like the cloaked figure had on the green.

Jessie gulped as the scene snapped to total darkness. Branches now partially obscured the image as though the camera had been moved to another location, but they were still looking at the field, and the ring of candles had already been lit. A cloaked figure paced around the circle momentarily before a glinting dagger appeared. It swooped down in a silent stab.

"She's sick," Jessie said. "Why would she do this?"

"It's not even like she could use that in the documentary," Ava whispered, rubbing tears from her cheeks. "Just for her collection."

"Sophia?" a strained voice said from behind them.

They'd been so engrossed in watching the scene unfold that they hadn't noticed Derek watching from the doorway. His face twisted with rage.

"Mr Knight, I'm sorry, I—"

"They're saying it was the director?" Derek choked, unable to look away from the screen. "She comforted me. Told me that everything happened for a reason, which is something Sophia would have said, but this is the reason? *This* is why my wife died? Not the land... not the gang... a documentary?" He pounded against the doorframe with a clenched fist and cried. "I'll kill her!"

Jessie found herself hoping that Derek would have the chance. She dialled Barker's number and pressed her phone to her ear, her rapid heartbeat matching the dial tone. They had the evidence they needed, and he was somewhere out there with a woman who would stop at nothing.

"Pick up!"

∼

Barker held his breath as he crept up the broken staircase, each creak and groan of the ancient wood whispering out through the abandoned house. As he took another step, his foot plunged through one of the rotted steps, and he stifled a cry, panic surging through him. He caught himself just in time, pulling his leg free with a jolt of pain that he ignored, his entire focus narrowed.

He reached the landing, his breath catching in his throat as his eyes fell upon a sight that stopped him in his tracks. A camera stood on a tripod in the middle of the first room with an open door. Its light beamed at him as it had this whole time. The sudden and overwhelming sense that he was being watched fell over him.

His eyes darted around, searching for Anwen, feeling her presence like a shadow in the room's corners. He caught a fleeting glimpse of movement—a swathe of black rushed past the room, barely visible in his peripheral vision.

With adrenaline surging through him, Barker gave chase, his every instinct screaming at him to leave. But he'd come this far. He pounded down the landing after the figure, his footsteps echoing in the empty corridor. A door slammed ahead, and he raced towards it, calling out Anwen's name.

Without warning, the door gave way under his assault, and he stumbled forward, falling face-first onto the splintered floorboards. Inches from his face, he stared through a gaping hole in the floor, a drop into the darkness that led down to the house's ruined kitchen. Groaning, he rolled over, pain flaring through his body. He was getting too old for this. Rain from a hole in the roof drizzled down on him as he blinked up.

And there she was.

Anwen's grinning face, triumphant and mocking, stared down at him from under her hood. Her eyes were filled with madness, and Barker realised he'd underestimated her from their first meeting.

Just like she'd wanted him to.

Jam on her chin.

Running late.

Hiding the instincts of a killer.

He had no time to react as she swung a thick tree branch at him, a savage blow that sent him reeling. As the world spun, Barker had fallen into another of her traps. He should never have answered that damn email. She'd just seemed to love his book, but as darkness started to close around the edges of his vision as he bumped back down the stairs, dragged by his feet, his final thoughts weren't about Anwen or his book.

He saw his family.

Julia.

Jessie.

Olivia.

And Peggy Brown.

See you soon, Mum.

24

Barker's head throbbed, the pain pulsing in a slow rhythm that seemed to echo in the distance. He blinked, his vision blurry, a beamed ceiling coming into focus. Soft jazz music played in the background, and for a fleeting moment, he wondered if he'd passed on to the afterlife. But then his surroundings began to take shape, and the familiar scent of his office crept into his nostrils. The afterlife couldn't be so bad if it looked like this.

But he wasn't alone.

He tried to lift his head, a sharp pain reminding him of the tree branch, and his eyes fell upon a circle of flickering candles on the floor. Terror washed over him, but he fought to keep it at bay. Fear couldn't control him now. He was inside his office, lying across his desk, and his gaze wandered to the figure in the room.

Anwen Powell.

Her black cloak flowed around her as she moved gracefully in a circle, her hands covered in chalk, scribbling lunar symbols on the floor around the candles. As Barker watched her mumbling to herself, the hairs on the back of his neck stood up.

She hadn't noticed him yet.

He assessed his options.

The door was there, but she was standing too close, the glint of the dagger she'd used to kill the others hooked to her belt catching his eye. His video screen for the camera doorbell was within reach, but even if he could press the buttons to call out for help, the tiny speaker would echo around the small yard, and she'd stab him before anyone could arrive.

The ceiling above creaked, and he imagined Sue going about her day as the café came to life. So close and yet impossible to reach. Anwen looked up as quick footsteps moved about after a tinkle of the bell. He knew that journey from the door, the backdrop to his days writing and researching in his office.

There was no way out.

He'd have to use his brain and his words.

Anwen's eyes snapped down on him, a twisted smile on her face as she realised he'd re-joined her in the conscious realm. She stopped scribbling and walked over to the camera by the leather sofa. The red light came on, but she left the dancing candlelight to illuminate her scene.

"And *action*!" she declared. "What do you think? Spooky, right? The viewers are going to love it."

Maintaining a calm façade, he dared to prop himself up on his elbows. She didn't shove him back down, so he cracked his neck, testing the waters as his head spun.

"Quite the creative process you've got," Barker began, his voice casual. "Remember when we were last in here, discussing the relationship between creator and creation?"

"Magical, isn't it?" Anwen said without a hint of irony. "The power to shape worlds, to guide destinies. Think of all those mystery writers you read with your mum as a child and how they shaped you."

The mention of 'child' made him think of Olivia, and his gut squirmed.

He had to get out for her.

"Think of all the little Barker Browns out there right now," Anwen said, stepping over the ring of candles, her usually soft features were hollowed by the shadow of the hood and the twirling flames. "It's hard to know how many your first novel inspired, but think how many *more* your second will reach.

Posthumous releases have that funny way of selling just a bit more, don't they? And who knows, maybe the novels you scrapped will make it out there? What a legacy you'll leave. Your mum would be so proud."

It took all of Barker's strength to bite his tongue. She knew where to dig to push his buttons. She moved close enough that he could have reached out and grabbed her if he wanted to. A vision of his hands around her neck appeared too quickly in his mind.

Anwen's crazy was contagious.

But they weren't wrestling.

They were playing chess.

"And what about your grandparents?" Barker countered, daring to sit up another few inches as she paced around the desk. "Do you think they'd be proud of you? Crafting gripping tales, no matter the cost?"

A flicker of rage crossed Anwen's face, her manic smile wavering.

"They always supported me," she hissed. "They wanted me to leave Portmeirion. They paid for my college courses, bought me my Volvo, and sent me off to make stories for the world. They knew my purpose was greater than dying in a small village like them. I needed to create. I have the gift to make people feel, and they saw that before anyone."

"And would they approve of the lines you've crossed?" Barker said softly, challenging her creative philosophy. "You've betrayed the essence of the naturalistic storytelling approach you loved. You've manipulated reality to suit your whims, and in doing so, you've lost sight of what makes a story truly compelling. Stories about truth, about the human condition—"

"And where do you think truth gets you in the streaming age?" Anwen's face contorted before she ducked to continue with her lunar scribbles. "Buried under the next content dump. And that's if you're lucky not to be deleted in the name of a tax write-off."

"Is that what happened to your last few?" he asked. "The toilet wipes? The ghost? Princess Diana?"

"How foolish I was to think that last one would be a sure-fire win, yet I couldn't find a single person to distribute it. One too many, they called it." She clenched her palm, snapping the chalk. Unravelling her fingers, she let the dust sprinkle over the final symbol of a full moon. "People want to be entertained and gripped like never before. You can't sit around waiting for the stories to come to you. You create them, but you can't create from thin air. You have to find a source. People still want the illusion of truth, stretched across ten fascinating episodes with twists and cliffhangers to make them look up from their phones for just a fraction of a second. And so, I found this village. I found you."

"And like you found Johnny at *The Peridale Post*?"

Anwen chuckled, still circling the desk like a shark circling its bait.

"Oh, don't take offence, Barker. You might have been the backup, but you're a better angle than that drip. You're the handsome family man. Former DI turned PI with books under your belt. And your wife! The super sleuth baker, always willing to stand up for what's right. And not to mention this village. A quaint little Cotswold haven like any other, but you don't need to scratch too deep beneath the surface to find the darkness. Could I have asked for a better setting with more perfect leads?" She bit her lip, holding back a smirk. "And me, the person to capture it all on film for the first time! This will be bigger than those fracking protestors and that damn fox. And I did enjoy your book."

"I'm flattered," he replied.

She tilted her head, looking at the plant in the corner. "What better way to end my film than with the star of the show, helpless in his final moments, sacrificed at the hands of the cult he failed to capture? Killed in the same basement as Astrid, the poor girl who inspired your book. It's the perfect climax."

"You're quite the director, Anwen, I'll give you that."

"You know," she said, walking over to the plant to

bat at the leaves, "I think I might dedicate this film to her. After all, her death has given us both so much."

Barker looked to the door again. He could make a run for it, but there was no guarantee he would reach the door before a dagger sunk between his shoulder blades.

"It's not too late to cut the film here," Barker tried instead. "You could hand yourself in. That would be a more noble ending to the film. I think your viewers would enjoy that just as much."

"This is *my* story," she said, her tone dark as she turned back to him, the plant stretching behind her like skeletal wings in the shadows, "and I'll direct it as I see fit."

Footsteps moved above still, but none rushed. If people were searching for him, his office would be the last place they'd check. The police would be trawling the forest, shouting his name into the void.

The battle for Anwen's soul had already been lost, but Barker couldn't give up.

"Isn't the blood of two innocent people enough on your hands?" Barker asked, his voice trembling for the first time as desperation surged. "You killed Arthur, you killed Sophia, all for a story? You used their lives and pain as nothing more than plot devices."

"Like you did with Astrid, you mean?" Anwen's eyes danced, her smile twisting into wicked peaks. "So what?

A lowlife arsonist? A woman obsessed with cults and colourful chunks of rock? They were expendable. Their deaths will mean more than their lives ever did." She leaned closer, her voice dropping to a conspiratorial whisper. "They brought it on themselves. I overheard Sophia and Derek whispering about Arthur lurking around the place, spilling secrets about the gang, the fire, and their land. And... I had a little help from a friend." She reached out and ruffled his hair, making him recoil. "I might not have known what they were talking about if my star didn't kindly fill me in on his Arthur Foster case during our little drive to the B&B. The stage was set, and all I had to do was hit 'record' and let the rest unfold."

"You did more than that," he said, nodding to her black cloak. "Unless this is the point you tell me you're part of the Cult of Lunara?"

Her laugh was cold and hollow. "The book was on her bed as though waiting for me. Imagine my delight when I consulted the lunar calendar she had pinned on her wall. A full moon! I told you my grandparents are watching down on me, guiding me."

"So, you found Arthur when he returned to the B&B and struck him with a garden gnome? How did you get him to the forest without being seen?"

"Oh, you are clever. A little old 'Weekend at Bernie's' magic," she said. "Grandad's favourite film. I just walked him from the direction of the pub, and he was so dazed that he didn't fight. A couple of people saw us. Villages like this gossip about what they think they saw. A poor, helpless wife dragging her drunk husband home. I put my cloak on when I reached the graveyard, tossed him over my shoulder, and the rest is history." She clapped her hands together, her eyes alight. "Oh, you should see the footage from when we discovered him, Barker! It's magical. The moon, your face, Julia comforting you. I couldn't have scripted it better."

The words were a punch to the gut, and Barker struggled to keep his composure. The monstrous nature of her crimes, the chilling ease with which she'd planned and executed them, the way she revelled in the suffering she'd caused, the dagger hanging from her belt—it was all too much to bear.

"You've lost your mind, Anwen," he said, his voice breaking. "You're worse than those you claimed to hate."

Her eyes narrowed, and for a moment, Barker saw a flicker of something—doubt, perhaps, or remorse. But it vanished quickly, replaced by the cold, calculating gleam of a killer.

"If you can't beat them," she said, her voice dripping with arrogance, "outdo them. When this is all over, when the world sees my masterpiece, they won't be able to look away."

Barker shook his head, his heart heavy with the knowledge that there was no reaching her, no saving her from the darkness that had consumed her.

"I think they'll see you for what you truly are," he said, unable to look at anything but the dagger. "A murderer, a manipulator, a lost and twisted soul. And your story will be nothing more than a tragic tale of ambition gone horribly wrong."

"I'm a visionary!" she roared.

"You're desperate," he replied.

Her face hardened as Barker's voice grew to match hers. Even if she wouldn't admit it, she knew he was right, and the fear in her eyes told him that she understood, at least on some level, the terrible path she'd chosen. It wouldn't save his life. But at least his words would haunt the rest of hers, like the figure haunting the video intercom screen out of the corner of his eye. Anwen started circling him again, and he dared to steal a glance. There was movement in the yard behind the café. Someone was out there. He noticed the panel with the buttons to open the door just out of reach. If he could get to it...

"Why kill Sophia?" he asked, his voice carefully controlled. "Something tells me you didn't cast her as

Ritual Victim Number Two by drawing names of the Knights out of a hat?"

Anwen sighed, a dreamy look in her eyes as she stared at the ceiling. "I wanted to drag things out for as long as possible to ensure I'd thrown everyone off my scent. But I started asking Sophia too many questions about the cult. Sophia's book hadn't been published, and I didn't realise how few people could access the information she'd uncovered. I tried to play it off by telling her I'd found a book in the library. She nodded along, and I thought I'd got away with it. But she confronted me that night while Derek was blubbering to Evelyn about the house burning down."

"So, you killed, yet again."

"It was easy to convince her to go into the garden so I could explain and *whack*!" She mimed the strike with glee. "This village is a ghost town after midnight, so I carried her right over and set up the field, and ta-da! A second ritual killing. Spooked everyone, didn't it? The fear, the intrigue—it's all been so delicious to capture. I've made Peridale my stage."

Barker's stomach turned, the sheer delight in her voice at the mayhem she had unleashed unbearable. He glanced again at the screen, and the figure was pacing as though wondering if they should press the doorbell. It wasn't an unusual sight for a new client, and Barker didn't want to drag them into it, but he didn't want to be sacrificed for the sake of Anwen's climactic scene either.

"So, what now, Anwen?" he forced himself to continue. "What's your endgame? Now that you know I know about the gnome, you must realise the police are onto you?"

"They can be onto me all they like. They have to catch me first. I snuck out of the B&B right under their noses. And I waited at the one place I knew you would come looking when the penny finally dropped. I couldn't have planned it better. And when I have my ending filmed, I'll sneak away once more to figure out how to get my film out into the world from the shadows. Maybe I'll keep the Lunara revival going for a sequel in another little village. Or maybe even a trilogy? People love a trilogy."

Her words tumbled out in a feverish rush, her eyes wild with manic energy. But Barker barely heard her. His eyes fixed on the door, his hand inching towards the button. He could feel her still ranting, her delusions going in one ear and out of the other as he nodded, his fingertips creeping across the cold polished wood. He pressed the button. The door clicked, but she didn't hear it. He had no idea who was out there, but the door was open. His heart was pounding, his palms slick with sweat. But he trained his eyes on her, his face impassive, waiting for the right moment to strike. Her ranting continued, her voice rising and falling. The door swung open.

"Barker, are you busy?" a familiar, sad voice called down into the office with a sigh as a foot creaked on the first step. "We need to talk. I have to confess something to—"

The mystery pacer came into view, squinting at the strange scene before him from underneath a black fringe. Mark's dark-lined eyes flitted between Barker and Anwen, with something clutched tight to his chest.

"Anwen?" he whispered, taking another step. "Is this for your doc..."

Anwen scrambled for the dagger, her face twisted with unwavering fury. She pulled it free, drawing her arm back high above her head. Mark matched her pose with whatever he'd been holding and launched it through the air with unerring accuracy. A book—an unpublished manuscript—hit Anwen square in the face, the pages exploding in a flurry around her. She staggered, and in that critical moment, Barker did what he'd wanted to do since he'd opened his eyes in his office to a second chance at life.

He sprang into action.

But his head injury betrayed him, his wobbling legs sending him crashing into the vinyl player. The needle scratched across the record, the hazy jazz underscoring Anwen's final scene jarring to a sudden stop. His vision swam as he righted himself, swaying like he'd just exited the most chaotic rollercoaster of his life. By the time he'd blinked away the last of the dizziness, Mark had Anwen pinned to the ground, the dagger held out of her reach. She struggled against him, muttering about her ruined ending, extinguishing the candle before her face.

"One too many people have already died in this basement," Mark said as Barker pinched the pressure points in her wrist to make her unclench her grip on the dagger. "Barker, it was me. I found your book. I leaked it. I owe you—"

"I owe you my life," Barker said, kicking the dagger under the sofa. "And you got your ending, Anwen. Who doesn't love one last twist?"

25

The rain was relentless, a cleansing downpour washing away the shadow that had engulfed Peridale since Anwen's ominous arrival. Julia, her fingers embracing a warm cup of peppermint and liquorice tea, stood with Barker and Jessie, their gazes fixed on DI Moyes and her officers as they escorted Anwen from the office.

Ava was poised at the alley's opening, her camera protected from the rain by Evelyn's large pink umbrella.

"Any last words for *my* ending, Anwen?"

Anwen's face was a blank canvas, a chilling void replacing the lunacy Barker had described. Silence was her only answer as she continued on her path, pausing at the sight of Derek Knight with Faith, Sam, and Nathan beside him. The broken family's stern expressions spoke of their fortitude.

Ava's voice rang out, sharp and challenging, "How about an apology to Rupert's family?"

Anwen's eyes glinted with a sinister spark as she looked back near the waiting police car. "Rupert would never have kept his mouth shut about my little cloak prank. You got away lucky, Ava. I was planning to kill you next. I own that footage. Just remember that. This is *my* film!"

"Shot on *my* camera," Ava said, her once meek voice steady and defiant. "Stored on *my* hard drive. I think you were right about this being an award-winning opportunity for me. Too bad you won't be available to attend the ceremonies."

"I'll see you in court!"

"Good luck with that." Ava's voice was a cool breeze as she flicked off the light and lowered the camera. "I'll send you a postcard from the premiere."

Julia had yet to let go of Barker. The forest search had been frantic, all to find Barker hidden under the café the entire time. In blissful ignorance, Sue had been absorbed in baking, waiting for customers too fearful to leave their homes.

Once word got around, the café would fill up once again.

"All's well that ends well?" Barker suggested, a hint

of humour in his voice, as the police car door slammed shut.

"Nice try getting away with that one," Jessie said.

"Both of you," Julia started, words of warning on the edge of her voice. "I'm just glad you're safe, but if you throw yourselves into danger like that again, I'll..."

"Sacrifice us to the moon?" Jessie offered with a cheeky smile, capturing the scene with her camera. "And now we know why you're the good cop, Mum. Once upon a time, you'd have been the one to run after a killer. That baby made you cautious."

"And me," Barker said. "Most of the time. Now that Anwen's crazy lens has gone, I can feel the insanity lifting. Not sure I'll ever look at my desk the same way, but it's hardly the worst thing that's happened down there, is it?"

"*Yet!*" Jessie pointed out. "You look just like Dot when you purse your lips like that, Mum. Anyway, I'd love to hang around and chat all day in the rain, but there's another puppet master that needs their strings cut."

Jessie set off down the alley as the police car drove away, and DI Moyes joined them. The three leaned on the fence, looking out at the field in silent reflection.

"Good work," Moyes said, breaking the silence. "That filmed confession will cut down on the paperwork."

"All Anwen's doing," Barker replied, "but I'm glad your first official Peridale case is over, Moyes. How was it?"

She laughed, dropping her head. "Bonkers enough that I'll sleep well tonight knowing it's over. All that effort for a documentary? If she'd stayed around, I'm sure she'd have caught something real."

"Desperation," Barker said. "She wanted to be the one to capture a Cotswold case on film, and I suppose she succeeded."

"The cult is only half of the case," Moyes said, pushing away. "I'm not sure we'll be able to arrest Greg Morgan without firm proof that he set the gang onto the Knights, but after looking at Jessie's map, I think we might take a few Crew members out of the shadows. And if another mystery catches your nose, try not to..." Her voice trailed away with a sigh. "I won't waste my breath. Get me another copy of your book, Barker. I need something to do now that I can finally relax."

Julia waved Detective Laura Moyes off, looking forward to doing the same. The nightmare was over, and the village could breathe again. The rain was easing, and the sky was clearing in the distance.

"What now?" Barker asked.

The rain stopped, the clouds parted, and the sun broke through, casting a golden glow over the field, but Julia couldn't stand there looking out all day. She could already hear the bell above the door jingling.

"I have a café to entertain," Julia said, kissing Barker. "And you have an office to clean up."

"One more thing," Barker said, pulling her tight. "We got so swept up in the day, I think we've forgotten something. *Happy birthday*."

~

Jessie's boots thudded against the sterile floor as she marched down the hospital corridor, the distant clamour of journalists growing louder with each step. In a sea of flashing cameras and tailored suits stood Greg Morgan, his grin wide as he held a pair of oversized scissors poised to cut the red ribbon barring entry to the new ward.

"Thanks to my hard work in securing the funding for this new neonatal unit," Greg declared with a flourish, "this fine hospital can now offer an even higher level of care to the community."

With a snip, the ribbon fell, and the crowd pattered with polite applause. Among the assembly of doctors and nurses, annoyance flickered in their eyes. Jessie didn't know if Greg had secured the funding, but she suspected his grand words were mere window dressing. Yet, the journalists were scribbling, the cameras clicking, all eager to immortalise Greg Morgan's latest triumph in their following issues.

Dante, from the *Riverswick Chronicle*, caught Jessie's eye and winked. She smiled back, her heart skipping a beat, as he turned his attention to Greg.

"Mr Morgan, this is quite the achievement," Dante declared, his voice dripping with faux admiration. "But, given what was uncovered in Peridale this morning, I'm sure our readers would love to know your thoughts on this shocking murder case?"

A hush fell over the corridor, every eye turning to Greg.

Greg's smile wavered, his eyes darting before landing on Dante. "It's a relief to know that the police have successfully carried out their duty and swiftly ended the case. And, of course, my thoughts and prayers go out to the families affected by this tragedy."

Jessie inched through the crowd, clearing her throat. Recognition flashed in his eyes, and he fumbled with his tie before scanning the other journalists, desperate for someone else's inquiry.

"Greg?" Jessie said, her voice laden with a deceptive smile, waving so he couldn't pretend to ignore her. "*The Peridale Post* has it on good authority that while you might not have killed those people directly, you were the one who put the local gang, the

Cotswold Crew, on to intimidating the Knight Family."

Greg's laugh was dismissive. "And why would I want to do that?"

"Because the Knight family owns two strips of land blocking the only road access to a fifteen-acre field that you, in your final days as a councillor, saw was put up for sale," Jessie retorted, her voice steady. "A field that hasn't been advertised for sale and has been dropping in value the longer it sits stagnant. A field that, oh, I don't know... wouldn't be able to be developed into something else without the access to the road blocked by the land the Knight family refuses to sell?"

Whispers rippled through the watching crowd, growing with more health officials and patients. Greg, the centre of everyone's focus, laughed again, that smarmy grin stretching further.

"A fantastic tale but wholly without merit. Now, are there any other relevant—"

Jessie's eyes narrowed as she pulled out the picture she'd printed, holding it up.

"So, this isn't you, then? Meeting with a member of the gang at the Fern Moore café?"

"That's preposterous!" Greg cried without glancing at the picture. "We should get back to the matter at hand."

But Dante persisted, "Sources close to the *Riverswick Chronicle* have revealed that the sale is about to go through any day now. As you say, you're merely an MP working for the people, but you still have plenty of friends at the council, right? And I quote," he cleared his throat, brandishing a pad. "'Given my extensive history serving as a councillor, I still have many contacts and am privy to numerous exciting developmental initiatives currently underway.'"

"I never said such a thing."

"Yes, you did," another journalist interjected. "I wrote the quote down myself at your recent library conference."

Greg flapped at his tie. The air was tense as the journalists leaned in, eager for more.

"That's enough!" Greg snapped, his voice cracking. "This press call is over."

With a hurried exit, Greg Morgan left behind astonished faces and whispers. Jessie caught Dante's eye, and they exchanged a knowing smile. The wheels were in motion.

"Wait up!" Dante called after her. "Nice work. Let's see how many of those seeds make it into print. Without proof, the Cotswold Crew story is just speculation, so *The Chronicle* won't touch it, but we'll get him eventually."

"Then we need to keep digging."

"Couldn't agree more," he said, speeding up to keep pace. "How about we dig over a drink sometime?"

Pushing on the revolving door, Jessie smiled before looking back. "I'll think about it. See you around."

Outside, she spotted Veronica leaning against the wall, watching Greg as he hurried towards a waiting car. Jessie realised where she'd seen Greg's dark stare before and why it had seemed so familiar.

"I see it went well then," Veronica said.

"Dodged every question."

Veronica nodded as though she'd expected as much. "That's my brother for you. He will never accept responsibility when he's done something wrong. The police have made their first arrest at one of the locations on your map. The gang will scatter, but it's a start. Maybe one of them will give him up."

"I doubt it."

"It's a start," Veronica continued, smiling. "We haven't just poked the hornet's nest, Jessie. We've given it a good shake."

Jessie's curiosity was piqued. "What's next?"

"I need to show you something back at the office," Veronica said, sighing.

"Is Billy's mural that bad?"

"When I left him, he was doing a fine job."

"So, what?"

"I received an email today with a draft of the plans submitted for planning consideration by the potential new owner. And oh boy, you won't like it, Jessie. And neither will your mother." Veronica offered a tight smile as she reached Jessie's Mini at the edge of the car park. "Greg doesn't want that land for himself. Even if he could afford to redevelop it, it would cast too much of a spotlight on him. But accepting more bribes to make buying it easier for one of his friends?"

Greg Morgan's car sped off, and Jessie knew it wouldn't be long until they met again.

"But the road access?"

"The easiest route," she said. "There's *always* another way."

"Who submitted the plans?"

"Isn't it obvious?" Veronica asked, yanking open the passenger door. "James Jacobson was never going to be satisfied with putting his stamp on the manor and the library, was he?"

26

Barker went down the path in the garden behind the B&B under the watchful eye of the next full moon. He found Derek Knight, Faith, Sam, and Nathan gathered around the rusting wrought-iron table that had hosted them once before. The atmosphere, however, was different now. Things were calmer with Anwen behind bars and the lack of threats from the Cotswold Crew members evading arrest, but their loss couldn't be ignored. An empty chair at the head of the table marked the absence of Sophia Knight.

His gaze fixed on the moon above, Derek sat with his hand resting on the *Lost Religions of the Cotswolds* manuscript.

"The builders started clearing away the wreckage

of our home," Derek said, patting the book's cover. "We will rebuild our lives, starting there. Things will never be the same, but my dear wife always held a braver view of death. It's coming for us all, isn't it?"

"But not tonight," Barker said. He turned his gaze upward, sharing the contemplative view of the moon with the grieving man. "What will you do with Sophia's book?"

Around the table, unease lingered like a shadow, a testament to the conflicting emotions that Sophia's manuscript invoked.

"I say burn it," Faith muttered, her knees drawn in. "It's done enough damage."

"It was Mum's art," Sam said, his tone firm yet gentle. "Publish it."

"It's quite good," Nathan offered. "I wish I'd read it while she was still here. She always tried to make me, and now I have many questions."

Barker observed the turmoil reflected in Derek's eyes as they shifted from the moon to Barker himself. He recognised the unspoken question as the Knight patriarch awaited Barker's assessment.

"Publish it," Barker said, echoing Sam. "In Sophia's honour. She put a lot of work into it."

Derek's expression softened, and with a thoughtful nod, he pulled out an envelope.

"And now it's time for your payment, Mr Brown."

Though hesitant about accepting the payment after the unresolved situation with Arthur, Barker recognised the family's understanding that he'd done his best and, in the end, saved them from being framed by Anwen. He tucked the envelope into his tuxedo jacket's inner pocket.

"And what of your land, Derek?" Barker asked.

"I promised my father on his deathbed that I would never sell it, and I'll keep to my word," he said with a defiant nod, casting his gaze off in the field's direction. "He never forgave the council for splitting up his farm with that road. It was rather spiteful of him to sell off all the sections aside from those two strips, but he knew the power the road access held. If they're in my ownership, nobody will be able to make use of those fields. We've received no more threats since the fire, so the noise it caused will protect us from future intimidation." He paused, his gaze shifting a few metres. "I informed the police of what was happening when I realised Arthur might have had ulterior motives. They claimed I had no proof and that I was an overprotective father. They had their chance to stop this."

Knowing how things worked, they would have dismissed the claims as a petty domestic issue without concrete evidence. But it explained why Derek didn't trust the police. Barker wasn't sure he would either if he'd reported something only for everything to go up in flames anyway.

"They haven't come after me for that money, either," Sam offered. "I imagine Arthur pulled it out and gave it back to them like the good lap dog he was before he torched the place."

"And I'll never know if any of it was real," Faith said in a small voice. "Over now, I suppose."

"At least we don't have to look over our shoulders anymore," Nathan said, his tone the most confident Barker had heard. "The four of us get a second chance to start again."

"And speaking of starting again, I have something for you, Nathan," Barker continued, reaching into the bag he'd brought. He retrieved the Ella Fitzgerald vinyl that had caught Nathan's eye during his visit to Barker's office. "The first of your new collection."

Nathan's smile held genuine appreciation as he accepted the gift.

"And Sam," Barker turned his attention to the eldest Knight sibling, his tone taking on a more paternal note, "I have nothing to give you other than some advice. Create art because you want to and love what you're creating, not because you seek fame and glory. Look at what happened to Anwen Powell." He turned to the last of the Knight siblings. "And Faith, I've seen enough 'bad boys' over my police career to know the women who linger around thinking they can change them don't end up with their happy ever afters."

His words settled on the night air, and with promises made, decisions reached, and farewells exchanged, Barker and the Knights parted ways. Returning to the B&B, Barker's thoughts wandered back to Evelyn's earlier words.

Healing was indeed a journey, not a destination.

The wounds left behind by Arthur and Anwen's actions would take time to mend, but Barker was content knowing that he'd played a role in nudging the process along a little.

Back in the sitting room, Mark sat by the bay window, his fingers dancing over the strings of his acoustic guitar, weaving a cheerful melody that filled the room. Their eyes met, and Mark's smile lit up the room. Barker perched on the arm of a chair, stopping the music.

"I never intended to exploit your mother's memory for profit," Barker began, his tone sincere, "but I recognise it happened either way. If you had told me not to go through with it, I would never have published the book."

"Thank you." Mark shifted on the chair, his fingers lightly brushing over the guitar strings. "Hearing about the documentary brought up memories I wasn't prepared to face. I shouldn't have taken that out on you, nor should I have leaked your book. I wanted you to know what it felt like to have your story stolen, but I know my mum's story isn't mine to claim. You lived through that time, as did everyone else in this village."

"All is forgiven. I owe you my life."

"Mum's birthday didn't help, and I was already emotional," he paused, plucking one of the strings with a decisive motion. "I'd just broken up with Richie."

"I'm sorry to hear that."

"We'd been together since he showed up last summer," Mark said, his voice tight. "But he shared his dad's plans, and when he refused to stand in his way... I couldn't support him."

Barker's curiosity stirred at the mention of James Jacobson. Vans had been frequenting the grand bungalow, still unoccupied. "His dad's plans?"

"I'm not one to gossip." Mark's voice was final.

Barker nodded, respecting the boundary in a village that often did the opposite, even if he was itching to know. He patted Mark's shoulder before sliding off the chair arm, and the gentle strumming resumed.

"By the way," Mark said, catching Barker's attention, "I read your new book before I leaked it. It's good, Barker. You should get it out there."

Barker's heart warmed at the endorsement.

On his way down the hallway, Evelyn swept down the stairs, her presence as captivating as ever in a deep blue kaftan adorned with sparkly moons and stars.

"Ready for the documentary premiere?" Evelyn asked, adjusting Barker's bowtie.

"I think so. You look wonderful."

Evelyn reached into her kaftan to produce a velvet pouch, pulling out a jagged pale blue stone and placing it in his palm. "Kyanite, for creativity. May your next novel flow and flow."

"Thank you, Evelyn, but I'm not sure there'll be another."

"That's not what the tea leaves said this morning." She winked. "Care for a cup? I've just brewed a fresh pot."

Barker's smile remained polite. "Thank you, Evelyn, but I think I'll pass."

In his office, Barker settled into his chair and opened his laptop. No matter how often Evelyn had volunteered to sage the place, memories lingered.

"I think Astrid nudged her son to come to you just when you needed him most," Evelyn had said when tending to her protective crystals.

He placed the Kyanite beside his laptop, staring at the two options on the screen:

'Publish book'

'Save as draft'

He hesitated. Izzy, his former publicist, had pointed him in the right direction with self-publishing. She'd even put him in touch with his old editor and cover designer to keep things consistent with his first release. She thought he stood a shot.

"What do you think?" he asked the framed photograph of his mother.

With a deep breath, he pressed 'Publish book', then closed his laptop. *The Body in the Time Capsule* would be online by morning. Maybe he'd celebrate by writing the first chapter of the follow up.

Evelyn had seen his next book in the tea leaves, after all.

Who was he to argue with that?

The Sacrifice Under the Full Moon…

∽

In Julia's Café on a crisp early October evening, there'd been a buzz in the air all day for the forthcoming screening. The usual tables and chairs had been rearranged to accommodate the makeshift theatre setup, with a red carpet trailing from the front door. Behind the counter, Julia stood alongside her sister Sue, their usual aprons exchanged for glitzy dresses that shimmered under the candles scattered around the café.

As Sue helped her with her pearl earrings, Julia wondered about her husband's whereabouts.

"Has anyone seen Barker? People will start arriving soon."

"Don't worry," Sue reassured her. "He'll be here."

Jessie was assisting Ava with the projector screen; the young camerawoman turned debut director was silent—no doubt with the nerves for her big night. In the weeks following Anwen's arrest, Julia and Barker had been filming more than ever to help Ava construct her version of the story. This shoot, however, felt natural, as Ava was only interested in the truth. Without manipulation, the shooting process proved rather pleasant.

Just as Julia was about to head out the back door to search for Barker, the beaded curtain parted, and Barker entered. Julia's heart skipped a beat at how dapper he looked in his tux.

"You look beautiful," Barker said.

"And you look rather dashing yourself."

"What a difference a few weeks make, eh?" Sue remarked, scooping out a spoonful of Eton mess; Julia had found irony in serving the dessert at the premiere. "I can see why Madwen liked them so much. They're very moreish."

"Madwen?" Julia echoed.

"It's what people have been calling her. I wonder how she's doing behind bars."

"Probably staging her next big comeback," Barker said, refusing Sue's dessert offer. "Hopefully, she's learning her lesson. If only I'd ignored that email."

"So, you've learned to ignore emails," Sue muttered through a mouthful. "Julia?"

Julia considered her answer as the first cars began to pull up outside. "I suppose I've learned that no matter how much I try to protect my family, they'll always do something that nearly gives me a heart attack."

"And I've learned that no matter what you two say you've learned," Sue interjected, sweeping the spoon between them, "you'll be off chasing something else before the end of the week."

Julia and Barker shared a smile, neither of them denying the allegation as Ava's select guests began arriving on the short red carpet.

Dot was the first to sweep through the door, her dress adorned with moons and stars twinkling under the candles.

"Would you look at me?" Dot announced with a spin.

"A celestial vision, my love," Percy said, in a more

straightforward suit, his red bowtie swapped out for blue.

"You look lovely, Gran," Julia said.

"I saw this fabric and thought to myself, this is the *essence* of star quality."

"Bit literal," Sue whispered to Julia.

The door creaked open again, and Ethel strutted in, wearing the same fabric in a dress of a different cut. Dot's was floor-length with a V-neck, Ethel's knee-length with a scoop neck. The room fell silent as the women sized each other up.

"Well, I think we can all agree," Dot said. "I wore it better."

"You wish."

"I can't believe you copied my dress." Dot's voice rose, her hands landing on her hips in an all-too-familiar pose. "Have you no shame, Ethel White?"

"Copied *you*, Dorothy? *Ha!*" Ethel mirrored Dot's stance. "I had the idea first, and you know it."

"This dress is worthy of an actress like me," Dot proclaimed. "My scenes made the final cut, didn't they, Ava?"

Ava smiled and nodded at Dot before turning around and pulling a very different face at Jessie as she subtly shook her head.

"Well, Ethel," Dot said. "You look... *lovely*."

"And you look... like you turned up."

"Oh, you witch!"

"Takes one to know one."

Evelyn glided in, dazzling in a kaftan made from the same fabric as Dot and Ethel's dresses. The room fell into another stunned silence.

"It looks like the stars have aligned, ladies," Evelyn said, having a very different reaction. "It seems we all have the same exquisite taste."

Dot and Ethel looked at each other and burst into shared laughter, to Julia's total shock, their bickering forgotten for the moment.

"And with that," Julia called, gesturing towards the chairs, "why don't we take our seats?"

But as Dot, Ethel, and Evelyn made their way in, the rivalry was reignited, with Dot and Ethel pushing elbows to get in front of Jessie's camera for *The Peridale Post*.

"I'd say that's progress," Sue said as Ethel and Dot posed together, each pulling more prominent poses despite Jessie pointing the camera at the floor. "They'll be having sleepovers next."

People soon took their seats, and after Ava's brief thanks, the lights dimmed, the crowd hushed, and the title card flashed up:

Madness Under the Moon.

Dedicated to Arthur, Sophia, and Rupert.

As the projector flickered to life, images of Julia

and Barker on their first perilous journey through Howarth Forest began to unfold on the screen. A night she'd rather not relive was now playing out for all to see, but Julia maintained her smile as Barker and Jessie took seats on either side of her. Julia found herself grateful for the distraction of Jessie's glowing phone screen.

"Have a look at this," Jessie whispered. She showed Julia a preview of an article she'd been working on with Veronica. They'd gone through dozens of rounds with lawyers, a battle in itself, to reach this point. The headline read: 'Unnamed politician uses gang to intimidate family?' "It's going to print tomorrow. Buckle up."

Julia's eyes widened, the implications of the headline sinking in. She glanced towards the screen. The scene was of Rupert positioning Julia and Barker in front of Howarth House.

"Have there been any more developments about the field behind the café?"

Jessie tucked her phone away, her eyes shifting away from Julia's gaze. "Not... not yet. We're still looking into it."

Julia's heart clenched with the uncertainty in her daughter's voice, but she found solace as Barker's hand wrapped around hers on her other side. Perched on his knee, Olivia was barely paying attention to the screen as it showed Barker creeping towards Howarth House moments before their harrowing discovery. From seeing a rough cut earlier in the week, Julia was pleased with Ava's clever use of editing to cut around all the gory parts.

"Did you publish your book?"

Barker inhaled deeply before he offered a single nod.

Julia's face broke into a smile. "I'm proud of you."

So much had changed since the previous full moon, and Julia was glad they'd survived the day without another sacrifice. The Cult of Lunara was back where it belonged in the depths of Peridale's ancient history.

In the here and now, with Barker's new book fresh out in the world and whispers that the field behind the café had sold, Julia didn't know what the future held. What she did know was that when the documentary ended and the tables were back where they belonged, she couldn't wait to open the café doors in the morning for what she hoped would be an ordinary, uneventful Monday.

Thank you for reading, and don't forget to
RATE/REVIEW!

The Peridale Cafe story continues in...

PUMPKINS AND PERIL
PRE-ORDER NOW! COMING OCTOBER 17th 2023!

Sign up to Agatha Frost's newsletter to be the first to hear about its release!

Thank you for reading!

DON'T FORGET TO RATE AND REVIEW ON AMAZON

Reviews are more important than ever, so show your support for the series by rating and reviewing the book on Amazon! Reviews are **CRUCIAL** for the longevity of any series, and they're the best way to let authors know you want more! They help us reach more people! I appreciate any feedback, no matter how long or short. It's a great way of letting other cozy mystery fans know what you thought about the book.

Being an independent author means this is my livelihood, and *every review* really does make a **huge difference**. Reviews are the best way to support me so I can continue doing what I love, which is bringing you, the readers, more fun cozy adventures!

WANT TO BE KEPT UP TO DATE WITH AGATHA FROST RELEASES? *SIGN UP THE FREE NEWSLETTER!*

www.AgathaFrost.com

You can also follow **Agatha Frost** across social media. Search 'Agatha Frost' on:

Facebook
Twitter
Goodreads
Instagram

ALSO BY AGATHA FROST

Claire's Candles
1. Vanilla Bean Vengeance
2. Black Cherry Betrayal
3. Coconut Milk Casualty
4. Rose Petal Revenge
5. Fresh Linen Fraud
6. Toffee Apple Torment
7. Candy Cane Conspiracies

Peridale Cafe
1. Pancakes and Corpses
2. Lemonade and Lies
3. Doughnuts and Deception
4. Chocolate Cake and Chaos
5. Shortbread and Sorrow
6. Espresso and Evil
7. Macarons and Mayhem
8. Fruit Cake and Fear
9. Birthday Cake and Bodies
10. Gingerbread and Ghosts

11. Cupcakes and Casualties
12. Blueberry Muffins and Misfortune
13. Ice Cream and Incidents
14. Champagne and Catastrophes
15. Wedding Cake and Woes
16. Red Velvet and Revenge
17. Vegetables and Vengeance
18. Cheesecake and Confusion
19. Brownies and Bloodshed
20. Cocktails and Cowardice
21. Profiteroles and Poison
22. Scones and Scandal
23. Raspberry Lemonade and Ruin
24. Popcorn and Panic
25. Marshmallows and Memories
26. Carrot Cake and Concern
27. Banana Bread and Betrayal
28. Eton Mess and Enemies
29. Pumpkins and Peril

Other

The Agatha Frost Winter Anthology

Peridale Cafe Book 1-10

Peridale Cafe Book 11-20

Claire's Candles Book 1-3

Printed in Great Britain
by Amazon